the democracy game

the democracy game

RILEY CHANCE

CP BOOKS

This is a work of fiction set in New Zealand's near future and the environment and context for the story is part extrapolation, part invention. Except for public figures, characters are creations influenced through the myriad of people I have met – any resemblance to whole persons is coincidental. The opinions expressed are those of the characters and should not be confused with the author's.

Published by Copy Press Books, Nelson, New Zealand 2023
Copy Press Books, 141 Pascoe Street, Nelson, New Zealand

ISBN 978-1-067010-06-5 (International Edition – Print-On-Demand)

Typesetting and cover design by Suzanne North, CopyPress
Proofreading by Stephanie McConchie, Focus Proofreading & Editing
Copy editing and literary input – Geoff Walker

COPYPRESS

Designed by CopyPress, Nelson, New Zealand.

{REAL**NZBOOKS**}

Distributed in New Zealand by Real NZ Books, Nelson, New Zealand.

'It is not possible for any thinking person to live in such a society as our own without wanting to change it.'

George Orwell – June 1938

CHAPTER 1

It was the right house.

The driver of the red, late model sedan grinned; the information was accurate. The journalist had tried to keep her address confidential, her number plate blocked, but one of the brotherhood had followed her home after a book launch – her type loved that sort of fluff.

Her car, an older model Ford Mondeo, was parked at the end of a dark driveway but enough streetlight penetrated for him to recognise it and read the number plate. Licking his lips, he imagined dropping her address into future social media posts. That would get her the sort of attention she wouldn't like.

Silently, using the hybrid car's battery power, he parked across the street from her house and turned the lights off. Settling in his seat, he surveyed the street ahead before using his rear-view mirrors to check behind. The street was silent as he anticipated it would be after 3am on a weeknight.

After watching for five minutes, just to be sure, he had driven away – the only sound was the squish of tyres on asphalt. Once clear of her street, he flicked on the headlights and drove to a quiet side street near Palmerston North's recently built pedestrian bridge on Dittmer Drive. Taking care to close his car door quietly, he checked his surroundings as his breath formed swirling clouds in the cold, still night. The suburban street was asleep, there were no witnesses. He nodded to himself – being cautious was not being paranoid.

Dressed in black from head to toe, he set off towards the tar-sealed track that ran alongside the Manawatū River. Instead of taking a direct route back to the journalist's house, he had planned a circuitous route, running along the river track before cutting through the Esplanade, the city's large park-like area with gardens and bush walks. Busy and alive during the day, the council closed the Esplanade to traffic at night, and with no street lights for comfort it would be uninhabited.

He moved quickly and stealthily. The track and Esplanade had been leafy and pleasant when he had tested his route. Pitch-black, it was foreboding. He forced from his mind the image of hordes of street people, doggers and rough sleepers watching, waiting to emerge from the bushes like zombies.

Exiting the Esplanade through a pedestrian gate, he blew out a long breath as he emerged onto the dimly lit Manawaroa Street. Passing the unattended all-night service station, he crossed a four-lane avenue and took a dark side street. There had been no cars around – he was alone and unobserved.

As he neared the journalist's house he slowed, looking around, checking for movement. If he saw anything or anyone concerning, his plan was to continue straight past her house. No one would challenge him at that time of the morning dressed as he was.

Stopping at her front gate, he checked the street a final time before sliding the note into her letterbox.

Smirking, he stared at the darkened house, imagining her reading it. If only he could be there to watch, to see her eyes widen, to see the fear. *Yes, we know where you live you bitch. You better pull your fucking head in – or else.*

As he went to leave, he noticed a pair of yellow eyes trained on him from under her car. Taking a careful step towards the cat, he held out his hand in encouragement. The cat emerged hesitantly at first, but as it gained confidence it stalked towards him, miaowing as it approached. In the still night, the noise sounded like the screech of an owl.

He waved his arms wildly and the cat darted back under the car. Blood pumped noisily in the back of his neck as he stood listening and watching. No light came on. The early-morning stillness remained undisturbed.

With a final glare at the cat, which the cat returned, he retraced his circuitous route, arriving unseen at his car. Allowing himself a final satisfied fist pump, he drove home.

CHAPTER 2

Three weeks earlier

An enthusiastic and dripping-wet retriever bounded through the door, taking no notice of Grace Marks – red-faced, in shorts and a sweatshirt from the gym – as she held the front door open like a bouncer. While she heard Roxy investigating her kitchen floor, Grace's partner Sean carted in an array of bags from his car, hurrying as best he could to avoid the cold, driving rain. It wasn't one of Palmerston North's finest winter evenings.

She went to hug him but he shrank away from her damp, sweaty embrace. 'Sorry, I need to wear this suit tomorrow,' he said.

Shrugging, she closed the door and followed him into the lounge.

'I take it as a vote of no confidence in my cleaning ability that your dog expects to find a meal on my kitchen floor,' said Grace. A reluctant homemaker at best, she was a journalist for Radio New Zealand – RNZ. She, like her colleagues, had expected to be part of the clumsily named, and now abandoned, entity Aotearoa New Zealand Public Media – ANZPM. The new state-owned enterprise, an amalgamation of RNZ and TelevisionNZ, was to be the government's response to strengthen public media in the face of the combined evils of misinformation, the pandemic, and multinationals, such as Facebook and Google, devouring advertising spend. Grace viewed the decision to abandon it as a victory for votes and short-termism.

'She's just trying to help,' he said, dropping his bags which made the house vibrate. Sean, a local family court lawyer, and Grace had been together for close to a decade. They had first met when he was her lawyer, helping her navigate what turned out to be a straightforward divorce. Divorced himself with two children either side of ten he shared the care of with his ex, he was a few years younger than her – though she didn't tell anyone how many. Although the dreaded five zero was in her rear-view mirror – a few years ago too – on a good day she could easily pass for forty.

Grace organised snacks for her children, who were allegedly studying in their bedrooms, and wine for the adults while Sean, having changed out of his precious suit, fed his always ravenous dog. When they had settled themselves on the couch and caught up about their respective days, she unpaused a news item she had queued.

'Did you want to show me this?' he asked.

Grace nodded as the newsreader, stylish and serious, took up the story. 'Protests were held in many cities and towns today in support of the ProtectNZ movement which has gained popularity in recent months. Covering the story for One News is Ryan Boswell.'

The shot showed people marching holding various placards in support of ProtectNZ. The placard the camera focused on contained a message frequently used by ProtectNZ protesters, *Climate change – the cure is worse than the disease.*

Boswell voiced over the shot. 'ProtectNZ has emerged from the ashes of rural lobby groups such as Groundswell which imploded due to its contentious relationships with Voices For Freedom and Destiny Church. Wider than the farming community, ProtectNZ claim they're focused on protecting ordinary New Zealanders and the New Zealand way of life.'

The image changed to a woman wearing a ProtectNZ T-shirt standing outside the recently erected security fence ringing Parliament. The close-up revealed the woman was a middle-aged Pakeha. Rather stating the obvious, the caption on the screen gave her the title *Protester*. In the background, a man with a megaphone was addressing the crowd.

An off-screen Boswell asked the woman, 'What's the key message you're trying to get across to politicians?'

'We're marching to protect the New Zealand way of life. We're not against climate change but it's only the well-to-do who can afford EVs and eat organic food at twice the price of regular food. Farmers, small businesses, and workers are the life blood of this country, and the Government is sacrificing them while countries like America, Australia, India, China and Russia carry on polluting. We want a government who cares about ordinary New Zealanders, not looking virtuous for the international media.'

The image lurched as two protesters pushed into the shot. Lunging towards the screen they yelled, 'Fuck off, fake news.'

Boswell, microphone in hand, jumped into the picture, positioning himself between the protesters and the camera. One protester tried to take Boswell's microphone, but the woman Boswell had been interviewing helped drag the protesters away. More people rushed to help the TV journalist.

A split screen replaced the action, the serious-looking newsreader on one side, Boswell on the other still holding his bright red microphone.

'We can go live to Ryan now he's relocated to a secure location. What happened?'

A nodding Boswell replied. 'Kia ora. You saw the altercation caught on camera, well that's an example of what's becoming a regular occurrence. I've spoken to other members of the media; many have said they've been subject to abuse, threats and hate mail sent through social media. Today's attack forced us to relocate behind the police cordon.'

'This isn't new, is it, Ryan?'

'No. Increasingly protesters are targeting the media and, I'm sad to say, we're becoming used to this sort of treatment. To be fair, it's becoming rare at ProtectNZ protests and, as you saw, several protesters helped us out of what was a tight spot.'

'What about the protest itself?'

'We've had reports of similar protests in most major cities and towns across Aotearoa. The feeling many people expressed to me was anger. Anger at having to sacrifice their lifestyles while wealthy New Zealanders and the international community do little.'

'Did any politicians address the protesters?'

'From the reports I've received, politicians from all the major parties have ignored the protests and ProtectNZ, though I understand that senior representatives of ACT and New ACT are having talks with the protest group.'

'Ngā mihi e hoa, stay safe Ryan. In other news, interest rates are rising again—'

Her nose wrinkling, Grace paused the newsreader and turned to Sean.

'Go on,' he said. 'What's your interest in the protest? Is it tied in to your investigations into the alt-right?'

'No, I don't think so,' she said squinting. 'There were the Groundswell protests, the misguided at best "Freedom" protests, and now ProtectNZ. What do you make of them? You're not quite the man-in-the-street, but you're close enough.'

Sean sipped his wine. 'People protesting to protect their interests, to protect their jobs.'

Grace stayed quiet.

'Ordinary New Zealanders are unhappy.'

'Ordinary?' She raised an eyebrow.

'Well, Groundswell were ordinary farmers, at least to start with. Until they jumped into bed with the crazies.'

'What about this new organisation, ProtectNZ?' asked Grace. 'Groundswell is the living dead now.'

He drank the last of his wine. 'Similar, I guess, but they seem to have a broader appeal with ordinary Kiwis.'

'Ordinary working-class Kiwis?'

Sean smiled. 'I know where you're going with this. You're like a ferret, sniffing out the wealthy – and a story.'

Grace held up her hands. 'I'm wondering why this latest political shower is fixated on locking in the status quo.'

Sighing, he looked at his empty glass.

She giggled. 'Answer me one more question, it's been bugging me. ProtectNZ, what are they protesting? I mean, who are the villains in their rhetoric?'

Taking a few moments to consider the question, he said, 'If they want to protect the New Zealand way of life, they're against those who want to change it. Does that make it the government?'

'The *current* Government? Or *all* governments?'

Sean spoke deliberately, as though assembling his thoughts. 'They're against those who want us to focus on taking action to combat climate change, that makes it all governments. New Zealand signed the Paris Accord and we've made commitments at various COPs.' He shook his head as though it didn't make sense. 'But, from what I've read, they're not climate change deniers.'

'They're not,' she said. 'For a so-called *astroturf* protest, it's surprisingly nuanced. They're not against climate change, they're against action to combat climate change.'

'Isn't that the same?'

Pouting, she said, 'There's a subtle difference.'

Sean took Grace's also empty glass and headed to the kitchen.

When he returned with their glasses refilled, she hugged him. 'Sorry, I didn't mean to grill you. You're at the top of my list of smart people I can bounce difficult topics off.'

Giving her a sideways glance, he said, 'How long's your list?'

'Immense, that's how clever I think you are.'

He rolled his eyes.

Grace added, 'Before we finish this most fascinating of conversations, I need to bounce one more idea off you.'

His face was a combination of resigned, pleased, and worried.

'I'm researching popularism. You know, how Boris, Trump, Bolsonaro, and other politicians managed to hoodwink vast sections of the population to vote for them. They make themselves appear as viable leaders, not what they are – shambling, knuckle-dragging morons.'

Sean gave the slightest nod of encouragement.

'Right. First, their support isn't the spontaneous explosion it appears. It's orchestrated and they share three core aspects. One, they appeal to' – she used her fingers as speech marks – "the people". Two, they're anti-elite. And three, they wrap their arms around their support base by making everyone else the enemy – the dreaded "other".'

'Sounds right,' he said. 'Trump, an effing billionaire, appealed to ordinary but dim Americans.'

'He wanted to "drain the swamp",' she said. 'Even though he was a billionaire, he managed to make his narrative anti-elite.'

'And the other was the do-nothing Democrats.'

'Them,' she said, 'and anyone who didn't look, talk and think like they imagined an American should.'

'White?'

'And a gun-toting Republican,' she added.

After a brief pause, he said, 'ProtectNZ, they're sure as hell appealing to ordinary New Zealanders.'

Nodding, she said, 'They're positioning themselves as the protector of the Kiwi way of life.'

'Are they anti-elite?'

Grace hummed a little. 'Groundswell was pro-farmer rather than anti-elite; they wanted to bury New Zealand's collective head in the sand. The "freedom" protests were a bin bag of half-chewed liquorice allsorts who ended up anti-government, anti-media and pro-whatever group would buy them a hotdog. But you couldn't classify either as populist movements.'

'They weren't even popular,' he added.

'But ProtectNZ,' said Grace, 'they're painting the middle class, those promoting action to combat climate change, and the educated, as the elite. The wealthy Tesla-driving middle class who ProtectNZ claim aren't suffering economic hardship.'

'It's clever, isn't it,' he said. 'I mean, to appear for climate change action but against the Green Party.'

Grace snorted. 'Clever, that's one word for it.'

'What was the third aspect again?' asked Sean.

'They paint people not aligned to their cause as "the other".'

'Are they pointing at other countries as the problem? Making them the cause of the problem and the source of inaction?'

'That's how I read it,' said Grace. 'It allows people to feel incensed. Why should our New Zealand lifestyle suffer when the Americans, the Chinese and even the bloody Australians are doing sweet fuck all?'

Sean laughed. 'The penny's dropped. Not spontaneous, organised. You're sensing a story. You're sensing, drumroll please, a *conspiracy*.'

Holding up her hands as if in surrender, she said, 'Look at Brexit, that was hardly an untainted democratic process. It took money, greed, political ambition, and a shitload more money to hoodwink enough people into believing that getting out of the EU was in the best interest of the average Brit. The problem is, when you say conspiracy, everyone thinks you're a nutter. Any organised attempt to pervert the course of a country's future so a small few profit is the dictionary definition of a conspiracy.'

'True enough. Although, using Brexit as an example, that means some conspiracies are legal, helping them to hide in plain sight.'

'Legal?' Grace's face soured. 'Maybe, because their intentions are impossible to prove, but what about ethical? And surely the public needs to know what's going on so they can make an informed decision.'

He nodded his agreement. 'When you wrote about the rise of surveillance, you needed evidence to make people take the issue seriously.'

'And when I had the evidence, detractors couldn't write off what I wrote as the ravings of a left-wing, Marxist, lesbian troublemaker. So, I've decided not to call it a conspiracy.'

'And?' he said, when she didn't elaborate.

'I'm calling it what it is – they're gaming democracy.'

Sean pursed his lips. 'Gaming democracy, I like that. It's catchy too.'

'I know, not *clumsy*' – she winked at him – 'for once. From now on my detractors will have to label me a left-wing, Marxist, lesbian, *game* theorist and general troublemaker.'

Breaking a short reflective silence, Sean asked, 'Do you honestly believe ProtectNZ is involved in something dark?'

Grace shrugged. 'I sure intend to find out.'

CHAPTER 3

Grace arrived in Wellington at half past eight in a dark mood. She had planned to take the Capital Connection, a commuter train that ran weekdays from Palmerston North, so she could work rather than stare at the brake lights of the car in front of her crawling along in first gear. When she arrived at the station, there were buses waiting and no train. Cramped into a claustrophobic seat, she sat next to a woman who had introduced herself as CEO of the local university. When Grace queried why a university needed a CEO, she explained it better reflected the nature of the role and, she had added with a broad smile, it helped with future employment options.

Grace, who had introduced herself only by her first name and said she was a writer, jotted down a note to follow up but she lost the two hours' work time she had hoped to gain, hence her dark mood.

Her sole appointment for the day was to interview Sebastian Ball, the leader of ProtectNZ, at 9.30am at his Murphy Street office. He would no doubt be in a suit, so she had dressed in business-consulting attire – black skirt, tartan tights, a crisp white T-shirt, black jacket, and black ballet flats – to ensure a clothing balance of power. It was a ten-minute walk from the station and, with half an hour to kill, she stopped at the café in the National Library building for a caffeine fix.

The odd politician, mainly backbenchers, and journalists used to frequent the café but not now. She found it sad the ill-conceived occupation of Parliament's grounds had altered the political precinct and landscape. New Zealand was one of the few countries where the public could mix and mingle with politicians and journalists. For the most part, everyone knew the rules and left people to get on with their days unmolested. How much would it change? Would the security fencing that periodically surrounded Parliament after the recent occupation soon become a permanent feature?

Seb Ball, as he preferred to be called, was not Grace's cup of tea, although she imagined she wasn't his either. He seldom gave interviews to the media, never to what he called "hostile" journalists, more often throwing missiles at them for "misinforming the public". It was his polite way of screaming "fake news", a tactic perfected by populist leaders worldwide. She had never dreamed he would let her interview him one-on-one, so she had never considered asking. That made today's interview strange because the interview request had come from his office. The email she received said he was *keen to meet the indomitable Ace Marks*. She had to look up the word in the dictionary – just to be sure.

Drinking her coffee slowly, she considered how the interview might run. Did Ball suppose he could win her over with the same charm offensive he had exuded through his tame media contacts? Were they hoping to reach a new audience through her – people who had so far ignored their message? For ProtectNZ it would be a risky strategy, but for Grace, it was a scoop that had fallen into her lap. It was the sort of opportunity journalists toiled for but seldom received.

Leaving with plenty of time in hand, so she could stroll rather than speed walk, she headed for ProtectNZ's offices. As she drew closer, she saw a crowd of people gathered outside listening to the recognisable figure of Ball, in a suit and tie as she predicted. Standing on the front porch of the building allowed him to look down on the pack of journalists as they competed to have their questions answered. The footpath was narrow, so they had coned off the car parks in front of the offices creating a journalistic mosh pit.

Grace watched the melee with professional interest. Nobody had informed her he would be speaking to the media outside his offices, but they must have informed their preferred media outlets. Journalists didn't roam around Wellington in mobs on the off chance they may catch a politician by surprise.

Her journalistic antennae vibrated, and, at the same time, a warning bell sounded in her head. Orchestrated – that word encapsulated the actions of ProtectNZ and Ball. She certainly wasn't naïve enough to think they saw her as anything other than a pawn with a part to play. A part that would help push their agenda, which was what? That was the real question, what did they want to achieve?

As she stood watching, Ball checked his watch. Holding up his hand as a final gesture, he disappeared into ProtectNZ's offices, two security guards following a pace behind. The media milled around checking their photos and recordings for useable content and their phones to see where they needed to head next.

Grace checked the time on her phone, 9.29am.

Orchestrated.

As she walked through the rapidly dispersing media a voice called out, 'You're too late, Ace.'

'Not early enough by the look of it,' she said, unsure of who she was answering as she walked towards the front doors.

'*You* won't get a warm welcome in there ...' The journalist's voice trailed away as the door opened as if by magic as she approached. She turned and gave the remaining journalists, who watched in confusion, a smug smile before she too disappeared into ProtectNZ's offices.

The tallest of the security guards, who were decked out like 1960s FBI agents protecting JFK, motioned for Grace to head towards the reception desk. She nodded but didn't move as she looked around, taking in the scene.

Decorated in a minimalist, faux-successful-corporate style, the office was a hive of activity. Past the receptionist's desk she could see at least a dozen people, trendily dressed even for Wellington, talking on phones or in small groups. It reminded Grace of a beehive, an actual one, not "The Beehive".

Grace made for the reception desk but Ball, who had emerged from an adjacent office, made a beeline for her. 'Ace Marks,' he said, his hand outstretched. 'Can I call you Ace?'

'Sure can,' said Grace, shaking his hand. His image had sharpened since he had risen to prominence. Gone was the caterpillar with his rounded face, developing jowls, corduroy pants, Beatles-era haircut, and accountant's disposition. In front of her was the butterfly: a lean, confident, suit-and-tie-wearing, bald but stylish merchant banker.

'Please, call me Seb' – he raised his eyebrows – 'not the name you like to use in your stories if that's all right.'

Grace smiled briefly. 'What can I say?' She had been following the rapid rise of ProtectNZ and had developed a nickname she occasionally used for him in her stories – Sleazeball. It was another reason she attracted more than her share of online hate and threats. It was also why his reaching out to her for an interview was unexpected.

'Let's see if we can't bridge the divide between us,' he said smiling. 'Coffee?'

'Thanks.' She didn't need another coffee, but it was an integral prop in business and political meetings.

Ball turned to the receptionist. 'Two black coffees, please Dean, no sugar. This way, Ace.'

Grace fell in behind Ball. *Orchestrated – and how the fuck does he know how I take my coffee?* She tucked the question away.

Ball led her to an office that tried hard to give off an old-world library ambience. Bookshelves with an array of ancient legal books covered the walls either side of a large bay window, its curtains pulled. Her nose wrinkled in response to the staged vibe the room gave off. It had all the correct elements for the effect they were striving for, mainly books, but it lacked authenticity. It was as if real estate agents had staged the room to impress buyers. When they had stitched up their victim, the room would dissolve back into an uninspiring meeting room.

'The view is of a construction site,' said Ball, answering the question he incorrectly assumed was the reason for Grace's expression. 'We've asked them to moderate their language but … Please, take a seat.'

A large wooden desk and vintage leather chairs added to the room's almost-a-library ambience. They sat opposite each other. Grace took out a notepad and pen and put her phone on the table between them.

'Do you mind if I record the interview? It saves me having to scribble notes and I can concentrate fully on what you're saying.'

'Not at all. That makes perfect sense.'

'How long do you have?' she asked, turning on the recorder app on her phone.

Spreading his arms, Ball leaned backwards. 'I'm not due anywhere until lunchtime, so until then I'm all yours.'

Grace smiled. *His aides have briefed him and he's feeling confident. Let's see how well they've briefed him.*

'Okay. First, why did you want *me* to interview you? I mean, there are loads of journalists and talk-back pedlars who share your views, shall we say. Why not old what's-his-name, the git with a sugar daddy who mistakenly thinks he's smart.'

Ball giggled more than laughed, as he ran a hand over his smooth head. It was a habit Grace had noticed from his television performances; he did it when he felt in control. In poker, it's called a tell.

'My team and I considered that you, a well-known and respected investigative journalist, would give me a fair hearing. You're right, I do talk with journalists more sympathetic, shall we say, to our position, including' – he raised his eyebrows – 'old what's-his-name, but we're preaching to the converted. Win, lose or draw, this interview will reach a different segment of society. At the very least, they'll be discussing the issues. That's all we want.'

'That's fair,' she said. 'I'm a professional. I won't twist your words, but you will need to answer *my* questions, not the questions you want me to ask.'

'That's how journalism works,' said Ball again opening his arms wide.

'Let's start at the beginning,' said Grace. 'You were a modest business success, a self-made man who made a pile in the real estate industry and you were smart enough to get out before the party ended. Why are you doing this?'

A serious look came over him. 'I've been lucky in terms of money, but there's more to life than money. A higher purpose if you like.'

Putting her elbows on the table, she leaned closer. 'If you wanted to run the "higher purpose" line, why invite me? Along with most of New Zealand who bothers to listen to you, I don't believe a word of it.'

Grace sat back and opened her arms, imitating Ball. 'Come on, Seb. Let's make this a real interview where you say what you think, not regurgitate your organisation's views.'

Annoyance flashed across his face, but before he could reply, a knock on the door halted their conversation. It was Dean bringing their coffees.

Grace cursed his timing. By the time he had left, Ball had composed himself.

'I was warned you don't take prisoners,' he said.

Grace stared blankly at him, staying quiet.

'Friends of mine, friends of the country as it happens, thought I could make a difference. They asked me to front the ProtectNZ movement because they, like me, believe passionately that politicians are needlessly sacrificing the New Zealand way of life while the major polluters of the world carry on unchecked. That's where the focus needs to be, not on beating up ordinary New Zealanders.'

'New Zealand should ignore climate change?'

'Ace, we're a fly on an elephant in terms of impact. We contribute one-tenth of one per cent of CO_2 emissions. That's the dictionary definition of a rounding error. China and the US combined contribute over forty per cent. Our best chance of saving the planet is pressuring them to act, not sacrificing ordinary New Zealanders in a futile gesture. A gesture that allows the better-off in the so-called team of five million to smugly drive about in expensive EVs.'

'That's a worn argument,' she said. 'If smaller countries all took the stance you want New Zealand to take, the world will burn irrespective of what the US and China do. There's the other sixty per cent of emissions, not to mention the more harmful methane emissions belched and farted the length and breadth of New Zealand. And if countries our size don't act, how can the world collectively pressure the US or China?'

'That's a worn argument too,' said Ball.

'No, it's not. You're trying to sell the past; convincing people we can recreate the 1970s.'

'I'm afraid we're going to have to agree to disagree.'

Looking at him hard, she asked, 'You do believe climate change is real, don't you? And that it's caused by humans?'

'Absolutely.' He ran a hand over his head. 'Parts of the media are trying to make us look like cow-cocky conspiracy theorists – it's pathetic. We know it's real; we know humans are the cause. What we're saying is that sacrificing ordinary New Zealanders' way of life isn't going to change what's going to happen except to doom most people in our country to years, if not decades, of economic and social misery.'

'It's not black and white,' said Grace. 'We could transition to a green economy.'

'And ruin the lives of ordinary New Zealanders.'

They sat looking at each other for a long moment. She realised one point he had made was right – they weren't going to agree, making the line of questioning futile. Boxer-like, she jabbed several questions around climate change, but Ball's responses were predictable – repeated variations of the same answer. Their stance was gaining supporters as it was alluring, and, at least from their perspective, it made sense. In a previous story, she had called it their "head-in-the-sand" strategy because her editor had made her change it from "head-up-their-own-arse" strategy.

'Let's move on from climate change,' she said, 'to me, that's a bit of a smokescreen.'

Ball's head tilted.

'Who do you' – a half-laugh escaped her – 'I mean, who does ProtectNZ represent?'

'You've heard me say it dozens of times: ordinary New Zealanders,' said Ball as he stroked his head.

'Who else?'

Ball shrugged.

'Come on,' said Grace. 'Your rich friends ask you to front their movement, you're representing them and *their* best interests. They'll expect a return on their investment – that sort does nothing for nothing.'

'My friends are acting in the *best interests* of New Zealand. Somebody needs to. Somebody needs to stop the sacrifice of—'

'Ordinary New Zealanders,' she cut in. 'I know, save it for your rallies. Who are these rich friends of yours?'

Ball smiled. 'The organisation's backers want to stay out of the public gaze. They don't seek recognition for their service to New Zealand.'

'How noble of them,' said Grace flatly. 'My bet is they're a bunch of the usual wealthy, conservative suspects who need to keep a low profile because, if the public knew who they were, they'd know for sure ProtectNZ was acting in *their* best interests.'

'That's your opinion, Ace and you're in a minority.'

Gritting her teeth, she was annoyed she had let him call her Ace; it sounded as if they were old friends. She continued to press, trying to push on the right button. 'Similar movements: Groundswell, the Tax Payers Union, the New Zealand Initiative and the Free Speech Union; the people behind those are mainly white, right-wing, rich' – she smiled, refraining from adding an expletive – 'men. I'll bet I'll find a subset of the same tragics behind your organisation.'

Unflustered, he said, 'They want to remain anonymous benefactors and I intend to respect their wishes.'

'I'm going to find out who they are,' she said with a raise of her eyebrows. 'It's what we journalists do.'

Shrugging, he said, 'Good luck, but you won't find the scandal you're hoping for. You'll be wasting your time, missing the *real* political action.'

Deciding it was time to change the subject, and throw a curveball, she asked, 'You lived in Auckland for a while, are you still a member of the Tara Iti Golf Club?'

Ball jerked as though she had slapped him. It was a handy tactic; throw questions from left field they weren't expecting to knock them off their stride. It also had the effect of keeping the interviewee unsettled, wondering where the next question was coming from.

'I don't see what my golf habits have to do with the situation.'

'It's a simple yes or no question.'

Taking his time before answering, he said, 'No. I've only ever played there as the guest of a member. But again, I don't see your question's relevance.'

'Human interest. I'm sure you want me to portray the real Seb Ball. Relaxing with his mates on a US oligarch's land where honest Kiwis can't afford to stand. Do they let women on the course? Apart from Lydia Ko when she played with Key.' His mouth opened but she didn't give him a chance. 'No matter. Where did your initial finances come from to establish ProtectNZ?' Interviewing 101 – once you have them off-kilter, ask the hard questions.

Ball twitched. 'How we were financed—'

'Have you put your own money into the movement?' Grace asked, not letting him finish.

She was starting to enjoy the interview. He had spent the last few months interviewed by hand-picked sympathetic, if not sycophantic, journalists who wanted repeat gigs. No one had pinned him on the ropes and, now he was there, he looked like he wanted to hear the bell.

'A little.'

'How much?'

'That's none of your business.'

'And the rest came from these friends you mentioned?'

His eyes wide, he leaned towards her. 'Now look here, Marks.'

Grace picked up her coffee and leaned backwards maintaining the distance between them. She watched Ball battle to regain control of himself, she gave him the time he needed. She didn't want the interview to end, not yet.

Running a hand over his head, he sat back. 'I was warned.'

Replacing her coffee, she pressed. 'I'm not here to dote on your every word. I'm interested in how you're financed and who's putting up the cash.'

'I can't divulge that information.'

'Fine, not telling me makes it more noteworthy,' she said looking at her notes. 'Are you still a practising Evangelical Christian?'

'You've done your homework. Yes, as a matter fact, I am.'

'There are a few of you around, aren't there – who knew? You've kept that on the down-low, why?'

'Because my personal faith isn't relevant to my role with ProtectNZ.'

'Not relevant?' She raised an eyebrow. 'How do you square away your Christian beliefs with the way rich people, the people you're representing, rape and pillage the planet for their own hedonistic ends? Not to mention gay and trans rights, abortion, or society's silence about domestic violence.'

Ball ran a hand over his head. 'I'm not going to discuss or defend my religious views. We don't have enough time to get into that topic, and, unless I've misjudged you, you've set views on the subject.'

'Let's drop religion – for today.' She asked her next question looking at her notes, not Ball. 'Are you, and your party, considering running for parliament?'

Grace looked up abruptly, catching Ball smiling.

Reverting to his all-business look, he said, 'I didn't expect you to ask that. All I can say is that I and ProtectNZ have no political aspirations at this point in time.'

'That sounded rehearsed. I think you meant to say yes. Which party will ProtectNZ align itself with?'

'We have broad support across New Zealand. So politically, if you'll forgive the religious term' – he chuckled – 'you could say we're agnostic. We expect that any government will listen to the voices of our supporters carefully; if they want to stay in power that is.'

Ball raised his eyebrows; she could tell he was back feeling smug and in control. Time to fire in another uppercut.

'How deeply is ProtectNZ affiliated with Hobson's Pledge?'

He appeared to look confused.

'Don't give me that look,' she said. 'You know all about Brash's nationalist echo chamber.'

'You're right, I can recall them. And we're not.'

A question he must have known was coming, he looked at ease with the subject. He was well-schooled, Grace had to give him that. Deciding to press, she said, 'No? I'm surprised. Isn't your organisation's line that we should view everyone as a New Zealander? Everyone's the same so we can rewrite history and erase the numerous racial injustices we've inflicted – it would be like they never happened. That "colour-blind ideology" is right up Brash's back passage, figuratively and literally.'

Ball laughed. 'Hobson's Pledge, as I understand it, is politically motivated. They want a world that can't, and shouldn't, exist. Economics drives our party's view. We want everyone treated as a New Zealander economically, irrespective of race, colour, creed, gender, or hairstyle.'

'I see the difference but' – she shrugged – 'it's the opposite side of the same coin.'

'That's your opinion, Ace, it's not mine. And it's not the view of our supporters who, as I'm sure you've noticed, come from diverse backgrounds.'

Grace nodded, then asked, 'Have you ever been a member of a white supremacist group?'

If Ball looked like she had slapped him before, this time it was like she had grabbed his balls and squeezed – hard.

'What?'

Grace stayed quiet, looking innocent. At least she hoped she did.

'I've never been anywhere near a white supremacist group.'

'What about an alt-right group?'

'Nor an alt-right group,' he said, his voice suggesting he was struggling to keep control.

'What about your business associates?'

'I have no idea … which associates?'

'Your reaction tells me I've hit a nerve. You tell me which associates.'

Ball scoffed. 'You're fishing.'

Grace shrugged. 'If you're going to run for parliament one day, you need to handle questions you don't know are coming. Have you seen the movie *Rounders*?'

'What? No.' He hadn't yet pulled himself back to the public persona created and polished by ProtectNZ's public relations team.

'It's about poker,' she said, 'but the messages are transferrable. Matt Damon said something like, "If you can't spot the sucker in the room within five minutes, you are the sucker."'

Ball shook his head and frowned. He didn't get it, but she had intended it to be oblique.

Standing she said, 'Thanks for the coffee. I've enough to write a story that will … inform the public.'

He leaned back in his chair, his eyes narrowed, staring hard at her.

'Don't get up, I'll see myself out.'

CHAPTER 4

Grace busied herself making coffee and listening to the TV crew setting up their equipment on her front porch. Putting the cups out on a tray, she had intended to add biscuits, but all the tin contained was two empty packets – the teenagers had struck again.

'Thanks, Grace,' said Abbey Wakefield, a Wellington-based journalist assigned to the story for the TV news. Their paths had crossed occasionally but they were, at best, distant colleagues.

Wakefield, stylish in black and white chequered pants and a red T-shirt under a warm black jacket, accepted a cup from Grace who had chosen semi-casual jeans and an upmarket hoodie for the interview.

'What have the police said?' asked Wakefield.

'Nothing much. They've taken photos, poked around the section, knocked on a few doors. But, as always, the messages appeared in my letterbox when the world was asleep. It's the same this time.'

'How are you coping?'

Grace made a face. 'Fine, I think. I mean, you know what it's like, Abbey. Drivel, lewd comments, and the odd emailed rape threat; it comes with the territory.'

'It does,' said Wakefield frowning, 'but it effing well shouldn't. I'm keen to do another exposé on the misogynistic attacks levelled at women in the media. We've highlighted it for years, but if anything, it's getting worse.'

'You're right, but I can cope with that. To survive we have to, don't we? But receiving hate mail in my letterbox is bad enough' – Grace pointed at her front door – 'but waking up to find dead man's hand nailed to my front door with a knife, that's a whole new level.'

Wakefield frowned. 'Dead man's hand?'

'You didn't know?'

'I thought it was just a nasty way to shock you. You know, a knife through an ace as a metaphor. What's dead man's hand?'

Grace told her the story of how the playing cards stuck to her door made up the hand that Wild Bill Hickok allegedly held when John McCall shot him in the back of the head – hence dead man's hand.

Wakefield's eyes lit up. 'I'm glad you told me. That makes it, well, you know.'

'It does jazz up the story,' agreed Grace.

'When was it?'

'Last night,' said Grace.

'No,' she said, laughing. 'I mean Wild Bill Hickok.'

'Oh.' Grace made an I've-got-no-idea face.

'Jess …' Wakefield turned to her camera operator who had her hand raised as she studied her phone.

'1876 in Deadwood. That's in South Dakota.'

'Deadwood! The story's getting better.' Wakefield stepped towards the cards pinned to the front door. 'A pair of aces, a pair of eights and a queen.'

'It's usually called "aces and eights",' said Grace.

'Aces and eights. Dead man's hand,' said Wakefield, getting familiar with terms she would soon be using in the story. 'We've set up the shot to have the cards in the background, if you're okay with that.'

'Sure. The police said they'd send a team later to take the cards and the knife and maybe check for fingerprints, but until then …'

Wakefield half turned. 'Jess, we'll redo the voice-over after we've got Ace in the can.' Putting her coffee on the table, she said, 'Right, let's get this done.'

The camera operator adjusted Grace's position until she stood near her front door, the cards visible behind her. While Jess positioned the microphone out of shot and turned on a portable light, Wakefield scribbled on her notes, presumably adjusting her report to make it sound as if she was familiar with dead man's hand and its story.

'Relax, Ace. Abbey will ask the questions and I'll record the whole interview. We'll cut it later.'

Taking in a deep breath, Grace shook her body gently to dispel any tension. It had been a while since she had been in front of a TV camera, but she didn't feel intimidated, rusty if anything. As for cutting the interview, that was how they rolled, and she had to trust them. As she was a colleague, and a victim (the media liked to paint people as either victims or villains), they would make the cut sympathetic.

Smiling broadly Wakefield asked, 'Why did you start researching and writing about the alt-right?'

Staring into the distance, letting her mind gather the threads, she said, 'The pandemic kicked off my interest. The alt-right were heavily involved in circulating conspiracy theories about vaccines. Why? That's not part of their agenda, so I went digging.'

'You've written several stories about the alt-right, how were they received?'

'Well, the stories stirred up those involved. They didn't like having their activities scrutinised. They like pushing their misogynistic racism anonymously and when I shone a light on them, they tried to crawl, cockroach-like, back under the nearest rock.'

'What's the fallout been like for you personally?'

Indicating the cards pinned on the door behind her, she said, 'This is the latest in a series of personal attacks. When I published the articles, I received an intense burst of online abuse including threats of rape to "straighten me out". I see them as unpleasant but infantile – attacks trying to stop me doing my job, doing what society needs, exposing them and their kind. I reported them to the police, but they can't do much with anonymous hate mail.'

Wakefield nodded but stayed quiet which Grace took as a cue to keep talking.

'Somehow, they found out where I live and started leaving notes in my letterbox, nasty stuff. I gave those to the police too. This morning I woke to find this.' She indicated the cards behind her. 'That means they came onto my property, they came within metres of my children, carrying a knife. I'm concerned it's escalating.'

Turning to her camera operator, Wakefield said, 'I'll voice over the next bit. Get a close-up of the cards.' She winked at Grace. 'I'll sound like an expert on dead man's hand.' Pausing, to make cutting the clip easier, she asked, 'What are you planning to do?'

'I'm not leaving the alt-right alone, that's for sure. In the current environment they feel emboldened, as though their views are acceptable. If I did stop, they'd win and that's not how democracy works. We, the media, are under attack and it's becoming targeted and nuanced. Aggressive sections of society want to weaken our ability to function, to expose them and their racist, bigoted, fucked-up ideas.'

Wakefield laughed. 'I wish we could run that, Ace.'

'Sorry, Abbey, let me do that again.' Grace composed herself. 'Sections of society want to weaken our ability to expose them, leaving them free to advance their agenda.' She waited a few seconds before asking, 'Better?'

Wakefield, not in shot, gave her the thumbs up. 'I know your thoughts on surveillance, but won't security cameras help the police catch them in the act?'

Grace frowned. 'I'm against monitoring our streets while the SIS roam around cyberspace on the fringes of the law. Besides, if I did install a security camera, they'd wear disguises or find a different way to get their message across. My plan is to identify all those responsible, nip this in the bud, but I may need help.'

'How are you going to do that?'

'Good question,' said Grace. 'I'm working on it.'

After another pause, Wakefield said, 'Great stuff, Ace, that's all we need. Jess, how was that?'

'I need a noddy,' she said. 'Keep chatting, I'll let you know when I'm done.'

As the camera operator moved to get the shot of them talking and nodding, where the term came from, Grace asked, 'Enjoying life in front of the camera, Abbey?'

Her face scrunched. 'It's not bad. The pace is relentless, and I get my fair share of shit thrown at me too. I'll do this until a spot becomes available on a gig like *Sunday* or *Q + A*. I might need to push Jack down some stairs,' she said with a wink. 'Are you really going after the alt-right or was that just a great sound bite?'

'I see my role as helping these people come out of the closet.' Grace returned the wink. 'It must be hell, having to pretend you're a human being.'

Wakefield laughed.

'We're good,' called out Jess.

'When you find out who they are, call me,' said Wakefield. 'We could have cameras there for the reveal – like *Catfish*.'

Grace half-smiled, taken by surprise.

Wakefield called over her shoulder, 'Take care, Ace,' as she headed to her car.

Watching them go, Grace thought, *Catfish? The journalistic world does need to embrace reality TV.*

CHAPTER 5

The Parapara Estuary twinkled as Alice Green, not her real name, stood on her deck in front of an easel, frowning. The winter day had been stunning and the late afternoon sun made it not too hot, not too cold. Painting, as an art form, was not coming easily to Alice. It took her hours, sometimes days, to make acceptable progress. She was getting better and the only way to improve was to keep painting. Her goal, which felt ridiculously out of reach, was to paint huge murals on buildings where everyone could enjoy them for free. When she had visited Christchurch on her extended tour of the South Island, she spent half an hour captivated by a girl's face painted on the back of a hotel.

In her previous life in the United States, she had made her art from discarded scrap, selling it under the pseudonym Norma Rules – NoRules. When circumstances forced her to abandon that life – when her assignment in New Zealand had gone pear-shaped – she had gone into hiding in the South Island, considering it an early retirement. She would have liked to return to her previous artistic medium, but she couldn't risk the possible connection. In the States her art had become collectable – and recognisable.

Checking the time on her phone, she saw it had gone five. The warm day had allowed her to wear a T-shirt and her favourite worn harlequin shorts, but when the sun disappeared, which would be soon, the evening would rapidly cool.

'That's enough for today. How's it coming, Indy?'

Indy, a small version of an American bulldog that she had rescued from the Nelson SPCA, ambled over to take a serious look. Instead of looking at the picture, she sat at Alice's feet staring up at her wearing her permanently puzzled expression.

'I agree, but I'm improving. Dinner time?'

Indy's tail wagged furiously, and Alice gave her head a scratch. She packed up and they headed inside.

Throwing a baggy black sweatshirt over the vintage 'Stop the Tour'

T-shirt she had bought from an art gallery, she organised Indy's dinner, opened a bottle of wine, turned on the TV and snuggled into her favourite cushion-filled couch with its panoramic view across the twinkling estuary towards Kahurangi National Park. After touring the South Island for eight months, she had returned to Golden Bay, leaping at the chance to rent a small fully furnished house with large windows on the edge of the Parapara Estuary. Not only did she find the location visually beautiful, it had a thriving arts community. There were too many anti-vaxxers for her liking, but she was keen to get involved in the arts community when her painting turned the corner and Covid was in the rear-view mirror – if it ever would be.

The day after she had moved in, she had sat on the couch, marvelling at the scenery but realising that she would go stark raving mad living alone. The next day she had gone to Nelson and come home with Indy, the most hopeful, sad-looking dog in the SPCA. Although she would have sworn it only happened in fairy stories, Alice had fallen in love with Indy at first sight.

Since settling into Parapara, her life had taken on a retirement pace. It was the polar opposite of her previous life as an agent for hire when Uncle Sam needed IT skills in dangerous situations but couldn't be officially involved. Now she painted, read, watched old movies and took Indy for a daily walk at the peaceful Milnthorpe Park. Once a week she headed to the roughly equidistant towns of Tākaka or Collingwood to stock up on supplies. Apart from the gentle changing of seasons, one week was much like another. Alice was happy enough, though she suspected this new life couldn't last for ever. It was idyllic – but was it her? And what about her past? Would it really let her go?

Sipping her wine and stroking Indy, who had joined her on the couch after demolishing her dinner in record time, Alice absentmindedly listened to the news as she stared across the estuary. The news seemed to be constantly on repeat since she had settled into her new life. Covid kept mutating, vaccines kept evolving and the world kept trying to rewind to 2019. The promises countries had made to limit climate change at the COP26 conference were, like wedding vows in Vegas, a good idea at the time that hadn't lasted as one-in-a-hundred-year weather events daily hammered parts of the globe. Two such weather events had threatened her new community since she had moved in but, so far, she had suffered no damage.

Russia's new leaders had refused calls to let the International Court of Justice try Putin, preferring to keep him confined near the town of Kyzyl in southern Siberia where photographers regularly snapped him horse riding bare-chested. They had their hands full trying to repair the damage he had caused both inside Russia and in Europe.

Crazy right-wing political parties were on the rise and finance ministers across the globe blamed the war, Covid-19, inflation, and the lure of crypto currencies for the financial mess they were making. They ignored the twin drunk elephants in the room – inequality and greed – snoring and farting with gusto.

She was listening, although it was more as background noise, when a news item piqued her attention.

'Coming up, Dan's here to look at the one-in-a-hundred-year weather bomb that's heading for Auckland, and journalist Grace Marks speaks out about the hate mail she's received after her investigations into New Zealand's alt-right. See you after the break.'

As the adverts rolled, Alice refilled her glass, deep in thought. She had kept an eye on Grace's stories, enjoying the journalist's recent 'open-heart surgery' on New Zealand's alt-right. Now it seemed that the alt-right was stalking Grace and the media thought their actions serious enough to feature on the news.

Snuggling into the couch, she increased the volume when the news restarted. After Dan had enthusiastically warned Aucklanders to keep indoors, smiling as only weather forecasters can at impending storms, Abbey Wakefield's story started. It centred on how the level of online hate mail, including rape threats, that Grace was receiving had markedly increased when she had started investigating the alt-right. Strangely, at least to Alice, the story made rape threats sound like an occupational hazard for female journalists. The concerning turn came, according to Wakefield, when someone started leaving notes in Grace's letterbox in the middle of the night. The story peaked with the fact that last night those responsible had stuck "dead man's hand" to her front door with a knife.

'Dead man's hand,' said Alice quietly.

Grace had looked natural in front of the camera, making the point that this sort of activity wasn't going to put her off investigating and reporting on the alt-right. The final words of the story were the ones Alice dwelt on: 'My plan is to identify all those responsible, nip this in the bud, but I may need help.'

Alice paused the news, picked up her wine and snuggled into the couch. She sat looking at the view as she digested the news item. Rape threats via email, posting notes in her letterbox, that was concerning enough. But using a knife to stick dead man's hand to Grace's front door, that seemed a serious escalation.

After starting dinner and unnecessarily tidying the lounge, she sat next to Indy. Staring at the stars that were beginning to dominate the night sky, she arrived at a decision. Turning to her dog, she said, 'Fancy a road trip to meet a friend of mine?'

Indy tilted her head.

'Well, she's sort of a friend.'

Recently arrived in the North Island, Marla Simmons watched the receptionist at Williams and Haricot reluctantly pass on her message. Having left her Alice Green identity in the South Island, she had dusted off an alternative identity, Norma Smith, for the trip. She and Indy had driven from Parapara to Palmerston North, crossing Cook Strait on the Interislander. Indy, who had to stay in the car during the crossing, gave Marla her saddest, guilt-inducing look when she realised she had to stay in the car. When they had arrived, she found her dog asleep, curled up like a cat on the driver's seat – she was fine.

The receptionist had tried his best to put Marla off. 'Mr Williams is *very* busy'. Marla's casual jeans and sweatshirt look clearly hadn't impressed the immaculately dressed and groomed young man. Used to operating in the US Army where assertiveness was vital for motivating action, she smiled politely but firmly insisted.

After giving her a cold look bordering on bitchy, he picked up the phone. 'Mr Williams, there's a *woman* at reception who *insists* she needs five minutes of your time.'

Maintaining his icy look, he asked, 'He wants to know what it's in relation to?'

'Tell him … I'm back from my South Island roadie.'

'Your *roadie*, right.' The receptionist closed his eyes as he relayed the information. 'Oh,' he said in disbelief as he hung up the phone. 'Apparently he'll be right out.'

Marla smiled warmly; there was no need to gloat. Being on the reception desk of an accounting firm was hardly anyone's dream job.

Seconds later Damien Williams, the lead partner of the firm, came hurrying along the corridor. Over the decades many professions have developed a uniform look, if not a uniform. Lawyers favour an expensive, upper-crust appearance – though at the exorbitant rates they charge, for what is mostly administration, there's no excuse for not dressing like a peacock. Accountants are comparatively the dull, brown night birds of the business aviary. In Damien's case, the look didn't match his personality. When he saw Marla he slowed, his face going through a range of expressions as surprise turned to recognition.

'Hell, Norma, I hardly recognised you with long blonde hair. The last time I saw you, you had a jet-black crew cut.'

Standing, she beamed and gave him a warm hug. Damien hadn't changed a bit, not even his suit. As she hugged him, she took the few seconds she needed to remind herself that for Damien she *was* Norma Smith – an ex-marine, divorced, who became stuck in New Zealand during the pandemic and decided to stay. She would need to keep alert, her skills as an agent would be rusty.

Taking a step backwards, she said, 'You look great, Damien. Slimmer?'

He laughed. 'That's your memory being kind. Do you have time for a coffee?'

'Sure have.'

In a café near his office, Marla filled Damien in on what she had been doing since they last met eighteen months before. Loosely accurate, she changed the names of places and made no mention of her renting a house in Parapara. She didn't like having to lie to him, but she also couldn't risk letting him, or anyone, know where she lived. Since she'd had to run from her former employer, she knew the US would be keen to get their hands on her – and not in a loving way.

'How come you're back? Is the travelling bug out of your system?'

'Not yet,' she said, not knowing whether that was the truth or a lie. 'I think being in the army, moving from place to place, has formed a lasting imprint. I'm here for a few days helping a friend.'

Damien's face fell. 'I take it you'll be staying with him while you're here?'

'No, I can't stay at *her* place,' she said. 'If you're still single, I hoped I could stay with you like last time. No pressure, I can always slum-motel it.'

Breaking into a broad grin, he said, 'I'd love to have the pleasure of your company again.'

'I have a favour to ask though,' said Marla.

His face turned serious. 'Go on.'

'I didn't take your advice. I found myself a companion.'

This was too cryptic for Damien. His face remained serious bordering on disappointed.

She put a hand on his arm. 'I've brought my dog with me. She's only little – Indy. You'll love her. She's house-trained and I'll make sure she doesn't chew your favourite blue slippers.'

His raucous laugh drew the attention of most in the café. 'Indy's welcome too. I haven't had a dog in years, but the section is fully fenced.'

'Damien, you're so kind. What time do you finish these days?'

He checked his watch. 'That reminds me, I better get back to the office, another boring meeting. I'll be home a bit after six.'

'Great. I'll bring over supplies and make dinner. We can spend the night in … if you like.'

Grinning, he said, 'I like.'

CHAPTER 7

Looking in her letterbox, Grace let out the breath she didn't know she was holding. Even though the notes arrived in the dead of night, it was a relief to find her letterbox empty. No threatening notes, bills, or threatening bills. She surveyed her street; it looked ordinary, boring even. That was partly the problem – it was easier to deal with a physical threat, no matter how intimidating, than a psychological one. She was dealing with a pack of spineless cowards who were nowhere and therefore could be anywhere.

Making sure she locked her front door behind her, she put her laptop bag on her desk before heading towards the kitchen and coffee. As she entered the lounge she stopped; the scene that greeted her was wrong. Nobody should be home. Her son was in Auckland, her daughter at university and Sean at work. The house should have been exactly as she left it – but the French doors were wide open.

Silently she picked up the self-defence container on the mantelpiece; she had placed three of them strategically around the house – just in case. It blinded attackers with pepper spray, coloured them with a fluorescent dye, flashed a strobe light in case you missed their eyes, deafened them with a klaxon and sent a text to Sean. It was pulp mayhem in a can. Illegal in New Zealand, she had bought three on the internet and was surprised when they arrived unmolested by customs.

Holding it in front of her, she felt a mix of scared shitless and fucked off as she stalked towards the French doors. Pausing when she reached them, she surveyed her backyard. It was as if she had walked into a horror movie that was ratcheting up the suspense. Her yard was unchanged except for the two sinister-looking wine glasses, one empty, and one half full, on the outdoor table.

'Is it that bad?'

The voice from behind her hit her like a hammer. Whirling around, in full fight mode, she was ready to let a stream of agonising spray into her attacker's face. But the owner of the voice stood well out of range. She stared at the diminutive figure.

'That looks dangerous,' said the intruder. 'I thought we could talk about it over a wine.'

'What?' said Grace. 'Who the fuck are you?' Even as she spoke, her brain was piecing the jigsaw together. While the build, posture and face were familiar, the long blonde hair, sunglasses, stylish black knitted top, ultra-fashionable navy suit and black low-heeled pumps were throwing her.

'You don't recognise me? Great. I tried to dress like a journalist, to look like a colleague, but I think I went too formal.'

It was the voice that allowed a calming Grace to complete the jigsaw. The same person but with short black hair, a leather motorcycle jacket over a plain grey T-shirt, jeans and red motorcycle boots emerged in her mind. A heavy groan escaped her. 'For fuck's sake, Marla, you took ten years off my life.'

'Sorry, but in my situation, I can hardly knock on the front door.'

Grace stared, trying to make sense of her visitor's reappearance. The last time their paths crossed, Marla had dropped off her laptop at the hospital where she was recovering from a non-accidental car crash. Framed and wanted by the police for murder, Marla had left a note for the sleeping Grace before she disappeared to the South Island. Grace had never expected to see her again.

'You can put the – whatever that is – down if you like,' said Marla. 'I'm not from the government, not anymore, but I *am* here to help.'

Grace looked at her arm as though it wasn't hers – ramrod straight and aimed at the intruder, her finger poised on the nozzle of the can. Lowering the can, she remained on guard. Marla was a former agent, soldier, and trained killer.

Pushing her sunglasses onto the top of her head, Marla said, 'You know I'm not here to hurt you.'

She did know that because, if the American was here to hurt her or worse, the scene would have played out differently. Putting the can on a nearby bookcase, she said, 'I don't understand why you're here. What's going on?'

She tensed as Marla walked towards her. The woman held a wine bottle in one hand and raised her other hand in a calming gesture. 'I brought wine. Let's have a drink while we chat and enjoy the sun, I've hardly seen it since I arrived.'

Laughing with relief, Grace said, 'I bloody well need a drink after this, you scared the life out of me.'

They settled themselves at Grace's cheap but serviceable outdoor table. Marla poured her a generous glass, topping up her own. They sat in silence for a moment, enjoying the wine.

'Let's cut to the chase,' said Grace. 'I doubt you're here for old times' sake, too risky. And, unless I missed the story, the police haven't charged anyone with the murder they think you committed. Are you here to tell me your life story? That I could use.'

'My life story?' Marla chuckled. 'That wasn't uppermost in my mind. I told you; I've come to help. I saw you on the news, dead man's hand stuck to your door with a knife. From online threats to that, I wondered what they'd do next. Then on the news you doubled down – you said you wanted to catch them all and nip it in the bud.'

'You're here to help me? That's … that's great. I could sure use help, but what if you're seen with me?'

'There's an element of risk,' said Marla, 'but I know what I'm doing, or what I did. For a start, you'll be pleased to know you're not under surveillance from the SIS or anyone else. I checked your car last night too, no bugs.'

'You've been sneaking around outside my house?' Grace raised her voice. 'Under my car?'

'Yeah. I had to make sure nobody was staking you out. I watched for a few hours. It was clear so I checked under your car before I headed home.'

'Home?' said Grace, her voice unintendedly shrill. 'You live in Palmerston North?'

'No,' said Marla calmly, 'I went to where I'm staying. It feels like home, that's all.'

Grace took a big slug of her wine. 'Sorry. I don't usually shriek. My brain's obviously struggling to comprehend what's happening.'

'Fair enough,' said Marla. 'I'm being ultra-cautious. I want to appear on as few surveillance cameras as possible. Despite your efforts, I don't know who might have access or whether the spy agencies are intercepting the camera feeds.'

'True,' said Grace. Despite both the US and New Zealand authorities saying they were not involved in the plan to integrate surveillance cameras, artificial intelligence and facial recognition technology in New Zealand, nobody trusted them. The American was right to tread carefully.

'How have your children taken the threats?' asked Marla.

'They're outraged. They would've made awesome vigilantes if they lived in a different time.' Her face turned serious. 'Their bedrooms are closest to the street, to the front door. They were home at the time.'

'I know, they covered that on the news too. That's also why I'm here. Professionals don't do dramatic threatening bullshit. This creep is an amateur, which makes him more dangerous.'

'How?'

'Because he'll get too confident, think he's a pro and make a dumb mistake. But' – Marla held up a finger – 'it'll make him easier to catch.'

'What will you do if you catch him?'

Marla flashed an eyebrow. 'The journalist smells a story.'

'I bloody well do,' said Grace grinning. 'I reckon there are two options. One, my story set off a lone nutter.'

'Hmmm.' Marla's eyes narrowed. 'Lone nutters are tricky but they're rare. Unlikely, but possible.'

'That's what I reckon. Two, my stories have pissed off the collective alt-right. They've organised one or more arseholes from their membership to play post-boy.'

Marla's eyes remained narrowed. 'That's more likely, especially with the "dead man's hand" play. Still amateur, but organised and careful. They want to warn you off, not land themselves in court where they'll be on public display.'

'So as much as I want to catch whoever's doing it,' said Grace, 'if it's organised, I want to catch their white, pasty-arsed leaders. That would be a story.'

'They can always find another foot soldier,' said Marla, 'but cut the head off the snake and things fall apart; the centre cannot hold.' In answer to Grace's confused look, she added, 'Yeats. It's a military saying.'

'I get it, apart from the Yeats bit. If we cut the head off the alt-right snake, everyone can sleep a little easier in their beds.'

Marla held up her glass. 'I'll drink to that.'

Grace raised her glass and they both drank.

'I anticipated this being a quick operation,' said Marla. 'I'd be home before I could leave the hint of a footprint. This is what we call operational scope creep. It makes it trickier, but interesting.'

'Have you the time to spare?'

'I sure have. I'll need a copy of the electronic and physical threats you've received and when they arrived.'

'Easy. How can we keep in contact without getting anyone on either side of the Pacific excited?'

'I'll establish a secure VPN and you'll need to install the Tor browser. Are you any better with technology, Ace?'

Grinning, she said, 'A few years ago I would've stared at you blankly, but my run-ins with the SIS mean I now know enough to be dangerous. I've installed the Tor browser; it makes the internet slow but it's good to know I'm invisible. And I'm all over "virtual private networks",' she said smiling.

'This should be fun.' Marla proposed a second toast. 'Here's to outing some white supremacists.'

Grace raised her glass. 'In a front-page feature.'

CHAPTER 8

For Marla, it was an insight into what it might feel like if she "settled down". She was sitting in the corner of Damien's couch, her feet on his lap, working on her laptop. Damien, with Indy curled up next to him, was watching one of the interminable spin-offs spawned by the reality TV programme *Survivor*. This show allegedly featured New Zealand celebrities, but she had never heard of them.

During an ad break, he muted the show. 'What a load of crap, I don't know why I bother.'

She looked up. 'Why do you?'

'I started watching because I like Amelia Kerr, I wanted her to do well. I should've stopped watching when they voted her off the island for not wearing a bikini. But you know, I'm invested now. I need to know who wins.'

'They voted her off for *what*?'

Damien chuckled. 'Not really, but those shows love their celebs looking trim with their gear off. Boosts the ratings.'

'And now you're hooked.' Damien made to defend himself but, before he could, she added, 'I get it. I got hooked on a series of *Married at First Sight*. Talk about tragic, but I needed to see the carnage, to get closure.'

Marla's laptop pinged. It was an email from Grace forwarding the messages from her late-night prowler.

'Bad news?'

Made aware that she was scowling, Marla relaxed and said, 'It's from the friend I'm helping.'

He frowned deeply.

Picking her words carefully to avoid revealing too much, she said, 'She's being stalked. I'm helping put a stop to it.'

'How?'

'First we have to find out who it is.'

'She doesn't know?'

Marla shook her head. 'It's not an ex-partner, that would be easy. It's an anonymous creep who wants to stay anonymous.'

'How bad is it?'

She couldn't let Damien know she was helping Grace Marks. If he put two and two together, she would be back to staying in cheap motels. 'Bad, he knows where she lives. Leaves messages under her car's windscreen wiper,' she said, bending the facts.

Grimacing, he said, 'That's not a comfortable feeling. How bad are the messages?'

She read one of the notes from the screen in a matter-of-fact tone. 'I'm going to rape you, strangle you and then rape you again.'

'Jesus, she needs to go to the police.'

'She has. They've been helpful, and they're concerned, but what can they do?'

'What can you do that they can't?'

'Do you remember I told you I was in the US Army?'

Damien nodded.

'I was in Special Ops. Part soldier, part IT geek. They sent me in when they needed technology skills in places where bullets were flying around. I figure I can use those skills to track him either online or the old-fashioned way.'

'You were like an FBI agent?'

'Kind of. Like me, she's an American living here,' she said, bending the story further. 'She's more a friend of a friend.'

His face radiated both interest and confusion. Marla stayed silent, deciding she had said enough.

'Can you track him from the email?'

She shook her head. 'She sent it to me as an image. It's untraceable.'

'What are you going to do?'

'I've looked through the anonymous online comments as well as the notes left in person – there's a pattern. Whenever my friend comments or posts online, two days later he – or I suppose it could be a she – retaliates. They take their time to compose their charming notes and deliver them when no one's around.'

'Interesting,' he said. 'It's not in the heat of the moment, it's deliberate.'

'Calculated and deliberate. My friend posted a short update on social media on Tuesday.'

'That means it could be tonight.'

'I'm heading out later to stake out her street. See who turns up.'

'What's your plan if they do?'

Shrugging, she said, 'No plan survives first contact with the enemy.'

'Helmuth von Moltke,' he said.

She was surprised he had heard of the Prussian responsible for that piece of military wisdom, receiving a grin for the look she gave him.

'And,' he continued, 'he didn't mean you shouldn't have a plan, only don't expect to carry it out blindly after it kicks off.'

'You were so not meant to be an accountant, Damien. You're right and I do have a rough plan in my head.'

Damien raised his eyebrows.

'First, presuming they use a car, I'll get the licence plate. That'll make it straightforward.'

'Not that straightforward,' he said. 'Every government department is ultra-nervous about giving out private information. You could give it to the police.'

'Remember, I'm an IT geek. If I can't hack my way in, I know people who can.'

He raised his bushy eyebrows. 'The mysterious Norma. But why not give it to the police?'

Marla couldn't afford to get involved with the police, though she couldn't tell him that. 'I'd like to have a word with them first. My friend thinks they're just the messenger, she wants to know who's pulling the strings.'

His face reverted to a concerned look. 'What sort of trouble is your friend in?'

'Nothing illegal but I can't tell you much more. I'd be breaking her confidence. You'll have to trust me, there's no danger for you. I'm on the side of the angels.'

He gave her a questioning but acknowledging look. 'And if they don't use a car?'

'That's trickier, though the most likely scenario is they'll have parked nearby. I'll see which route they take and plot a course to get in front of them. They'll be looking over their shoulder, worried about who's following them, a car in front of them shouldn't register.' In response to his look, she added, 'I know, it's not foolproof. I might follow them on foot.'

His frown deepened.

'I've done it before. Don't let my looks deceive you.'

'Good point. I've only known you as an attractive, clever tourist. It's hard to imagine you in fatigues toting a machine gun.'

Winking, she said, 'I can dress up for you if you like.'

Damien's eyes widened for an instant. 'No thanks, you might look too intimidating for me to – well, you know.'

'You haven't had any trouble that I've noticed. Eager I'd say.'

Blushing, he asked, 'What time are you aiming to head out?'

'People stay up watching TV or reading until midnight. Early risers get a head start on their day around five. My gut feeling says this person is ultra-cautious. They want to remain anonymous, so I think they crawl out from under their rock between one and three. I'm aiming to be in position around midnight, to be sure.'

Checking his watch, he said, 'Three hours to kill, fancy ...?' He raised his eyebrows.

'If you're sure you're "up" for it,' she said with her own eyebrow raise.

CHAPTER 9

Night-time stakeouts in winter were challenging.

In her anonymous 2014 silver Honda Fit, Marla parked in the same location where she had staked out Grace's house eighteen months before – on the apex of a bend where she could watch activity on Grace's street from a safe distance. Then it had been daylight and she'd had to pretend to be talking on her phone when Grace had driven towards her position. Now, well past midnight, the overhanging branches of a huge tree blocked the orange street light, leaving her position in mottled blackness – it was perfect. To blend into the night, she had dressed in black, her long blonde hair pulled into a severe pony tail and tucked into her hoodie. It was cold but she had experience of Nebraskan winters and was wearing numerous layers.

She picked up her camera, to which she had attached a 24-70 mm night lens with an ultrasonic motor. Along with painting she was dabbling with photography and had bought the telescopic lens in Dunedin. With little light pollution to contend with at Parapara, after several nights of practise on the beach she had been able to take amazing photos of the star-filled night sky. Indy, who accompanied her on these nocturnal art classes, wasn't a fan of the dark and stayed glued to her leg.

From her secluded position she planned to photograph the rear number plate of cars turning into Grace's street and the front number plate of those driving towards her and out of the street. If they carried on through the intersection, towards her position, she planned to ease out of sight while they looked left and right for traffic. Humans were hard-wired to notice movement; it was an evolutionary trait that saved us from becoming an easy dinner for a predator.

If they arrived on foot, she would use the additional time to plot an intercept course. She had borrowed a windscreen shade from Damien to use so the light from her phone didn't attract attention. When it came time to move, she could reverse around the corner or head straight ahead, lights on or off. With respect to von Moltke's wisdom, she had options. That's if they turned up.

One o'clock came and went. Damien had suggested she take a thermos of coffee to help stay awake. Right now, she would have loved a hot drink but, as she pointed out, where would she go to the toilet? On the way she had filled her car with petrol and bought several chocolate bars, though she hadn't yet touched them.

Over the next hour she photographed eight cars. None had stopped near Grace's house, and none was a repeat visitor possibly casing the street. Stakeouts were ninety-nine per cent tedium. To keep her mind active, she was listening to a Lee Child audio book whose hero, Jack Reacher, seemed to be getting taller, his chest wider and his hands bigger with each book as though he was morphing into Andre the Giant.

Seven cars, a worse-for-wear couple on foot, no activity near Grace's house and two chocolate bars later, three o'clock came and went. Marla finished the last of her chocolate at 3.30am. It looked like a washout. The sweet spot of city slumber was ending, soon alarms would blast early-morning workers out of their beds to service the city's constant demands.

As she went to put her seat back to its normal position, a car turned into the far end of Grace's street, driving slowly. Marla picked up her camera and watched the car park across from Grace's house. She took multiple photos of the driver as they got out. The figure, who was wearing high-viz gear, stretched before opening the boot of their car, taking out a bag and going into what must be her house.

Marla's chuckle turned into a loud yawn. 'Bugger.' As soon as she saw the high-viz jacket, which would have been an odd choice for an anonymous stalker, she knew it wasn't them. After stretching herself, clicking her neck and picking up the empty wrappers, she drove back to Damien's house. Stakeouts were like fishing, you needed patience to catch the big one.

After spending most of the morning in bed, much to Indy's annoyance, she took her dog for a long afternoon walk. In the evening they went out for dinner. She filled Damien in on the boredom of her stakeout, he filled her in on his boring day meeting rich business-owning clients who wanted to pay as little tax as possible without risking jail.

Once again, around midnight, she was in position. And once again, after photographing random cars and people, she abandoned the stakeout when the woman living opposite Grace returned home. Most people lived their lives on repeat. If she watched this scene long enough, she would get to know the pattern of the street's life intimately – as in Hitchcock's movie *Rear Window*.

Marla spent a similar day, except that she cooked dinner, before settling herself for night three. It followed the same pattern as the previous two nights – random cars, a few people on foot and no suspicious activity near Grace's house.

Until 3.05am.

Twenty-five minutes before Grace's neighbour was due home, a single headlight, too faint to be a motorcycle, came around the sweeping corner behind her position and silently whistled past. Marla watched, a small laugh escaping her, as a helmeted figure dressed in black rode away from her on an e-scooter.

Without a doubt, this was her quarry.

She took a dozen photos, though she knew they wouldn't help. Watching through the lens, the rider slowed at the intersection before accelerating towards Grace's house. Riding onto the footpath, the distinctly male figure slowed and stopped next to Grace's front gate. After putting a small item in her letterbox, he turned back towards her, his dim headlight bouncing on the uneven road.

Ducking down, staying low, Marla let him sail past. She had toyed with the idea of improvising and trying to jump him, but it was a low-percentage play – too much could go wrong. It meant that if he escaped, he would never return.

In her rear-view mirror she watched the rider turn left into a side street. Once he was out of sight, she counted to three before starting her car, performing a fast, tight U-turn, and setting off in pursuit, her lights off. The side street curved to the right and, as he wasn't in sight, she accelerated. The street ended in a T-intersection, and she braked hard, edging around the corner where she could see.

The rider had gone through a red traffic light and was rushing down a dimly lit street. The wide four-lane avenue was devoid of traffic as she followed through the red light, headlights still off in case he glanced backwards. Her advantage was that e-scooters didn't have rear-view mirrors.

Just when she thought she had the pursuit in hand, the headlight of the e-scooter disappeared. Expecting he had gone around a bend, she kept following at the same pace. Without her headlights on, the road ahead appeared black, as though she was heading towards a tunnel. As she neared the point where he had disappeared, she had to brake hard because a pair of large iron gates blocked the dimly lit street.

The sign on her left told her the Victoria Esplanade lay beyond the iron gates. Switching off the engine, she got out feeling resigned – she had lost him. The night was still and quiet; the only noise the city could manage was a low, slumbering hum. She gave the gate a mild kick, it was more than solid. The heavy chain and padlock that secured the gates glistened with dew; he hadn't touched them. Besides, it would have been a clumsy escape plan and taken several minutes to unlock, go through and relock the gates.

Either side of the gates looked impassable for an e-scooter, but when she checked she found a wide-open pedestrian gate hidden in the shadows. That made sense as an escape plan. As soon as she was through the gate, an inky darkness enveloped her. She stood still, listening, waiting for her eyes to adjust. The only noise was the gentle rustling of leaves; the sound of an escaping e-scooter long gone.

Using the torch function on her phone, she walked along the path which opened out onto a pond. Skirting around it she was soon standing on a smooth tar-sealed road, perfect for an e-scooter. At around 25 kph, the rider would have been long gone before she arrived at the gates.

She gave an admiring grunt. Smart. Professional? Unlikely.

Back in her car, Marla used Google maps to reconstruct the route he had taken. The Esplanade was a large park bordered on one side by the Manawatū River. There were two entry points for cars, but because a track ran beside the river, there were dozens for pedestrians or alt-right dickheads on e-scooters. He could have gone a hundred different ways.

She was confident he didn't know she had followed him; this was a pre-planned route that he had thought made tracking him impossible. It didn't feel professional, he was dropping hate mail on an e-scooter after all, but he was smart and careful.

As she drove to Damien's house, Marla reflected on the positives from her night's work. She now knew the method the man used to drop his notes into Grace's letterbox. And he would likely use the same method in the future. It was the smart play – if you were one hundred per cent sure you hadn't been seen. If he was being chased, unless the pursuer was on a faster e-scooter, the route through the pedestrian gate was the perfect getaway.

It was, however, the thinnest of bottlenecks – for an ambush.

CHAPTER 10

The young server sported a dubious-at-best pornstache that he must have cultivated lovingly for weeks. Marla ordered two Americanos and received a confident-but-hopeful eyebrow raise as acknowledgement before she headed to where Grace was sitting. The café they had arranged to meet at was one she had previously reconnoitred, selecting it because there were no internal security cameras. As a further precaution, she watched the comings and goings for five minutes after Grace arrived to make sure no one was tailing her.

'I ordered you another Americano,' she said joining Grace.

Grace stared at her before she rolled her eyes. 'You've seen my SIS file. The whole world seems to know how I drink coffee.'

Marla gave her a wink. 'It always pays to do your homework before joining the fray. I kept a copy, ran through it before I arrived. Still prefer chardonnay?'

'Who doesn't?' said Grace. 'From your message, it sounds like you saw this being delivered.' She passed Marla an A5 piece of yellow paper folded in half.

'I did,' she said studying the note but not opening it. Before she stole into Damien's bed, she had sent Grace a message warning her that there would be another note in her letterbox, asking her to bring it along.

'I'm sensing disappointment,' said Grace.

'You are.' She took Grace through the method they had used to deliver the note, the over-confident server bringing their coffees in the middle of her story. She stressed that now she knew their operation, her task was easier.

Opening the note, she put it on the table face down to hide the message. 'It's an A4 piece of paper cut in half. That edge' – she ran her finger along the long side of the note – 'isn't straight.'

'Is that material?'

'Do you have A4 yellow paper in your house?' asked Marla.

'Sure. The kids have accumulated all the colours of the rainbow over the years.'

'Exactly. Parents have coloured paper. It's not an absolute, but it's suggestive.'

Grace sipped her coffee, letting her continue.

'I didn't get a close look, but your stalker's male and has an e-scooter. They're not uncommon, but it's not a mode of transport I'd associate with the alt-right.'

'Definitely not,' said Grace. 'So, borrowed? Maybe he's a parent who doesn't want anybody, maybe even his partner, to know what he's doing.'

'He's venturing out in the middle of the night,' said Marla. 'Would you notice if Sean ducked in and out around three in the morning?'

'I would bloody well hope so. It's Sean who sleeps like the dead, not me.'

'That means, assuming we're dealing with a hetero-stereotypical male, that his partner either knows or she's not on the scene.'

'It'll be a she,' said Grace. 'He's an alt-righter. There's no place in their tiny brains for any relationship other than male-female, missionary-position, female-orgasm-an-accident.'

Marla stifled a laugh. 'I always thought journalists would make handy detectives. It's a similar skillset.'

'But does it help?'

Marla wrinkled her nose. 'A bit. I get the impression this guy has plenty to lose, hence the caution. He's in the alt-right scene but he wants to stay away from publicity. I mean, if he did want to show his face, he and his mates could stand outside your house with placards, hurling abuse at you and the media's unfair treatment.'

'There are plenty who think the media are dishonest,' said Grace. 'Another of Trump's gifts to societies across the globe, media distrust and hatred. He's the arsehole that keeps giving.'

'That means,' said Marla, keeping the conversation focused on the immediate problem, 'if we can find out who he is, we might be able to lean on him.'

After a short silence, Grace asked, 'Are you going to read the note?'

'Yeah, but I already know what it's going to say, roughly.' She turned the note over and read it dispassionately. *Unless you crawl back in too you're hole youll miss you're childrens weddings.* It was like the other notes Grace had received, misogynistic, insulting with appalling grammar, but this one contained a direct threat.

A disgusted grunt escaped Marla. Her military training had allowed her to keep assignments at arm's length, to not allow any aspect to get under her skin. That was preferable but, after the morning's events, she was feeling a personal stake in the fight. She turned the note face down.

'Same old same old,' said Grace.

'It is, but the threats of violence are escalating. This is the first time they've threatened your life if you read between the lines. And he is so shit with grammar.'

'I didn't think you'd notice,' said Grace. 'He is, at least, consistently shit – I wondered if it's deliberate. You know, make him seem illiterate when he isn't. And you're right, it's the first time they've actually threatened me, though I read it as another scare tactic.'

'How much online abuse are you getting?'

Grace shrugged. 'To be honest, I wouldn't know because I don't read most of it. We've been trialling a system where a moderator reads our online messages and all the posts and comments that clutter our inbox. The idea was they'd bin the drivel, leaving us with the interesting stuff.'

'Sounds like a useful system.'

'It was, but after a week the interns and students hired to do the moderating wanted out. They couldn't handle the constant garbage they had to read. You can't blame them. God knows how content moderators working for the big social media platforms survive.'

'From what I've read, they don't,' said Marla. 'What happens with your email now?'

'I ignore ninety per cent of it. It means I miss the odd intelligent comment, but to get those would be like trawling the sewer for gold.'

'I can imagine,' said Marla. 'I've kept an eye on your online activity. It seems that when you publish a story, or post on social media, they, whoever *they* are, pounce.'

'That's how it works. A troll sees my story and posts a comment to alert their followers and they pile in. They're like ants; one finds the chocolate, lets the colony know and soon there are hundreds.'

'Apt analogy, although they sound more like cockroaches.'

'Anonymous cockroaches that need squashing.'

Marla drummed her fingers briefly. 'Anonymity, that's their shield. I'd bet some of the online comments come from the cock on the e-scooter. You wouldn't know because you don't read them, and besides, his message isn't for you, it's for the other roaches in the woodpile.'

'It's called a dog whistle,' said Grace, 'but it seems cockroaches have ears too.'

'What if we "out" these people?' asked Marla.

'Dox them?'

'Sort of. Doxing is usually malicious; in this case, it would be righteous. Let's stick with "outing". The point is, would naming and shaming work?'

'I think so, especially if they're prominent somehow. Internet trolls throw shit because they can stay in the shadows. But, how? Can you track them electronically?'

'No,' said Marla. 'If a crime's been committed, the police can get the records from internet service providers and the SIS can access the information if they've a warrant. The problem is, these people haven't committed a crime, and even if they have, the police don't know whose records to check. And if they used a Tor browser, they're untraceable.'

Grace laughed. 'They're hiding behind the laws that protect privacy. How fucking ironic is that? And the same tools you use to make sure you're invisible are available to them – and me.'

'That means our best bet remains catching the e-scootering postie.'

'Have you worked out a plan?'

'I have. What say you post that note online as an example of the abuse you're getting. Write something like – this journalist ignores the infantile actions of alt-right creeps *driving* around, playing post-boy in the middle of the night.'

'I can sure do that. You think it will get an immediate response?'

'Not immediate, but in a day or two. Make sure you mention "driving", it'll help convince him he's a genius. Apart from that, if you want to get a message to me, use the VPN I set up.' She sang the next words. 'When he goes down to the woods again, he's sure of a big surprise.'

Grace tilted her head.

'I'll be the one having a picnic,' said Marla raising her eyebrows.

CHAPTER 11

In front of flashing cameras and cheering supporters, Seb Ball was in his element. ProtectNZ's *Saving New Zealand* road tour was in full swing, the crowds swelling at each stop. Standing at the side of the Michael Fowler Centre's cavernous main auditorium, away from the main media contingent, Grace watched the lurid display with fascination. It reminded her of North Korean scenes where everyone clapped fanatically to lessen their chances of getting on a re-education list, or worse. The difference was that this crowd seemed genuinely over the moon to see Sleazeball in the flesh.

It was a risk attending a ProtectNZ rally. Following the populist playbook, they targeted mainstream media outlets, calling them a corruption New Zealand needed to "sort out" – whatever that meant. When they said, "the media", what they meant was anyone who didn't agree with their position, and Ball had singled Grace out for special attention. Ever since she had interviewed him, and didn't play ball, he had gone out of his way to highlight her as an example of how socialism was corrupting the media. His supporters lapped it up, but all it told intelligent people was that he didn't know what socialism was.

Consequently, she had come to the event in a long, dark wig and dressed in keeping with the crowd in jeans and an old FCUK T-shirt she had dug out of her drawers. No one was likely to recognise her because everyone was staring at the stage and their bald leader. About a third of the crowd were recording the event on their phones, which allowed Grace to take photos of the crowd without looking as if she was taking photos of the crowd.

Over time, she had witnessed the followers of ProtectNZ morph. Originally, like the incongruently named "freedom protests", they had attracted every group that had a beef with the government: farmers desperate to disavow their part in climate change, anti-vaxxers, ban 1080 devotees, Hobson's Pledge supporters, alt-right groups, Nazis and white supremacists, Covid deniers, anti-fluoridation zealots, 5G conspiracy theorists, anti-media campaigners, traditionalists and, bizarrely, Trump supporters – Grace called them collectively "The Dorothys" in her stories, a *Wizard of Oz* reference to the fact they seemed unaware that they weren't in Kansas. ProtectNZ was the latest "thing" this rabble wanted to swamp. To take ProtectNZ seriously was to join the lunacy, and most mainstream organisations and lobby groups wisely stayed away.

But the nutters were gone. ProtectNZ had not only ignored them, they had given them no quarter and the great unwashed who followed them had slunk back to their various fringe political parties and sad echo chambers. Now the audience was frighteningly mainstream which allowed the lobby groups and the conservative media to add their weight.

Their popularity put the collective media, Grace included, in an unenviable position. The media had to cover them, but the act of reporting on them also promoted them. When she wrote a story based on her interview with Ball, shredding what she called "the populist nonsense ProtectNZ was trying to harness", the deluge of emails, comments, posts and tweets was insane. ProtectNZ was demonstrating the time-tested adage that all publicity is good publicity.

The worse aspect was that Ball was no Trump. He wasn't a billionaire, misogynistic narcissist. From a safe distance, he was personable. He spoke well and didn't focus on himself the entire time. His performances were scripted – orchestrated as Grace was fond of observing – but Ball played his part well. Keeping away from the controversial political poles, he sailed a line down the middle appealing to people on both sides of the political spectrum.

The crowd quietened. After the tedious introduction of ProtectNZ's local representatives, who each felt obliged to say a few words, Ball took over. He loved playing to an audience. His voice and the choreographed crowd reaction melded into a beehive-like drone. Because she had heard it before, Grace had to physically shake herself to concentrate on what he was saying.

'I don't need to remind you' – he gestured to the crowd – 'that as a country we risk economic ruin unless we, the people, act to stop this insane socialist agenda.'

The crowd roared its agreement.

'Our livelihoods and our lifestyles will be unrecognisable. The industries that put New Zealand on the world stage will be decimated. And where will that leave us? We'll be riding e-bikes, eating overpriced imported plant-based burgers and who knows who'll be sponsoring the All Blacks, maybe China.'

The crowd uttered a collective groan.

'I've talked to ordinary New Zealanders – and I've listened. Honest, hard-working Kiwis trying to run businesses, painted as enemies of the people, as climate change deniers. They've told me they're tired of listening to, and having to vote for, politicians who have forgotten who they're representing.'

A chorus of outraged voices agreed.

'I can remember the days when the arrival of tractors at Parliament made *all* politicians nervous. Not today. Not today.'

Closing her eyes, she listened while Ball bounced from issue to issue, trying to cover the frustrations experienced across the economy, the law and government policy. Restrictions on tree felling; the corporate tax rate; limits on herd numbers; water restrictions; house prices, fines for contaminating groundwater; the price of petrol; the price of fertiliser, the Emissions Trading Scheme; and the ultimate dog whistle, any issue that involved co-governance.

Grace tuned out of Ball's speech; the messages didn't change. Soon enough he would conclude the event with the usual appeal for people to join and donate. She was more interested in the crowd – who was in it and why. Ball was in Wellington Central; it was as far from his logical support base as she would have thought possible, yet hundreds had turned out. And the crowd was a diverse mix of people. Half looked as if they'd come from rural areas, but there were as many dressed like they were off to the opera.

Interviewing a sample of the audience would make interesting copy but it was too risky, at least tonight. Maybe a colleague could do the interviews, an intrepid young journalist wanting to get amongst the action – a new face they wouldn't instantly tar and feather. She tucked the idea away as Ball finished speaking. The crowd yelled their support and stomped their feet. With a final wave, Ball and his entourage disappeared backstage. The crowd mercifully quietened as they filed out. Grace didn't fancy inching along in a crowd in which many would be unvaccinated, so she stayed leaning against the wall as the crowd thinned.

Then pandemonium broke out.

It started with a sound, a single bang from behind the stage. It sounded like a car backfiring or a single loud firework, except that the noise wasn't right, and the situation was all wrong. Modern cars seldom backfire, and who lets off a single firework inside the Michael Fowler Centre?

The sound ushered in a split second of silence. The crowd collectively froze mid-stride to listen and work out what was happening. The piercing scream that followed a second later confirmed that whatever was happening, it wasn't good. Prior to the Christchurch terrorist attack, many people might have rushed backstage to help. But New Zealand had changed.

The scream set off a cacophony of noise and movement as people surged for the exits. Grace pushed herself hard against the wall as people pushed, jumped over seats, and jostled to get out. She considered yelling for calm, but no one would have heard or taken notice. The crowd had developed tunnel vision, they all wanted to get out the nearest exit.

As people pushed past her, Grace edged the other way until she was clear of the agitated crowd. It wasn't that she had a death wish, but equally, she hadn't heard another gunshot, if it was a gunshot. If it was a terrorist-style attack, there would have been similar screams to the one that started the stampede. Pulling off her wig and taking in a calming breath, she headed towards the stage and the exit Ball and his entourage had taken.

Nearing the front of the auditorium, now littered with assorted ProtectNZ paraphernalia, she was alone. People were still battling to exit the auditorium, although the commotion was lessening as people got away. No one noticed as she climbed the steps onto the stage. Agitated sounds came from behind a set of curtains on the other side of the stage. She crossed the stage silently, opening the curtains just enough so she could slip into the room unseen.

The scene she came upon was frantic. In the middle of the melee of people dancing around in circles was Ball, lying on the ground, writhing and holding his shoulder. She could hear him repeating, 'This wasn't meant to happen.'

'It's okay, you're going to be okay. Stay quiet,' said a man to Ball as he tended to what Grace assumed, given the sound she had heard and the blood on the ground, was a gunshot wound to his shoulder. Around Ball numerous people pushed, panicked, and ordered each other about when they weren't getting in each other's way.

To make herself heard above the chaos, she called out forcefully, 'I'm assuming you've called an ambulance.'

Another brief period of silence ensued as everyone, Ball included, turned to look at her as though she had intruded on their private party.

'Of course,' snapped a no-nonsense woman and the chaos resumed. Grace recognised her from the rally. She had stood behind Ball on stage with a way too enthusiastic "I've-drunk-the-*Flavor Aid*", smile.

'It doesn't pay to assume,' said Grace as the woman bustled towards her. 'What happened?'

'Sebastian's been shot,' she said holding back tears. 'They were waiting for him.'

'They?'

The woman's face changed to confused. 'Who are you anyway? What are you doing here?'

'It's Grace Marks,' said a groaning Ball. 'The left-wing journalist.'

'Just journalist, actually,' said Grace.

The woman, who had turned towards Ball, looked back at Grace with her face twisted in anger. 'Why are you here? Haven't you caused enough trouble?'

Nimbly sidestepping around the woman, having had enough of whoever she was, she moved closer to Ball. His wound looked nasty but not life-threatening, not that she had any experience with gunshot wounds. Like most people, her entire knowledge had come from movies and TV shows.

'Come to see what your *comrades* have done?' Ball hissed through clenched teeth.

If this was what it seemed, an attempted political assassination, Grace was aware she had walked into a momentous incident in New Zealand's political history. If it was a politically motivated attempt on Ball's life, New Zealand would never be the same again. The scene was, however, low-key and ordinary. Ball was bleeding, but it didn't appear serious. People milled around, waiting as the sirens grew louder.

'This is the first time I've seen you speechless, Marks,' Ball hissed.

Grace shook herself back to reality. 'What's there to say? I hope you're not badly hurt. Help is on the way. Comrades? You think everyone who doesn't put money first is a communist but now's not the time to get into that.' Looking around she asked, 'Where are your security guards?'

He coughed in obvious pain. 'I didn't think I needed them, not in Wellington.'

At that moment, police burst into the room and took command of the scene. Grace left them to it and edged away to the periphery. An ambulance team arrived a minute later, and eventually Ball was stretchered away. The ambulance crew's unhurried actions confirmed Grace's suspicion – Ball was going to live and she wasn't sure how that made her feel. But if he didn't make it – what a story!

The police insisted everyone remained at the scene so they could take statements. While they waited, the no-nonsense woman came over to Grace while she was sitting on the floor, capturing her thoughts while events were fresh in her mind for the story she would be filing. Journalists need luck and she was in the right place at the right time.

'You're the cause of this,' said the woman, her eyes wide. Grace pegged her for late forties; the clothes were businesslike but closer to bureaucrat than banker. She was likely a key part of the team that helped Ball look slick.

Looking at her neutrally, Grace said, 'No I'm not.'

'Yes, you are. You've whipped up hate against Sebastian and you wrote those terrible lies.'

Grace momentarily closed her eyes. 'Listen, lady, I know you've had a shock so I'm trying to be polite. If you leave me alone, we'll both get on much better.'

'I will not leave the likes of your sort to—'

'Fuck off,' Grace said barely below the level of a shout.

Everyone stared at her before a new voice broke the silence.

'You sure know how to piss people off, Ace. Is it a gift?'

Grace turned to the familiar voice coming from the doorway.

A tall woman stood framed in the double doors, dressed in a black suit with a crisp white shirt. The lights in the room cast her face in shadows, but Grace knew who she was. Getting to her feet, she said, 'I thought you might turn up, JP. The SIS, one step behind the action. Some things never change.'

CHAPTER 12

The strident woman continued to look daggers at Grace as they each waited for the police to interview them. After enduring as much of that as she could handle, and having filed a brief report for RNZ on her phone, she left the room. To keep warm and occupied she had completed a third slow lap of the deserted Michael Fowler Centre auditorium.

Her phone, which she checked every few minutes, told her it had crept past 10.30pm. The shooting had occurred after the rally finished, around 9pm. For the last ninety minutes she had been waiting for the police and, as SIS agent Jenna Parata was on the scene, the domestic terrorism unit of the SIS, to interview her.

She sent another text to Sean – *Still waiting. Won't be home until well after midnight, don't wait up. Hope kids weren't too demanding.*

His reply came within a minute – *All good here. Hope they don't arrest you.* He added a winking emoji.

'They've done it before,' she muttered.

While she waited, she kept an eye on developments in the news. The local media websites had extensive coverage of the shooting and her story was the lead on the RNZ website. If Ball survived – and the hospital had listed him as "serious but stable" – he was going to become a hero of the people if the online reaction to date was any indication.

She checked other media sources, but they had simply rehashed her story to make it sound as if they too had been on the scene. They added no new information and no mention of anyone involved in the attack which meant no one had claimed responsibility. The police said they planned to hold a press conference in the morning. That meant a long night ahead for many, including the ones waiting to interview her.

'Grace Marks?' The voice came from a young, male, uniformed police officer. 'We're ready for you now.'

'About bloody time,' she said under her breath.

A police detective – it was their attitude more than their clothes that made them stand out like dog's balls – and the SIS agent had established a temporary interview room in a backstage dressing room. The police officer indicated a chair for Grace before leaving, closing the door behind him.

The agent subtly winked at her as the detective commenced. 'For the record, you're Grace Marks, a journalist?'

'Yes. How come you left me until last? Professional discourtesy?'

The detective ignored the gibe. 'I'm Detective Sanderson. My colleague, who I can't name at this juncture, is here because this incident may be classified as an act of domestic terrorism.'

Grace pouted as she stared at Parata. They had come up against each other on several occasions and had developed what Grace considered a professional friendship. The smart move was to stay quiet, let the process continue, but having to wait for so long had aggravated her. 'Your colleague is Jenna Parata, a lead agent in the SIS's domestic terrorism unit.'

The detective, surprised, turned to the agent.

Lifting a calming hand, Parata asked her, 'How long after I left the hospital did it take you to find that out?'

'Thirty minutes, but I was heavily concussed.' When two rogue American agents had run her off the road in an attempt on her life, she had woken up in hospital and Parata had arrived to question and debrief her.

In answer to the detective's look, Parata said, 'It's all right, we've history. Too much bloody history as it happens. Arrive at a shooting and she's invariably hovering near the victim.'

'You make me sound like a vampire. How did the interview go with that woman by the way?'

The agent sniffed. 'You're lucky she's not in charge.'

The detective, regaining his composure, interrupted. 'Let's get back to the shooting, I want to get home before it's daylight. You're here as a witness, not a journalist, Marks.'

Grace gritted her teeth. 'Am I under arrest?'

'Let's not turn this into a pissing competition,' said Parata. 'We just want to know what happened. Take us through it, Ace. As I know you're going to cooperate, I'll let you ask a couple of questions at the end. Give you a head start on your journo rivals.' Parata made an it-will-be-fine gesture in response to the detective's look. 'She knows what we can and can't feed her.'

Leaping at the deal, Grace took them through what she had seen from the time she had her dinner to until the police arrived.

'Where did you stand?' asked the detective. 'Our team checking the security camera feeds hasn't identified you in the crowd.'

'I was wearing a wig.' To prove it, she took it out of her bag.

The detective's eyes narrowed. 'Why?'

'Because,' she said, 'Ball paints the media, and me in particular, as an enemy of the people. I didn't fancy having a bunch of right-wing dickheads harass me.'

Turning the screen so they could all watch, he played a security camera feed of the crowd. 'Show us?'

She pointed to herself, leaning against the wall.

'You blended in well,' said Parata.

'When you're normal, looking like a git is easy. It's the gits who try to look normal that stick out.'

The detective fast-forwarded the recording, pausing it when the crowd started to panic. 'You didn't move until after the shooting,' he said.

'Disappointed?' asked Grace.

'I am,' said Parata, flashing Grace an eyebrow raise.

'Can you recall anything out of the ordinary at the rally?' asked the detective.

Grace shook her head. 'Moronic, right-wing bullshit, but it was their standard song and dance show.'

The agent sniggered. 'I can see why you wore a disguise.'

'What about when you went backstage?'

Replaying the evening's events, she said. 'I didn't see what happened. When I arrived, the attackers had gone. Ball was groaning on the floor. Everyone was in a state of mild panic. After I had dodged around the woman commandant, I remember asking Ball where his security guards were. He said he didn't think he'd need them in Wellington.'

They listened intently, staying silent.

'I was keen to find out what had happened but I didn't get a chance, not with that woman throwing her weight around. I assumed the would-be killers had escaped down the stairs that I could see past where Ball was lying. With his entourage flapping about, I started composing a story to file, then you turned up. That's pretty much it.'

'Cast your mind back,' said Parata. 'Did any aspect of the scene you encountered strike you as odd?'

Even though it was only two hours ago, it was late, and Grace was struggling to recall events with clarity. 'It all happened so fast, let me look at my notes.' Frowning, she read her hard-to-decipher notes. Towards the end, her eyes widened.

'That's right. When I arrived at the scene, Ball was twisting on the ground in pain and muttering "It wasn't meant to happen". Something like that.'

'It wasn't meant to happen?' repeated Parata slowly.

Nodding, Grace said, 'It could've been shock, but even at the time it sounded' – she wrinkled her nose – 'wrong.'

CHAPTER 13

Marla didn't think the e-scootering postie would turn up the morning after Grace had plastered his note all over social media, but she decided not to take the chance. She spent another fruitless night on a fruitless stakeout, this time in a different location.

The following night she wasn't to be disappointed.

Fifty metres from the pedestrian gate he would in all probability emerge from, she sat in her car in an unlit part of the street. Dressed in black, she had parked facing away from the gate so she could watch in her rear-view mirror, lessening the chance of him seeing her as he headed to Grace's house.

At 3.05am a wide-awake Marla whispered 'Jackpot,' as she saw a light flickering in the trees. An instant later, the headlight of his e-scooter came into view as he rode confidently through the gate. Sitting low in her car, she watched him cruise silently past, sail through a red traffic light after the briefest pause and disappear down the same side street.

As predicted, he was following his tried and trusted route – why wouldn't he? She couldn't fault him for that. It was a solid plan if you expected the only danger would come from the under-resourced local police.

In approximately five minutes he would return, that was more time than she needed. Throwing her warm coat onto the passenger seat – she needed to be nimble – she grabbed her small operational bag. First, she Blu-Tacked a piece of paper over her rear number plate. Walking briskly to the pedestrian gate, she tied a black rope she had found in Damien's garage across the opening at what she calculated was his chest height. She didn't want to injure or kill him, she wanted him to land in a heap at her feet.

From the bag, she took out the Glock 19 she had taken from two CIA agents who had tried to frame her for murder. It wasn't loaded. She intended to use it as a theatrical prop. If events didn't run to plan, she had her army training to fall back on. She might be rusty, but self-defence training never left you. Finally, taking two long zip ties out of the bag, she positioned herself behind a large gum tree twenty metres from the gate. It was ideal cover.

Two minutes later she watched a faint headlight cross the avenue and head towards her position. Pushing her back against the tree to make sure she was out of sight, the quiet whine of the e-scooter cut through the night as it approached. She mentally ran through the steps as they would unfold. He would ride past her position, slowing as the gate was narrow and the path ahead pitch-black. She would fall in behind him unseen. Then, as per von Moltke's advice, it would depend on what happened when he hit the rope.

Taking a deep breath in through her nose, she watched as he passed her position, slowing more than she had expected. Marla waited an extra beat to ensure he wouldn't see her when she sprang in behind him. As predicted, he had no chance of seeing the black rope, riding into it relaxed and, until that moment, carefree. The rope caught him across the chest, stopping his upper body. Inertia meant the e-scooter and his legs kept travelling forwards. Like a child on a swing, his legs arced upwards before gravity took over and he landed flat on his back, the e-scooter clattering into the darkness.

As he was no doubt trying to work out what had happened, Marla jumped astride him, the unloaded Glock pointed at his head. With the world around them black, she could see the fear in the whites of his eyes. He was in no danger of dying – but he didn't know that.

'Roll over or die. I won't say it twice.'

Struggling to comprehend what was happening, he didn't move. She kicked him in the ribs with her heel, not hard but hard enough so he obeyed. He rolled over reluctantly and, after putting the Glock in the back of her pants, she dug her knee into the small of his back and zip-tied his hands then feet together. As she expected, he was powerfully built – the alt-right loved pumping iron.

Rolling him over, she roughly dragged him to the gate, propping him in a sitting position with his back against the metal bars. His eyes opened even wider when she took a knife out of her other pocket, unsheathed it, and brought it up to his face.

Bending close, she whispered, 'Don't move a muscle.' She slid the knife blade between his face and the helmet strap, the metal of the blade would feel like ice. His eyes screwed tight as the pressure increased until the strap gave way, and she pushed off his helmet.

'For fuck's sake,' he hissed. 'Why didn't you unclip it?'

'My way's more fun. Relax. If I wanted to kill you, you'd be dead already.' Marla used the knife to cut the black rope from the gate, throwing it towards her bag still by the tree.

'What do you want?' he asked, his voice raspy. The fall had knocked the wind out of him.

'In a perfect world, you not to be on the planet. Which pocket is your wallet in? I don't want to touch you any more than necessary, your type is worse than Covid.'

He stared at her.

Marla kicked his feet, spinning him so he was staring into the pitch-black Esplanade. 'I don't like asking twice.'

'Front right pocket but …'

'But what?'

Glaring angrily, he stayed quiet.

Kneeling, she put her left hand around his throat while she took his wallet out of his pocket. With a disgusted grunt, she said, 'Gross. You could've warned me you'd wet yourself.'

'Fuck you.'

Standing, she shook her head, saying to herself, 'I didn't think I'd need gloves.'

He licked his lips. 'There's no money in it … bitch.'

'Your arsehole personality is returning, how charming. I should warn you, I'm not the blushing kind, I'm the kick-you-in-throat-to-shut-you-up kind.' Emptying his wallet, she arranged the items on the footpath in a neat pattern. As she had expected, he was confident enough to carry ID. Taking out her phone, she set the camera app to flash as the orange streetlight filtered through leafy trees made them impossible to read. She took two photos of the cards, two photos of the side of his head as he twisted to hide his face and two photos of his scowling face after she kicked him and said, 'I'm going to take your photo. It's over to you how much pain you'll be in when I do.'

'I thought this was a robbery,' he said. 'What are you going to do, Marks? I've got a family.'

'I'm not Marks, you moron. And you should've considered your family before you became an obscene, threatening offence to society' – she looked at the neatly lined up cards – '*Regan Western.*'

She enjoyed the look on his face as his situation dawned on him.

Retrieving his e-scooter, which was heavier than she had expected, she asked, 'Who does the scooter belong to?'

He stared at her.

'Come on, I want to go to bed. You've already cost me too many interrupted nights.'

'It's my daughter's.'

'Fuck,' said Marla, putting the scooter onto its stand. 'I was going to confiscate it but it's not your daughter's fault she has a moron for a father.'

'Who are you? What do you want?'

'I'm your worst nightmare because half an hour after I wake up tomorrow … today, I'm going to know all about you. Where you live. What you do … or should I say *did*. People don't like working with racist criminal scumbags.'

Even though he was clearly scared, Marla saw he was struggling to keep his anger in check. He was probably a person everyone considered a great guy, except those who knew him. To them, he didn't have to pretend, he could be himself – an arsehole.

'And it's not what I want,' she continued. 'It's about what I'm going to do.'

'And what's that?'

The fact he managed to make his words sound threatening annoyed Marla. She bent close to him. 'I can see why your wife left you.' His eyes flashed with anger but, before he could open his mouth, she added quietly, 'Listen carefully. What you're doing is going to result in exposure, humiliation, and a chat with a judge. I'll settle for putting you on display, but I'd prefer your bosses. I'm giving you forty-eight hours to consider your future. If you don't want to play ball, I'll hand your details over to Grace, the police and the SIS at the same time.'

Stepping back, she carefully checked her surroundings before picking up the rope. He glared as she used her fingertips to pick up his damp wallet and cards. Smiling, she tossed them over the chain link fence into the inky black.

'You fucking bitch,' he hissed. 'I'm going to—'

He didn't get the chance to finish his sentence, her kick, not hard but aimed at his diaphragm, cut him short. As he fought for breath, she bent over him again. 'You need to sort out your anger issues. If I thought there was the remotest chance you would become a threat' – she theatrically took out her knife – 'let's just say wetting yourself would be the least of your troubles.'

She pushed him over with her foot as he struggled for air. Putting her knee into his back again, she used the knife to cut the zip tie around his feet. 'I'll be in touch, and you can tell me what you've decided. Oh, and I'd think carefully who you tell about our tender exchange. I mean, how much do you trust your friends? I'm sure they're not the type to double-cross an associate because he fucked up. Just because they usually do doesn't mean they will. Or will they? In my experience, those with money and power do whatever's needed to keep their money and power.'

Marla stood warily, ready in case he decided to be stupid. He didn't. As she walked to her car, she could hear him spluttering as he tried to get air into his lungs. As she drove away, she watched him in her rear-view mirror as he struggled to his feet. It would take him at least half an hour to free himself and find his belongings. By then, she would be snuggled in with Damien and Indy.

Instead of turning left towards Damien's house, she turned right at the lights. It was a minor misdirection more out of habit than necessity. When she was around the corner, out of sight, she pulled over to remove the paper from her number plate. The police pulling her over was not the way she intended the morning to end.

Yawning, she headed to Damien's house with the intriguing thought – *Who was Regan Western going to be?*

CHAPTER 14

Agent Parata flashed her credentials at the police officer guarding Seb Ball's hospital room. Dressed in what passed for a uniform for SIS employees – a black jacket, white shirt, black trousers, and sunglasses – she was about to enter the room but heard an agitated voice on the other side of the door. She listened intently but the words were too muffled for her to make out the conversation.

Parata had joined the SIS after waking up one morning knowing with clarity that she didn't want to live and die in an accounting firm. Starting as a surveillance officer, where she learnt the ropes, she had soon moved into an operational role. Now, seven years later, she was the lead agent in the domestic terrorism team. The work, the odd hours and the secrecy suited her current lifestyle. She told friends and possible romantic candidates she had a job as an investigator for Inland Revenue – that killed work as a topic of conversation.

She entered the room without knocking – it was a four-bed room with the other three beds left unoccupied as a precaution. Ball, sitting up in bed with a phone to his ear, glared at her. His face was red and, judging by the look on his face, he wasn't happy with whoever was on the other side of the conversation. She raised her eyebrows in response.

'I need to go. We'll discuss this later.' Terminating the call, he looked up at her, still glaring. 'What's the meaning of this? You can't barge in here unannounced.'

Taking off her sunglasses, she said, 'Kia ora, Mr Ball. Who were you speaking to?'

'What's that got to do with you?'

'I don't know yet.' The agent flipped open her credentials, holding them briefly for him to see. 'I'm curious about why you're angry. I mean, you've just survived an assassination attempt, I expected you'd be, what – relieved?'

Running a hand over his head, he said, 'You're right. I guess it's the …'

Looking out the window, without turning around, she asked, 'It's ... the what?'

'You know, the shock of it all. Why would anyone want to shoot me?'

She spun around. 'Shoot you? You don't think they tried to kill you?'

'Well, yes, of course. But why?'

Shrugging casually, she scrutinised his reaction. 'It's not my place to speculate why, I'll leave that to the police. I'm with the domestic terrorism unit.'

'You think they were terrorists?'

'Until we have more details, it's hard to know. They weren't boy scouts though, were they? You're a bit of grey area. You're not a politician but the movement you're leading is political. The question in my mind is, were they random nutters or was it an attempt to' – taking out a packet of chewing gum, she popped a piece into her mouth – 'influence the political landscape?'

Ball shifted in his bed awkwardly but stayed quiet.

'How's the shoulder?'

He moved it, grimacing at the effort. 'Sore, but they tell me there'll be no lasting damage.'

Pulling over a chair, she asked, 'What can you recall? Take me through what happened.'

'I've already told the police what happened.'

'I know, you can tell *me* now.'

Ball exhaled theatrically. It made him look like an unhappy child who wants to leave the table but his parents have said no. Chewing slowly, she sat emotionless, studying Ball's body language.

As he was about to speak, she took her phone out of her jacket pocket. 'You don't mind if I record our conversation?'

'Is it really necessary?' Ball looked a combination of annoyed and uneasy.

'I take rubbish notes. This way I won't miss a word.' Parata finished with what she hoped was a winsome look.

'If you must.'

Turning on the recording app, she said, 'Start with how you arrived at the venue.'

Ball briefly closed his eyes. 'We were ahead of schedule, and I was hungry, so we had dinner at a restaurant near the Michael Fowler Centre.'

'What time was that?'

'Around six.'

'Go on,' she said.

'Over dinner, we chatted about the evening and upcoming events. We headed to the Michael Fowler Centre around seven fifteen.'

'Did you have a security detail?'

He shook his head. 'We thought we wouldn't need them, not in Wellington.'

'We?'

'Well,' said Ball licking his lips, 'me actually.'

'Just you?'

'I've never felt unsafe in Wellington. I thought them an unnecessary expense, so I gave them the night off.'

Parata stared at him for a long moment. 'How did you go into the venue?'

'We went in the front. It was a chance to say hello to supporters. Shake hands, kiss babies. PR stuff.'

'Which way had you planned to go in?'

Ball frowned. 'I'm not sure. Usually, we'd arrive by car and go in the back way.'

'Which was the way you were leaving when they jumped you? Was your car at the back of the Michael Fowler Centre?'

'That's right,' said Ball slowly.

'Take me through what happened from the end of whatever it was you were doing.'

'Now listen, are you trying to be offensive, agent whoever-you-are?'

'Agent Parata.' Ball was right, she was. It was an old tactic, push the right buttons to see if you could shake information loose. The sequence of events around the shooting struck her as odd. When Grace had mentioned what she heard him say at the scene it had added to her suspicions. 'And no, I'm here to find out what happened, that's all.'

Ball stared at her. 'Someone tried to kill me, I do not need your attitude right now.'

'Fair enough, Mr Ball. What happened after you finished?'

Taking his time, he took her through the end of the rally, posing for photos on stage before his manager ushered him offstage and they headed towards the exit.

'Your manager is Ms Pilkington?'

'That's right.'

She refrained from commenting about the redoubtable Ms Pilkington, figuring Ball might explode. 'No security detail, so you walked in front?'

He took his time to answer, his face pinched, before he nodded.

'Take me through what happened.'

Ball had the sort of look people have when they're not sure what to order from the menu but the server is hovering. 'It happened so fast. Two men – I think.'

'You think?'

'One could've been a woman.'

'You couldn't tell?'

'They were wearing motorcycle helmets and leathers. The one in front was a man, no doubt. He was waving a gun in my face. The other one stood a pace behind, obscured. To be honest, the gun had my full attention.'

'He was *waving* the gun?'

'Sort of like this,' he said demonstrating with his uninjured arm. 'I guess he wanted to make sure everyone knew he was armed.'

'What did he say?'

'It was hard to make out through the visor, but it sounded like, "You're a disgrace to society."'

Parata had to bite her lip to maintain a poker face. Besides, it was the same story he had told the police. 'Who were they?'

'Sorry?'

'I mean, did you recognise anything about them? Were they wearing any insignia?'

'Ah. No, nothing. They were in black; their helmets were black too. Is that significant?'

She shook her head. 'What did you do?'

'I called out for everyone to be calm.'

'I believe you said, "I've got this."'

Ball wet his lips. 'That sounds right.'

'Got what? What did you think was happening?'

'Two activists trying to spoil the rally.'

'Dressed in black waving a gun?' she said. 'Activists want to be recognisable, that's the point, isn't it?'

Ball winced as he adjusted his position. 'As I said, it happened in a blur.'

'Fair enough. You said, "I've got this". Everyone stayed behind you. What happened then?'

He looked at her blankly. 'He shot me.'

'How far away was he?'

'I stepped towards him. Maybe two metres, a bit less.'

Her eyes widening, she said, 'That close?' She already knew this from his police interview but wanted to press.

Ball spoke slowly. 'I think so, yes.'

'You're lucky to be here. I mean' – Parata held out her arm, her hand mimicking a gun – 'if he holds the weapon at arm's length, the barrel's what, half a metre away. Hard to miss at that range. Did he sound nervous?'

He nodded. 'His voice was high-pitched, he sounded panicky.'

'That would explain it,' she said. 'A couple of mis-dressed activists, panicking because they brought along a gun.' Before Ball could speak, she added, 'Carry on?'

Drawing in a deep breath, he blew it out unevenly. 'I hit the ground. Sonya, Ms Pilkington, screeched and they ran off. Tony, our business liaison, tried to help me but he didn't know what he was doing. Luckily, I wasn't bleeding badly.'

'Luckily,' echoed Parata, causing Ball's eyes to narrow. 'According to what you told the police, they used the stairs to get away.'

'That's right.'

'Nobody chased them?'

Ball shook his head. 'Everyone was in shock. Besides, who chases after armed attackers?'

Parata nodded in agreement.

'Have the police caught them?' he asked.

She scrutinised his body language, unsure. 'Not yet, but there are a few CCTV cameras around. The police will find them – if they're activists.'

'Why if they're activists?'

'Because, despite what TV shows imply, you don't have to be that slick to avoid identification – if you know what you're doing. A couple of panicky activists should fit in the amateur category.'

Ball stayed quiet.

Tapping her phone to stop the recording, she said, 'Thanks Mr Ball, you've been super helpful.'

'You're welcome,' said Ball, noticeably relaxing.

As she reached the door, her hand on the door handle, she turned around. 'Oh, that's right. Why did you say, "This wasn't meant to happen"?'

'Did I?' Ball's forehead wrinkled.

'Several times apparently, before the ambulance arrived.'

'I was in shock. I had no idea what I was saying.'

'Interesting. I'll pop back – if I need to clarify anything.'

CHAPTER 15

Regan Western sold cars. He worked for a dealership in Feilding, a town Marla discovered was fifteen minutes from Palmerston North. Selling cars must be profitable because he owned a large house in the town on Fraser Drive, a location real estate agents might describe as "suburban bliss", a term she considered oxymoronic.

It had taken Marla a matter of minutes to discover Western's life history because he had voluntarily plastered it over numerous social media sites. Born and raised in Feilding, he was divorced with three children, his ex-wife was a leading real estate agent in the town. The divorce part fitted with his nocturnal activities. He was also a big follower of rugby and, if you followed the "right" breadcrumbs, of all thing's alt-right.

It amazed Marla that these infantile twerps posted pictures of themselves in closed groups thinking they wouldn't become public. The best piece of social media advice she ever heard was to treat what you put online, including email, as visible to everyone, including your mother. If people heeded that simple advice, they wouldn't post selfies of their private parts or Hitler-look-alike photos. It wasn't rocket science but it was wisdom seldom followed.

She had given him the weekend, a full forty-eight hours, to stew. Now, from where she had parked, she had a clear view into his office using the telescopic lens of her camera. His official title was sales consultant, which was simply an overinflated term for car-shark. As she was watching he left the car yard, returning ten minutes later with a takeaway coffee and brown paper bag, the sort they used for pies or savouries. She let him have a bite of what turned out to be a sausage roll before ringing him from a burner phone with a programmed temporary number.

By the time the receptionist had put her call through he had demolished the sausage roll.

Wiping his mouth with the back of his hand, he said, 'You've got Regan.'

'I do believe I have. Is that Regan Western, the car dealer?' Marla had the call on speakerphone so she could watch him through her camera.

'Sure is. Are you looking for a new car?'

'No, an e-scooter – for riding at night.'

He sat bolt upright.

'No, it wasn't a dream, Regan. I'm real. The question is, Regan Western, have you decided who's appearing in court?'

'Listen here—'

'Oh, I'm listening,' she cut in, 'but not for much longer.'

'You haven't any evidence it was me.'

He was right but he couldn't know that.

'Do you think I got lucky when I tied the rope across the gate?' Before he could reply, she added to her bluff. 'Or maybe I've watched, videoed and photographed you enough to know exactly where and when to tie the rope.'

'Fuck. I need time to think.'

'Even if you could think, you've run out of thinking time. I want names. Your one chance to avoid starring in your own headline is for the people above you to star instead. If you lie, if the names are bullshit, I pull the trigger – figuratively.'

Western digested this in silence as Marla scrutinised him. His body language wasn't what she had expected. He should have been a study in lose-lose decision-making, but he was sitting with an air of confidence he had no right to have. Interesting.

'Fine,' he finally said. Marla watched him pick up a piece of paper. 'But I'm not doing this electronically, leaving a trace. I'll meet you at six o'clock Wednesday, at The Lookout on Highfield Road.'

Marla's eyes narrowed. 'How long will it take to get there from Wellington?'

'By car, a couple of hours.'

'I wasn't intending on walking,' she said, enjoying her subtle misdirection. 'I'll find it. How are you going to give me the names?'

'I'll write them down and put them in an envelope. You have your passenger window open, and I'll pass them over. You put all the evidence you have on a flash drive and do the same. I do a U-turn, and hopefully that's the last I'll see of you.'

'That sounds like a plan.' She clicked off before he could add a comment that might piss her off. He hung up but she saw he kept holding the piece of paper. He used a mobile phone to make a short phone call, no more than twenty seconds. Leaning back in his chair he ran his hands through his hair.

Putting the camera in her lap she said to herself, 'That was way too easy. He had a plan. He didn't care about copies of the files. He makes a call to say, what?' She let her mind digest possible scenarios. Whatever plan he had developed, he thinks it's running and that I'm coming from Wellington to fall for it.

Looking through the camera, she saw he was now outside in the lot, looking like he didn't have a care in the world, talking to a young woman busy cleaning the cars. When he finished talking to her, he slapped her on the arse and laughed. Marla grunted but the cleaner took the abuse in her stride, at least she appeared to. She likely had to, to keep her job. Turning the hose on him would be a quick way to whatever unemployment system they had in New Zealand.

Marla plotted a course to The Lookout on Highfield Road.

CHAPTER 16

Agent Parata and Detective Fergusson, the lead detective on the inquiry team investigating the shooting of ProtectNZ's leader, stood on the spot where it had happened a week before. The Michael Fowler Centre was empty, and the centre's manager had reluctantly given them free rein to inspect the area. The investigation hadn't uncovered any leads to date, and they hoped a collective walk-through of the scene might shed new light.

They looked around, weighing up the scene.

'What do you reckon?' asked Fergusson.

'You're the detective, Detective.'

Snorting a laugh, he said, 'The security cameras have given us jack. Have your team dug up any information you're' – he licked his lips – 'sitting on?'

Parata shook her head.

'That's interesting in itself,' he said. 'It means it was well planned. Security cameras, as you know, are bloody everywhere. Let's do a walk-through; you be Ball.'

'Thanks,' said Parata.

'You're standing there, I'm …'

She pointed. 'Witnesses have you emerging from behind that curtain.'

Standing where she had indicated, behind a set of curtains to the left of a set of stairs leading down, he checked his surroundings. 'They chose well. They had a perfect view.'

'No one was backstage,' she said. 'Only Ball and his entourage had planned to exit this way. They could afford to wait; time was on their side.'

'They wouldn't want to wait for too long,' he said. 'If they didn't know when he was finishing, it would add risk.'

'If,' said Parata, flashing an eyebrow.

Fergusson nodded. 'Right, you're walking towards my position.'

Walking slowly, she said, 'You spring out. The witnesses weren't sure, but most likely a man and a woman, the man in front. Ball's walking in front of his entourage, they confront him.'

Pretending to hold a gun, the detective said, 'I wave the gun around, call Ball a disgrace and shoot him – in the shoulder. Ball hits the deck, lands at my feet. Shock keeps everyone rooted to the spot while we' – he turned around and pointed to the stairs – 'make our escape.'

Parata stepped closer. 'If the assailants knew what they were doing, and given there's been no sign of them, it looks like they did, how'd he miss?'

Fergusson raised his arm to imitate holding a gun. 'Unless he was incompetent with a gun, it's not possible from that range. And he'd know he missed. Ball's groaning on the floor and there's no hole in his head. If they wanted him dead, he would've fired again.'

'Conclusion?' she asked.

'Amateur and lucky with the security cameras seems unlikely. So, they only meant to injure him, maybe scare him – not kill him.'

'The shoulder's a good choice,' she said. 'I talked with a colleague, few vital parts to hit. It can go wrong, but you'd be unlucky. Have you identified the bullet?'

'It was a nine millimetre. Too common to trace but we're trying.'

'A low-calibre hard-nosed bullet,' said Parata. 'Less likely to do extensive damage.'

'Correct,' he said. 'Okay, Ball's on the ground, panic ensues. The assailants leg it down the stairs.'

They took their time descending the stairs, looking for possible angles.

Near the bottom, Fergusson pointed to the large glass windows on their left. 'They're on public display now, but ...' They carried on to the bottom of the stairs. 'Seconds later they're hidden in this foyer.'

Indicating the all-seeing orb mounted in the ceiling, she said, 'There's the sole camera that recorded the action after the shooting. They didn't hang around. Exited the building and turned right, out of sight of the camera. Have your team studied the images?'

'They have. Confirmed the one in front was male. The other one – they're not sure.'

'Really?'

'The images aren't crisp, and their motorcycle leathers were loose, and with a helmet on' – he made a go-figure face – 'their best guess is a solidly built female.'

Jenna puffed out a breath.

Outside, they stopped on a pedestrian crosswalk.

'They reach the Commonwealth Walkway. From here they could've gone either way,' said Fergusson. 'Or, as this water feature is dry, they could've headed to the back of the building and then gone left or right.'

'Four options,' she said. 'Then they disappear on a motorcycle into the Wellington night.'

The detective nodded. 'Our money's on the back of the building. Plenty of secluded places to park a motorcycle and plenty of options to take to get away.'

'Makes sense. Well planned and, if you accept the plan wasn't to kill Ball, perfectly executed. But why? It's a risky PR play.'

They stood contemplating the scene as Wellingtonians bustled past, each looking like they were on their own vital assignment.

The agent blew out a frustrated breath. 'What are you going to do now?'

'Keep away from the media for a start,' he said. The idea of talking to the media made Fergusson look ill. 'With no leads, we'll go over what we have, see if we've missed anything. What about you?'

'While it's classified as a potential act of domestic terrorism, I can stay on it. Use the service's resources, but where do I aim them? Are you following Ball? He and his organisation, they're the ones who have gained from this.'

The detective rolled his eyes. 'My boss has advised me to … tread carefully around Ball.'

Parata grunted in disgust.

'I know, but Ball would shout "police persecution" from the rooftops. How would that play in the media? My boss doesn't want the commissioner landing on her like a ton of bricks because we're hassling the alleged victim. Until we have evidence, he's off-limits. Can you put eyes on him?' the detective asked, looking hopeful.

Her eye's rolling, she said, 'That would be fun, but no. He's off-limits to us too. The media can pressure him if they smell a story.'

'Even they'll need more,' said the detective. 'Marks was at the scene, she heard what he said, but it's all speculation. It would be a dodgy story to run.'

'She has a habit of turning up at murder scenes,' said Parata.

Fergusson shook his head. 'Coincidence, there's no link. She's a journo with a nose for when political shit is likely to hit the fan – but I don't like coincidences.'

Taking out her chewing gum, Parata said, 'Neither do I.'

Highfield Road was an uphill one-way street, three-quarters of a kilometre long, The Lookout was halfway along on the left. On each side of the road, and at the end, was farmland as far as the eye could see. There were no escape roads, it was perfect for a trap – for the unsuspecting. When Marla reconnoitred the location, she had stood on The Lookout surveying Feilding and the countryside thinking – they must think she got lucky last time. Did they seriously think she was going to drive into their obvious ambush?

If they did, the other consideration was – to what end? In her game there were two possibilities, intimidate her or kill her. Given the seemingly moderate stakes involved, the kill option seemed excessive, dangerous, and risky. But, as Western would have informed them, she was no push-over, they must be planning a show of force. That raised the stakes. That took them from a band of hillbillies to a nastier level, a darker level.

On the Wednesday arranged, she left Damien's house with Indy and her Glock 19. At 5.45pm she parked on Lethbridge Street, putting Victoria Park, a large, flat playing field, directly between her and Highfield Road. By taking a short cut through the church bordering the park, it would take her ten minutes to walk to the Highfield Road turn-off on West Street.

At 5.50pm she set off, putting her plan into operation. She was wearing a peaked cap with her long hair loose, so it helped obscure her face, a hoodie, and ultra-tight, bum-sculpting three-quarter leggings – she was aiming for a flirtatious, obvious look. On the safe assumption that Western's colleagues would be men, she wanted them fixated on her arse, not her face. In the mini backpack she wore was her Glock, fully loaded in case events soured. Completing her cover, she had Indy on a retractable lead trotting along several paces in front.

The sun had set an hour before, the streetlights bathing the scene in an orange glow. Before she stepped onto West Street and into view, she took out her phone, put in earbuds and started the video recorder app.

To anyone looking, she was listening to music as she walked her dog; what she was doing was videoing her journey in HD.

Walking along West Street she saw what she expected because it was how she anticipated they would have laid the trap. Sitting alone and obvious, there was a car parked on the left side of West Street, fifty metres before the turn-off to Highfield Road. When she had checked the area there had been no cars parked on West Street because there was no reason to park on the street. Every driveway was long enough to cater for three or four cars.

The driver was intently looking at his phone as though he was reading an eBook as Marla walked past, grooving to imaginary music. She recorded the car, its number plate, and as much of the driver as possible, without looking as if she was recording him. The car was a rough-looking, dated Toyota. The driver, also rough-looking, had a shaved head, tattoos on his neck and, even though it was cold, a muscular, tattooed arm hanging out the window. He didn't look like the reading type and, unless he was gay, he would be perving at her arse as planned. If he was on a job, he would keep his mouth shut – not a giveaway but it added to the picture. Although assumptions were dangerous, she was confident he wasn't the brains of the operation, his role would be as an enforcer.

Her calculations were running as planned. Seconds before 6pm she was approaching the turn-off to Highfield Road. She was prepared to hold position if needed by seemingly attending to Indy, but it wasn't necessary. A shiny red sedan slowed as it made the turn into Highfield Road. It might as well have posed for her recording as it quietly eased around the corner, the driver accelerating up the hill towards The Lookout. She didn't look to see who was driving; whoever it was would be on the recording, but it would be Western heading to the drop-off, hopefully shitting himself.

Marla carried on walking behind Indy, seemingly oblivious to the trap she was walking through. Around fifty metres past the turn-off, she sighted the second car. She hadn't seen it until she was level with it because it was parked in the Victoria Park car park which was well below the level of the footpath. Orange street lights illuminated the car park allowing her to take clear images of its number plate but not the driver – the car's interior was too dark. It wasn't technically a car – it was a huge, shiny black ute.

When she had passed through their amateur ambush triangle, she walked across the park towards her car. In the middle of the park she stopped, took out a ball and let Indy off her lead. They would wait at least fifteen minutes, maybe longer, before realising she wasn't going to show – or that she had played them.

With Indy starting to tire – she kept losing the ball in the dark, running in ever-increasing circles trying to find it – and the ute still in the car park, Marla headed to her car. Driving the short distance to a second planned location, she parked behind the church she had walked through earlier. Sitting with her back against the church's wall of remembrance, invisible from the road and the neighbouring houses, she took out her favourite new toy, a DJI First-Person-View drone. It was an expensive toy, but it had allowed her to take stunning aerial photos of the South Island and, in situations such as this, it gave her an operational edge.

After checking the black masking tape covering the drone's lights was secure, so it didn't stand out like a beacon, she put on the control goggles. Sounding like a colony of angry bees, Marla commanded it to climb, the noise receding as it soared. Soon, she was looking at Victoria Park as if it was a map, able to see the three cars in play.

Now it was about patience. If her instinct was correct, and they intended to rough her up significantly, any weapons would be with the rough-looking enforcer. He would follow her up Highfield Road to close the trap. The third car might join the party or hold in place, depending on their plans and who was in the car.

At 6.25pm she watched Western and the enforcer's car headlights flick on almost in unison. They quickly converged on the parked ute. She grinned, her plan was running smoothly, and she was moving one step up the alt-right food chain. The man in the ute wouldn't be the alpha in their hierarchy but he wouldn't be far away.

She zoomed in to watch their brief conference at the ute driver's window, but the drone was too high for her to learn anything. Then the two cars drove away, the ute stayed put. The cars sped off in opposite directions around Victoria Park. They had put two and two together – they had realised the woman walking her dog was their target. Had she stayed at her previous position, they would be converging on her in a pincer movement. That was the art of covert operations, staying one step ahead – always. The two cars stopped in the middle of the road, presumably to exchange a few words, before they drove sedately back to the car park.

This time only Western got out. He leaned in the ute driver's window for a few seconds before all three vehicles left the car park. Western and the ute headed towards town; the Toyota headed in the opposite direction. As much as she would have liked to track the ute, suspecting it wouldn't stay in Feilding she would lose it anyway. Locking the drone on the battered Toyota, she set it to track. It didn't have much work to do – five minutes later it entered the driveway of a house on the outskirts of town.

Because of the noise it made, it was too risky to manoeuvre the drone lower. Instead, she zoomed in on the house as best she could. She watched him get out of the car with a bag, unlock a small shed, drop the bag inside before relocking the shed and entering the house by the back door.

Commanding the drone to return home, she took off the goggles and used a burner phone to work out the address – it was a property on Roots Street West. She dialled 1-1-1.

'Which service do you require?' asked the operator.

'Police.'

'Hold the line.' The operator's voice was calm, unhurried.

A second operator came on the line. 'What's your emergency?'

Marla used a low, slightly frantic voice. 'I saw a man with a gun on Roots Street West. I watched him; he hid it in a shed at the rear of the property.'

Marla could hear the clicking of a computer keyboard.

'Roots Street West, Feilding?'

'Yes.' Marla walked towards the church as the drone's buzzing grew louder.

'Do you know the number of the property?'

After passing over this information, she hissed, 'Shit, I think he's seen me—'

She terminated the call while the drone landed obediently from where she had launched it. She shut it down fast, silencing the angry bees.

She performed a 360-degree environment check to make sure the noise and her activities hadn't drawn any attention. The scene looked closer to midnight than seven o'clock, the street lights illuminating a scene of suburban tranquillity. The only eyes on her were Indy's, who sat in the driver's seat watching her every move.

Kissing the drone, she said, 'I wish we'd met before. You're the best two and a half K I've ever spent.'

Having reclaimed the driver's seat from a reluctant Indy, Marla checked on her map app for a place from which to observe the action. It was too risky to get close enough to watch the action directly, so she drove to a dairy where she bought a packet of chips and a soft drink. Rugged up against the cold, she sat at a battered, wooden picnic table outside the dairy, sharing the chips with Indy. The neighbourhood must be challenging because the owners of the battered, ugly picnic table had chained it to the pavement.

With satisfaction she watched two police cars, lights flashing but sirens off, bear down on her position before turning into Makino Road. Hopefully there was one less alt-right fucker on the streets, or at least armed. Having had time to reflect, it was concerning these morons had no qualms about using armed violence when they felt their operation threatened.

The question was how to take the step up the alt-right ladder? And what to do with the duplicitous Western?

CHAPTER 18

Shutting her laptop, Grace grunted in disgust. Ball was once again loving the media limelight after what he was calling his "near-death experience". Pro-ProtectNZ pundits emerged throughout the media, hand-wringing that an attempted political assassination could happen in New Zealand. Ball's manager – she had learnt the no-nonsense woman was a certain Ms Pilkington – led the crying and gnashing of teeth. What annoyed Grace was that most of the media were lapping it up. Ball's face was becoming as recognisable as the Prime Minister's.

Grace knew how the media worked, its insatiable hunger for eyeballs and clicks, but she also knew where that could lead. Privately held and publicly funded media companies were under pressure to get readers looking at their stories, driving revenue and relevance. Few people bought newspapers, which had the undesired side effect of making the corporates who spent millions on online advertising the media's masters. Compounding the situation, as the world had demonstrated for decades if not centuries, sex and sensationalism sells better than balanced reporting. That was the catch-22 for editors worldwide, including publicly funded outlets such as RNZ. Giving controversial people and groups coverage was good for business but it also gave respectability and fuel to what were dangerous wildfires. CNN may have blamed viewer demand for their extensive coverage of the Trump shitshow, but would he have become president without them? The media were an integral part of the game.

'Can I get you the dessert menu?' asked the server.

Wrestling with her better self, she shook her head. 'Just the bill, thanks.'

Having missed lunch, she was having an early dinner at the restaurant where Ball had eaten on the night the still-at-large assailants shot him. It was an appropriate venue as she was in town for his first press conference since the shooting. Normally she wouldn't come to Wellington for a press conference, which ProtectNZ simulcast on technology's waning death star Facebook, but she suspected this one would be interesting – they usually weren't.

Adding to her suspicion, Ball was melodramatically holding the press conference in the Michael Fowler Centre, metres from the spot where the shooting had taken place. ProtectNZ had scheduled the press conference for 5pm so, after paying the bill, she strolled towards the venue. As she was about to enter the Harbourview Lounge, the venue for the press conference, a strident voice rang out.

'She's not allowed in.'

Two uniformed security guards lumbered in front of the door, blocking the way. Grace turned slowly, her eyes rolling, she knew who owned that voice. Speaking as though she was addressing a child, Grace said, 'It's a press conference, Pilkington. I'm a member of the press.'

Ms Pilkington bustled forward, her hair in an impossibly severe bun, anger rippling across her face. 'Since the *incident*, we've increased security. Journalists, and I use the word loosely, like yourself invite trouble. We have taken the decision—'

'Move left a bit, Ace,' called out a male voice from behind them, interrupting Ms Pilkington's speech.

Grace couldn't tell who it was, the large camera he was aiming at them hid his face. The TVNZ logo on the camera told her he was a *de facto* colleague coming to her rescue. 'This'll make a great shot, ProtectNZ selectively barring journalists. Keep it rolling, Ace, I have the two goons framed behind you.'

Ms Pilkington's eyes flared as her face reddened. 'Turn that camera off, you're not allowed to film out here.'

The camera operator made a noise like a gameshow buzzer, then said, 'Sorry, you're wrong there, darling.'

Taking her cue, Grace asked, 'Ms Pilkington, is ProtectNZ denying access to journalists from media outlets it deems as unfavourable?'

'What? No.'

Her colleague emerged from behind the camera. 'Bugger, no story then. Let's go in, Ace. I need to check out the light.'

The two security guards glanced nervously at Ms Pilkington, who hesitated before nodding, her face radiating displeasure. As they walked past, her colleague winked at Ms Pilkington, increasing her scowl.

'Thanks, Zack, I owe you a drink,' she said as they walked past the relieved security guards.

'You certainly do. What did you do to rub her up the wrong way?'

'Not fawn over Ball's second coming.'

Laughing, he headed away to set up a suitable shot.

ProtectNZ had decorated the room in their typical style – a collision between a Donald Trump rally, a religious conversion event and, with so many images of Ball dotted around, a hair-loss convention. Behind the lectern, raised so Ball could preach from on high, was a wall of New Zealand flags interspersed with the ProtectNZ pull-up banners. The room was three-quarters full of the usual assortment of recognisable media identities. Grace found a seat near the back so she could survey the room.

In front of a huge banner of Ball shaking hands with a farmer was the lectern, partly obscured by microphones and cables. Blatantly mimicking the movie *Citizen Kane* but on a budget scale, ProtectNZ had meticulously cultivated this image of Ball preaching in front of himself – a man of the people.

The TV media, hoping to catch the eye of the *Dancing with the Stars* producer, dominated the front seats with the remainder of the room organically formed along the established media pecking order. Behind the TV division sat the journalists Grace most readily admired. They dived deep into their investigations, writing stories of substance. Once upon a time, these journalists dominated the media, including the front rows, but the dramatic decline of newspaper sales, and the rapid increase of inane social media platforms, had squeezed many out. In the back rows, where Grace felt most comfortable, sat the newbies and freelancers.

A colleague in the second row waved out, signalling for her to join her. Grace shook her head mouthing, 'I feel safer here.' Her colleague laughed.

She checked the time, five minutes until kick-off, though Ball would be fashionably late.

As she was taking the measure of the room, a tall woman quietly slipped into the seat next to her. Grace kept looking straight ahead, ignoring the newcomer.

'Kia ora e hoa,' said the woman. 'I figured you'd turn up.'

Turning her head slowly, Grace said, 'I didn't think you'd need to be here, JP. Aren't you watching and listening from those?' She indicated one of the numerous security cameras in the room.

'Of course. I enjoyed watching Pilkington try to get you thrown out. It reminded me of watching you fall off the treadmill.'

'How did you learn to suck the joy out of life? Was it part of your SIS training?'

Ignoring her, the agent said, 'I'm here to keep an eye on proceedings, that's all. Political assassination sits within my brief.'

'Have you, or the police, made any progress?'

The agent shook her head. 'No useful descriptions of the attackers, they knew where the security cameras were and ...' She stopped mid-sentence.

'And?'

'The most basic starting point. We've ruled out random activists so, unless the two would-be killers had a personal beef with Ball, there's no *obvious* motive.'

Grace huffed. 'I would've thought every second New Zealander had a motive. Certainly, anyone who's met him.'

Parata stared at her.

'Yeah, okay,' said Grace. 'Motive to kill him is a bit of a higher bar.'

'Kill him?' said Parata shaking her head. 'It looks like they only meant to wound him.'

'*What?*'

Giving her a confirming eyebrow raise, Parata said, 'They knew what they were doing and shot him from a range of half a metre.'

Grace went to stretch her arm in front of her like she was holding a gun to visualise the scene. Parata's hand shot out, gently easing Grace's arm back down. 'Use your imagination, Ace. Or wait until there aren't so many twitchy security guards watching.'

Grace looked around as she nodded.

'I've heard it said a few times recently,' said Parata, 'it's not how politics usually works, at least not in New Zealand. Outside the Warren Commission, there isn't a group with an obvious motive or who obviously benefits from trying to take Ball out of the game. Maybe the Green Party or Greenpeace, but it hardly fits with their ethos.'

'What's the Warren Commission?'

The agent half-shrugged, half-smiled. 'It's our internal name for the collective conspiracy theorists. You know, a warren is where—'

'Oh, I get it,' said Grace interrupting. 'JFK and the Warren Commission. It's clever, subtle even – for the SIS.' As the agent's gaze hardened, she continued. 'Someone has to benefit; someone will have a motive. From what you're saying it's too well organised to be randoms from the *Warren Commission*. I might use that, cite the SIS.'

'You're funny. I'd better get back behind the scenes. I'm not meant to show my face too much.' Parata stood up but leaned down and whispered, 'As to who benefits. I said there isn't an obvious motive; but look around. Why are you all here?'

Grace watched her leave noiselessly, unnoticed, which was a good effort for an attractive woman over six feet.

As she took in the room, her eyes came to rest on the larger-than-life image of Ball and the farmer – Ball's image appeared to be leering intently at her alone. The word was already out; he would be announcing that, along with a range of ProtectNZ candidates, he would be running in the upcoming election. ProtectNZ the organisation would become ProtectNZ the political party.

All ProtectNZ's actions appeared orchestrated but, if what the agent had hinted at was right, had Ball agreed to be shot? Surely not. You would have to be bonkers to willingly let someone shoot you for a few points of publicity and Ball wasn't bonkers. What if it went wrong? There had to be another answer.

As Grace was chewing over the unjoining dots, Ball emerged from behind his image and took his position at the lectern. Judging by the look on his face, he was surprised by the silence, that the journalistic community didn't leap to their feet and applaud. He might have forgotten this was a press conference, not a made-for-the-faithful rally. The well-practised confident look and head rub returned when he saw the TV cameras.

'Welcome everyone, thanks for coming along to what is an exciting time for ProtectNZ and ordinary New Zealanders.'

Beaming at the audience, all he got back was a sea of poker-faces.

As he read his prepared statement, he kept looking up expecting a reaction he wasn't going to get, not from the media. Had he ever given a real press conference? Everyone in the room knew what he was going to say, so unless he had a bomb to drop, they were waiting impatiently to ask questions. The time ProtectNZ chose, five o'clock, put time pressure on the TV journalists to get broadcastable content they could run in the evening news.

As distributed, or leaked, Ball announced ProtectNZ would become a political party. They would be standing candidates in as many electorates as possible in the upcoming election. That they planned to announce their list of candidates within three weeks. Ball added that several current politicians had expressed an interest in "waka-jumping" and becoming part of the ProtectNZ party.

Surveying the silent crowd, he ran a final hand over his head before announcing, 'I'll take questions now.'

Before TV's talking heads could fire off their questions to secure their sound bites, Grace called out, 'Which political heavyweights are jumping into your waka? I hear Grey, Baker and Tamaki are keen to grab a *hoe*, but I doubt they know how to paddle. And if you put those egos in a waka, it'll sink!'

After a moment's silence, the media erupted into laughter.

Ball's eyes narrowed when he picked her out of the crowd. 'I'll take questions from serious journalists.' The media stopped laughing and started sniggering. It was like being in a school assembly and the principal was being a twat.

The moment didn't last. Soon he was fielding questions from the left and right but mainly from the political centre. He was in his element. Grace had to wait for twenty minutes until the media had spent themselves. She found it tiresome yet funny to watch alleged adults, who rated themselves a cut above the pack, throwing tantrums when made to wait their turn.

After the TV teams had hurriedly decamped having secured their sound bites, Grace waited until the press conference was all but over before she called out as though she was in an episode of *University Challenge*, 'Marks. Radio New Zealand. What's your party's stance on immigration?'

She sensed Ball would have liked to dismiss her question, call time on the press conference. But the room stayed quiet, waiting for an answer.

He grinned artificially. 'Once we have bedded in our team, we will be looking at the key portfolios, including immigration. Our initial focus, however—'

Cutting him off, she said, 'Yeah, ordinary New Zealanders, you've said that a dozen times. What about your stance on Te Tiriti? How many of your candidates are associated with Hobson's Pledge?'

'As I was about to say,' Ball almost yelled before he caught himself. 'What I can say is our candidates will come from, and represent, ordinary New Zealanders.' Before Grace could launch a follow-up question, he said, 'Thank you for coming,' and stepped away from the podium, Ms Pilkington ushering him away. Before following him out of the room, she paused to give Grace a withering glare.

Giving her a cheery wave in return, she muttered under her breath, 'Cow.'

Zack, the camera operator who had helped her through security, stopped on his way out. 'Ball's an odd one, isn't he? Politically, he looks and sounds like the love child of Key and Luxon.'

Grace's laughter caused heads to turn.

'It looks like he's going to be around for a while, you might not want to piss him off too much, Ace.'

Shrugging, she said, 'Politicians – can't live with them, can't live *with* them.'

It was the camera operator's turn to laugh as he headed out the door.

CHAPTER 19

Indy licking her face woke Marla at 8.20am. She allowed herself to surface gently; Damien must have left for work and Indy had decided she had waited long enough for breakfast. After attending to Indy and using Damien's new barista-grade coffee machine to make a decent long black, she used her Tor browser to access an IT hacker's forum called X-Anon.

The first time Marla became aware of the group Anonymous, the forerunner to X-Anon, was when it came into prominence for its actions against the Church of Scientology. It wasn't an organisation as such, it was a loose collection of hackers with similar world views that started on the infamous platform 4Chan. Creating an online presence under the name "Beast Girl", she had developed a range of useful contacts in the IT hacking world over the years – at the time they loved she was deep inside the US military machine.

When US authorities arrested several Anonymous members, a subset of serious hackers formed X-Anon to distance themselves from 4Chan and its now-defunct darker spinoff 8Chan. They used the site to share hacks, boast, and help each other when required. Their primary goal was to remain in the shadows. So, for example, they never claimed responsibility for their cyber-attacks on Russian oligarchs or the attacks which helped destabilise Lukashenko, Belarus's despised dictator.

In a dark part of the dark web, on an X-Anon news board where users advertised "jobs" they needed doing, she posted the message – *Need to run New Zealand licence plates of alt-right arseholes – anyone?* After checking out a few links, she signed out. She would receive an alert if anyone posted an answer.

Running late, after a two-minute shower, she left to meet Grace. New Zealand was a member of Five Eyes and shared intelligence with its partners, including the US. Now she was out of the intelligence community she had no way of checking the status of surveillance operations, meaning she needed to travel anonymously whenever possible. Ironically, it was Western on his daughter's e-scooter who reminded her that they were a suitable, anonymous mode of transport. The e-scooter system in Palmerston North was ideal. After establishing and funding a bogus account on a burner phone, Marla could ghost her way around Palmerston North at a brisk 25 kph.

When she arrived at the café, Grace, who already had a coffee, was staring at her laptop. Paying cash after ordering a coffee, she sat opposite, wondering when cash wouldn't be an acceptable form of payment. Then every transaction would be recorded, analysed, and on-sold – society was seemingly oblivious to the dark side of the technology.

'Just a sec, Marla.'

Smiling, she shook her head. One day she was going to forget who she was. For Grace she was Marla, for Damien she was Norma and in the South Island she was Alice. Only Indy knew she was all three. After a minute, with Grace still staring at her laptop screen, she asked, 'What's so interesting?'

'What? Sorry, rude of me. I was looking through the crap doing the rounds on social media.'

'I was under the impression you shunned social media.'

'I do, but RNZ subscribes to this fantastic service that trawls through domestic and international news, even the social media sewer, and sends an email with links to articles, posts, and blogs of interest to you. It's like a personalised morning paper without the adverts.'

'Sounds helpful,' said Marla. 'You'd drown if you tried to do it yourself. How do they know what content interests you?'

'They started me on their generic New Zealand journalist profile. I gave them feedback on the content they delivered, and, over time, they tweaked it. I think they employ people to do it, it's too hard for algorithms.'

Marla considered this. Computer algorithms could be inhumanly smart, but a human brain could make leaps and connect unconnectable facts. In other words, people could be instinctive, which was, as she was aware, impossible to programme no matter how clever the pointy heads. 'That makes sense, and if they have a team curating content for journalists—'

'Over time they develop economies of scale,' said Grace, finishing

Marla's sentence. 'Everyone has to make a dollar. That's like gravity, an uncontested law of planet Capitalism.'

Marla smirked. 'For an ex-business consultant, your views are getting more and more left.' Grace opened her mouth, but she didn't give her a chance to speak. 'Anyway, did they include a link to the arrest of an alt-right dickhead in Feilding last night?'

Grace shook her head.

'May I?' she pointed at Grace's laptop.

It didn't take Marla long to find the post she had seen earlier. Even though his profile picture was small, his haircut, T-shirt with its offensive image, the fact he loved showing off his muscles and tattoos, and the I-am-a-loser attitude written over his face – it was the enforcer from the ambush.

Grace looked surprised when Marla returned her laptop. 'Facebook, I'm loath to go into that morass.' She read the post. 'It doesn't look like they arrested him. He's posted that the police had violated his rights because they "stole" his guns. Is this your handiwork?'

Marla raised her eyebrows. 'I can't be sure, but it's likely he intended to use those weapons they confiscated to scare me off – or worse.'

'You're making progress,' said Grace, her eyes wide. 'Are you, are we, in danger?'

'Not yet. They have no idea who I am and that's the way it's going to stay. Besides, as you know, I don't exist in New Zealand.'

'You cover your tracks well,' said Grace. 'Every now and again, when I'm between stories, I do a little digging, to see if I can find a trace of you.'

'It's good to know you can't. When I'm ready to tell my story – and I'm not ready yet – I'll get in touch. Right now, given these people seem happy to resort to violence, our attention needs to be on them.'

'This guy looks nasty,' observed Grace, 'but I can't imagine he knows much more than his own name. Have they used him to drop the notes in my letterbox?'

Marla shook her head. 'He'd be as subtle as an elephant.' She took Grace through her ambushing Western to the previous night's failed ambush they'd hoped to spring on her.

'Bloody hell,' said Grace. 'They're more organised than I thought. E-scootering at three in the morning. I assume you know who they are, are you going to tell me?'

'I don't know who was driving the ute, I'm working on that. I think he's our link to what I hope is the top of the tree. The fuckwit on the e-scooter, his name is Regan Western. Ring any bells?'

Her face twisting as her mind searched for a connection, Grace eventually said, 'Nope.'

'His name never came up during your alt-right investigations?'

'I can look through my files, but I think I'd recognise the name. Who is he?'

'If you didn't know, an average citizen. A sleazy-looking car dealer from Feilding; divorced with three children.'

Grace scribbled a note. 'Do you have plans for him? I mean, can I approach him?'

After a brief pause, Marla said, 'Yes, but I don't have any evidence unless you count grainy photos of a dark blob on an e-scooter outside your house. *He* thinks I have evidence, that's all we need.'

'No photos I could use in a story?'

Marla shook her head.

Grace harrumphed. 'We – journalists, that is – are like the police, we can't act without evidence.'

'You're not talking about all journalists,' said Marla. 'Some use what they read on toilet walls as anecdotal evidence.'

'I love the analogy,' said Grace grinning. 'Social media – the new toilet wall.'

'You could use that in a story.'

'And I will,' Grace said. 'Those journalists you mentioned, they're not real journalists. They're what I term "earnalists".'

'You like that term,' said Marla, 'I saw you use it in a story.'

'Thanks for noticing. Back to the point: what can I, what can we, do without evidence?'

'Not much,' she said. 'I doubt we can squeeze too much from him, not without significant leverage. We know he posted the notes, and he was happy to be an accomplice to violence. What do you think?'

Grace pursed her lips. 'It'd be handy to lean on him, make him an informer, but the alt-right are all in on their homoerotic, musclebound all-male fantasy. What would his "friends" do to him if they found out he was a rat?'

'Given the state of the hired muscle with the weapons, it would be grim.'

'What about the ute driver?' asked Grace. 'Do you think he knows you saw him?'

'Yep. It dawned on them that they'd seen me, but by the time they acted, I was watching from a different location. The same play won't work a second time but, if I was in his shoes, I'm not sure I'd let my superiors know what had happened. Not yet.'

'See if you could handle it yourself?'

'Exactly. I'd beef up security, physical and IT, and see who contacted me. They know I'm not with any law enforcement agency.'

'I wonder who they think you are?' said Grace. 'If you were them, what would you think?'

'If they danced around me? Trained operatives certainly. But that wouldn't make sense unless Ace Marks has her own private army.'

They sat quietly with their coffees, each running through the options. Grace broke the silence. 'What are we trying to achieve? It's the question I used to get business clients focused when they were running around like chickens with their heads cut off.'

'How often were they like that?'

'You wouldn't believe. Idiot CEOs prefer bigger idiots who don't make them look bad. Consultants, like I used to be, have a mantra to remind us to play the long game – milk the cow, don't rip its tits off.'

'Nice,' said Marla. 'In answer to your question, you were in trouble, and I came to help. My focus is removing the threat this alt-right group poses to you.'

'And I'm trying to expose them to public scrutiny. New Zealanders need to know about the society we're living in, not the society they'd like to think we're living in.'

'Will exposing them so the police and the public know who they are, finish them?' asked Marla.

Grace's brow furrowed. 'I would hope so but only maybe. If we could prove they were involved in criminal activity, we could put a few inside for a spell.' After a slight pause, she added with an eyebrow raise, 'And give me a great story.'

Marla's bag buzzed. Taking out all three phones she was carrying, she smiled as it was a response from the post she had put on the X-Anon site.

'How many phones do you need?'

'A few,' she said, 'to stay under the radar.' She paraphrased the message on her phone. 'I can buy ten authorised RealMe logins for the Motochek system for five per cent of a bitcoin.'

'If I knew what motor check was and how much five per cent of a bitcoin is worth, I'd let you know whether it's a bargain.'

'Moto, no "r", chek, no second "c", is your motor vehicle registration system.'

Grace rolled her eyes. 'Misspelling words isn't clever.'

'It's an IT thing.'

'Well, IT "things" should learn English.'

'Anyway,' Marla said, cutting in. 'With a car dealer's RealMe login, we'll get the owner's personal details.'

'Should I have an issue with you acting outside the law?' Grace asked herself, before shrugging. 'Nah. The SIS, not to mention the wealthy, they do what they like. Your actions are levelling the playing field. Will they, the car dealer that is, know you've used their login?'

'I assume my actions will create financial charges, but I can't imagine it's much. If they check, which I doubt they do often, they might realise it wasn't them. They might complain and change their password. That's why they're offering ten.'

'How did they get them from RealMe? That's a government system, it should be more secure than a bank.'

Reading the message, Marla said, 'They usually like to give you the details of how they hacked systems, it's like a badge of honour.' After a short pause, she said, 'He or she said it took seven minutes to hack into two car dealers' systems to, in his or her words, "liberate the information" from internal emails. They didn't touch the RealMe system.'

'Jesus, it shouldn't be that easy. And what's five per cent of a bitcoin?'

Marla tapped on her phone to check. 'About 800 US dollars. That's not bad, it was a lot more.'

'Can you afford that?'

'Sure. I can use the logins for maybe a year until they change their passwords. You never know when I might need to track down an arsehole who needs reminding that dumping their rubbish in the country is not fucking on.'

'Can you check the number plates now?'

'No, it's too dodgy on a burner phone; I'd prefer a secure VPN and a Tor browser. I can bring my laptop around later if you're going to be alone. We can find out who they are and work on a plan. There's no point acting independently, not now that it looks like they're organised.'

'Today works. If you're gone by five, nobody will see you. Do you want a lift?'

Shaking her head and smiling, Marla said, 'It's best if we're never seen together. Besides, on my e-scooter, I can make sure you're not under surveillance.'

It wasn't raining but the sky was threatening as Marla, wearing her Thule laptop backpack, crossed town to Grace's house on a hired e-scooter. It would take an hour for them to run the number plates, work out who they were dealing with and develop a plan of attack. She arrived at 2.15pm, after she had spent fifteen minutes reconnoitring Grace's and the surrounding streets to make sure no one was keeping watch. It gave them a ninety-minute margin of safety before Grace's children or partner might arrive home. That meant she would also beat Damien home, giving her time to take Indy for a walk before making dinner. She was doubling as an agent and a homemaker and, if she was honest, enjoying both roles.

As arranged, Grace had left her side gate open, allowing Marla to ride to the back of the house out of sight from the street. The French doors were unlocked so she went inside and set up her laptop on the dining table.

'Jesus,' said Grace, coming into the lounge and seeing her sitting quietly at her dining table. 'Make a bit of noise, would you?'

'I was trained not to.'

Bringing over two glasses of water, Grace said, 'It's a bit early for wine, isn't it?'

'Are you asking or telling me?'

'I'm convincing myself.'

'Water's fine,' said Marla smiling, turning her attention back to the laptop while Grace dragged a chair around so she could see the screen. 'I'm running a check to make sure I'm an internet phantom.'

The progress bar hit one hundred per cent and changed to a large green tick.

'We're good to go,' said Marla, as the login screen for the NZ Transport Agency online services appeared. 'The logins I bought are individuals who work for car dealers. This guy, Mian, works for Vehicle Direct Limited.'

Marla's fingers danced over the keyboard as she logged in and entered the number plate of the battered Toyota. In a matter of seconds, the screen displayed the registered owner's details.

'That's interesting,' said Grace. 'Geoffrey Western – must be a brother. Can I take a screenshot with my phone?'

Marla went to agree but caught herself. 'No, write it down. Who knows who'll be looking at your photos in the future? Or now?'

'True.' Grace retrieved pen and paper from her office. 'The benefits of having children who grew up before the world succumbed to devices. I've enough paper to last me a lifetime.'

After Grace had copied the first Western's full name and address, Marla entered what she presumed was Regan Western's number plate. The result wasn't what she expected. The dealership owned the car which meant Western drove it as a perk. 'I know his address if you want it.'

Grace pushed the paper to Marla who added Regan Western's address after retrieving it from one of her phones.

'And now for the big one.' Marla entered the number plate of the large, black ute. The screen refreshed in seconds.

The ute was a Black Edition Mitsubishi Triton. All the details of the vehicle were there: chassis number, colour, gross vehicle mass and a myriad of legally required but, for them, pointless details. What disappointed them was that the owner was also a car dealership, in Wellington.

'Bugger,' said Grace.

Marla shook her head. 'You Kiwis like that word, I heard it all the time when I was touring the South Island. Does it have another meaning here?'

Grace's giggle confirmed it didn't.

'Anyway,' said Marla, shaking her head to clear the unhelpful thought, 'I hadn't anticipated that being a dead end.'

They paused their investigations when they heard the unmistakable, and unexpected, sound of the front door opening and closing. They looked at each other, Grace's eyes wide. Marla made a calming gesture as confident footsteps approached them.

Tensing, ready for action, there was nothing Marla could do except wait and see who it was. Besides, a noisy entrance and loud footsteps wasn't the MO of most agents, and the police would have knocked.

A suited male sauntered into the lounge smiling and holding a bottle of wine. It was Grace's partner Sean; Marla relaxed.

A flash of disappointment crossed his face. 'Hey, Grace. Sorry, I didn't know you had a visitor.'

Deciding the best approach was to take command of the situation, Marla stood, and in her best neutral accent, she said, 'You must be Sean. I'm Norma, a journalist from Wellington.'

Marla shook Sean's hand while Grace watched on, her mouth open.

Going over to Grace, he kissed her on the cheek. 'I won't get in your way. I dropped by to put this wine in the fridge. It's, ah … for later.'

Regaining her poise, Grace said, 'Thanks Hon, any special reason?'

'Elle has her protection order, her ex decided not to contest the application.'

Jumping up, she hugged Sean. 'That's fantastic news, she'll be rapt.'

'She was. I nearly ran out of tissues.'

Grace explained to Marla that Sean was representing Elle in a nasty case of psychological domestic violence. She explained how she had used Elle's story for a preliminary article on the hidden scourge of domestic violence in New Zealand and how the justice system, in her view, was complicit by making wealth a condition of access. 'I wrote that it was another clear example of laws written by males for males.'

While Grace was talking, Sean put the wine in the fridge. 'Anyway, I'd better get back to the office, leave you two to your story. What are you working on?'

Marla answered. 'It's an angle on the alt-right story Ace is following. Right now, it's looking like a spaghetti western, but we'll get there.'

After flicking a glance at Marla, Grace beamed. 'We sure will.'

'Sounds positive. Grace likes getting dirty with society's lowlifes. I'm glad she has a colleague in the fight.'

They sat listening to Sean leave, closing the front door behind him.

Looking at her with a did-you-really-say-that look, Grace said, 'Spaghetti western, you're a scream.'

Marla grinned. 'He's in tidy shape. I didn't get to meet him last time, though I wasn't planning on meeting him this time.'

'It won't be a problem,' said Grace. 'Will it?'

'No. If I've a problem with anyone it's you, Ace,' she said with a wink. 'I'm sorry I was here to disrupt your afternoon rumble though.'

'My afternoon what?'

'You know,' she said giving her a knowing look. 'He comes home with a bottle of wine hoping to' – she used her fingers as quote marks – '"celebrate". You didn't see the look in his eye?'

'No, he's not like that.'

Marla made an oh-really face.

'Well, he's not usually.'

'If I wasn't here, he would've bent you over the table.'

'Piss off,' said Grace. 'The children might have come home.'

They laughed for what seemed like minutes. When they had gathered themselves, they sat in quiet contemplation.

Grace asked, 'Was there a shot on the video that could help identify the driver? Maybe you could get it put through Clearview AI?'

Marla's face scrunched. 'It was too dark and the window was up. Even if we had a clear image, Clearview AI's saturation in New Zealand is probably low, at least now.' When she was a US contractor, she had access to Clearview AI's digital repository that contained billions of images of people's faces scraped from every corner of the internet.

'Looking at the state of Regan's brother, I doubt he'll know much about the operation,' said Grace. 'That makes the car dealer our one lead.'

'And we've no concrete evidence,' said Marla. 'You couldn't expose him if you wanted to and, even if you could, it wouldn't make a dent in their organisation.'

'Agreed, Western's not the story. It's bigger than him, at least a couple of rungs higher. But how are we going to get him to talk now? Let alone give us his boss's name.'

'Maybe we don't need to. We could get to him through his phone.'

'Can you hack into it?'

'Not hack,' she said. 'I'll need to reacquaint myself with how the technology works, but there's a vulnerability in the mobile phone infrastructure.'

'New Zealand's?'

'The world's.'

Grace shook her head.

Marla explained. 'Most of the mobile world operates on agreed standards. It's why you can ring Greenland directly from your mobile.'

'Do I need to understand this?'

'Yes, if you're going to use it in a story and not sound like a hick.' She continued, ignoring Grace's suppressed smirk. 'The standard is called the "Common Channel Signalling System number seven", shortened to SS7.' Marla could see Grace's eyes glazing over. 'Basically, there's a hole which countries, including those in the Five Eyes alliance, delight in exploiting. But anyone can do it too with a few items available in stores where geeks shop. I'll get my contacts to set it up, it'll be quicker.'

'I think I get it,' said Grace. 'But in case I haven't – how will it work? You know, in practice?'

'For a short period, we'll be able to see and hear everything he does on his phone. We can't leave it open for long, it increases the chance of detection and we'd get blocked.' A plan was developing while she spoke. 'We need to work out a thirty-minute window when he's likely to contact his higher-ups.'

'How are we going to know that?'

'Because he'll be panicking, desperate to contact his boss because you will have just left his office.'

Grace stared at Marla. 'Me?'

CHAPTER 21

Grace watched Alexandra Moore pick up her desk phone.

'Regan, can you pop into my office for five minutes? Bring Carol too.' Grace heard a muffled 'Sure' before Moore, the manager of the dealership where Regan Western worked, hung up.

'They'll have lots of great stories you can use, Ace,' she said.

'Brilliant,' said Grace.

In less than a minute a beaming Carol bounced into Moore's office. Western entered confidently, took one look at Grace and stopped in his tracks. Moore introduced Carol to Grace before turning to Western, who looked as if he expected Grace to take a large, wet fish from behind her back and slap him.

'Regan, this is Ace Marks. She's a journalist, I'm sure you've heard of her. Ace, this is Regan Western. He's been with us for over ten years.'

Grace, still standing after shaking the woman's hand, extended her hand. 'Regan, have we met before?'

Shaking her hand without meeting her eye, he said, 'No, we haven't met.'

'You're sure? I'm usually good with faces.' She sat in the middle of three chairs, forcing him to sit next to her. 'It'll come to me.'

Moore carried on, her face reflecting that she was aware of an awkwardness in the room. 'This is great news, team. Ace, who has become quite the famous journalist, is writing a column about businesses in the region.'

'You know,' said Grace, 'local interest stuff to help the profile of the community. It's not all international plots and chasing local alt-right subversives.'

The women chuckled, but Western looked as though he might vomit.

'Grace is looking for interesting and amusing stories of car sales. What people have traded in, our well-known clients and what's happened to cars we've sold.'

'Your dealership services both rural and town markets,' said Grace. 'There should be loads of stories our readers would enjoy.'

Carol's eyes lit up. 'We've had several All Blacks over the years, is that the sort of story you want?'

'Perfect.'

'One time …' Carol tilted her head. 'Can we mention names?'

'Sure can. We may need to get approvals, but we can deal with that later.'

Carol nodded enthusiastically. 'I remember one dad, wealthy as, wanted the oldest, most beaten-up trade-in we could get so his daughter knew about starting at the bottom.'

'That sounds ideal,' said Grace. 'If I could get your business cards?'

'I have them here.' The manager's eyes gleamed as she handed over three business cards.

'Thanks, Alex.' Grace took her time looking at each card. 'Regan Western. Nope, still can't place you. Did you go to school in Wellington?'

A pale Regan shook his head, saying flatly, 'Born and raised here.'

She stared at Western. 'It'll come to me, but in the meantime, if you could capture your recollections, I'll be in touch.'

She stood. 'Don't get up, I can find my way out.'

After she left, Grace drove the one minute it took to get to Kowhai Park, where she had dropped Marla with a backpack full of technology twenty minutes before. She found her sitting on a park bench in the weak sun surrounded by hopeful ducks.

'How did it go?' asked Marla.

Giving her the thumbs up, Grace said, 'They loved the idea of free publicity. I'll do the story too. It's easy filing and I can hand it to the local reporters. It'll run well when they're short of copy plus they'll owe me a favour.'

'And Western?'

'Looked ill the entire time. When will you find out if he contacts his boss?'

'As soon as he does. My contact, "FuckQ", is eavesdropping on his mobile number for the next' – she checked the time on her phone –

'twenty-five minutes. He or she will send through any messages or audio files.'

'Fuck you?'

'That's my contact's screen name. It's spelt fuck with the letter q. Q being the made-up phantom at the centre of the QAnon horseshit.'

'Clever,' said Grace. 'Of course, it could be a straightforward "fuck you". I thought the Q drops had stopped?'

'They have, but the conspiracy theory lives on in the minds of the deluded.'

'What if Western doesn't bite?' Grace asked.

'I've wasted my slither of bitcoin.'

'I know you said money isn't a problem, but bitcoins certainly don't grow on trees.'

Marla smirked. 'No, with the amount of power used to create them, they're *killing* trees. I'm sweet. I've squirrelled enough away. It won't last for ever, but for five or so years I'll be fine. Who knows what I'll be doing after that?'

'Do you miss your work?' asked Grace.

Taking her time before answering, she said, 'I don't miss being an agent. I did that because I could, and the money was incredible. Weirdly, I miss the camaraderie of the army, of being in a team where the goal was tangible. Keep the country safe, even though we were screwing over other countries. Outside the army, the world seems all me, me, me, me, me. If you want me to give a toss, what do I get? What's in it for me? That's why I'm here now. It felt the right thing to do. I don't give a fuck that nobody's paying me.'

'Sometimes someone needs to do something,' said Grace. 'That's why I found my way into journalism. I could've stayed consulting, earning five times the money helping government departments tick boxes that did fuck nothing except keep ministers happy.'

Marla frowned. 'Fuck nothing?'

'Have you not heard that story?'

'Is it another of your Kiwi sayings?'

Grace shook her head. 'It's a David Niven story from Hollywood.'

'David Niven?'

'Am I that old?' said Grace with a sigh. 'Never mind, a story for another day. Where was I? That's right, that's why I like chasing stories that make an actual difference, not only the ones that pay the bills – though I do like paying the bills.'

'Do you think there's a big story in what we're doing?'

Grace tilted her head. 'You never know. It's like playing poker, you never know when you're going to uncover a royal flush. I mean, who is Western's boss? Imagine if it's an MP? Woah, there's a serious story.'

Marla laughed, 'I love your optimism.'

In response to a bleep from her laptop, Marla checked her inbox.

'Well, well. My slither of bitcoin may have struck gold.' Showing Grace her screen, she said, 'Western sent a text.'

Grace leaned closer. 'What a charmer he is. "The bitch came to my work. What should we do?" Did you get the number he sent it to?'

Marla gave a single, unenthusiastic nod.

'What's wrong?'

'Given he was careful enough to keep his name off the vehicle register, the phone will be a burner.'

Ducks milled around, hoping for food, while the women sat in silence.

Marla's laptop beeped again. 'He received a call from the same number.' Opening the audio file, they both leaned in to listen.

Without preliminaries, the caller asked Western, 'Marks or the bitch that ambushed you?'

'Marks.'

'What did she do?'

'Pretended she was writing a story about local businesses. Bitch smelt like a cheap whore.'

An outraged Grace opened her mouth but stayed quiet.

'Said she'd be in touch,' continued Western.

After a short period of silence, the caller said, 'We can't discuss this over the phone. I'll liaise with our friends to work out the best approach. Have you told anyone else about this?'

'No one.' Western's voice was an octave higher.

The caller broke an awkward silence. 'Let's all meet Friday at eight, I'll send through the location. Make sure no one follows you. They've caught you out once.'

The audio file ended with a click.

'I smelt like a cheap whore? Western is one C U Next Tuesday,' said Grace.

Marla sat quietly.

'Well?' asked Grace.

'I'm not sure. This guy is ultra-cautious. Why would he risk poking his head above the parapet a second time?'

'We're assuming it was him last time,' said Grace. 'Who do you think "our friends" are?'

Shrugging, Marla said, 'Probably more alt-right creeps.'

The ducks scattered as Grace stood. 'I could do with a coffee. It'll help me think.'

Packing away her equipment, she said, 'Let's head back to Palmy.'

Grace winced. 'Don't say Palmy, it makes where I live sound like an Australian who watches *The Wiggles*.'

Marla sniggered, 'I take it *The Wiggles* is a kid's show.'

'It's brilliant if you're under ten – age or IQ.'

At a small café on the outskirts of Palmerston North, Grace ordered two Americanos and a sausage roll while Marla inspected the café, satisfying herself no security cameras were recording their visit. They chose a table away from other diners. The cheap table and chairs, faded pictures, and peeling wallpaper suggested the food must be great; nobody would come for the ambience.

Leaning across the table, Marla whispered, 'Interesting choice, do they know what the word barista means?'

Grace rolled her eyes. 'Give it a chance. Anyway, let's concentrate on Western's meeting. You said in the car it could be a set-up. Why?'

'If I was them, I'd see Western as a weak link.'

'What would your former employer do?'

Marla raised her eyebrows.

'You'd kill him?'

'I wouldn't, but the people I used to work for would without a second thought. These people won't be as ruthless, that's not possible, but if the stakes are high enough … That's what's bothering me.'

'Go on,' said Grace taking a bite of her sausage roll.

'You've written stories about the alt-right, but they weren't earth-shattering.'

'Weren't they?' Grace tried to look indignant as she wiped the pastry from around her mouth.

'You know what I mean. Dropping hate mail in your letterbox was an overreaction, so was nailing dead man's hand to your door. And setting a trap for me? I mean, why take it to that level? There's more in play than we're seeing, and it centres on you. You're the one they decided to target.'

'I hadn't considered that.' Grace used a wet finger to pick up the pastry crumbs from the table. 'I've two other stories running in the media. I ran an exposé on real estate firms and how their actions contributed to the housing market's collapse. You know, people losing their houses while the company owners' swan around the world.'

Marla crinkled her nose. 'I can't imagine that's a part of this, though there are loads of wealthy people in the property industry.'

'Politically, they're right of the alt-right.'

'It's still a stretch. What's the other?'

'I'm monitoring the ProtectNZ movement. You know, they've grown in popularity of late using populist techniques to appeal to ordinary New Zealanders.'

Leaning a little closer, Marla said, 'You were there when their leader was shot.'

'Yeah, but the threats had started weeks before that.'

'How long have you covered them?'

'A few months, at least. They looked like another conspiracy crazy train, but they became more coherent and therefore worth keeping an eye on.'

'We've assumed you're getting this attention because of your investigation into the alt-right. What if it's because of your interest in ProtectNZ. Or maybe it's both?'

Grace snuck in another bite. 'It could be. It's widely believed ProtectNZ is in bed with the alt-right, but nobody's found any evidence – yet. I've mentioned the connection in my stories though I've been careful to say it's conjecture. But what about Western and his brother? They're *sieg heilers* for def.'

'It could be a coincidence or maybe convenience,' said Marla. 'They're perfect cover if an organised group wants to shut you down. Use a group of dozy white supremacists, make it look like you're under attack from the alt-right, but actually …'

Continuing the logic, Grace added, 'ProtectNZ could be trying to stop me nosing around in their affairs. Either directly by intimidation or indirectly by getting me fixated on the attack from the alt-right. But really? They must know it's a risky strategy, trying to intimidate a journalist.'

'It's ill-conceived but they might have judged it a no-risk play. I mean, some journalists would be put off and they weren't to know they were going to have the tables turned on them. They thought they were harassing a soft target – a single journalist.'

'Also,' said Grace, 'I dismissed it at the time as too far-fetched, but JP hinted that Ball, the ProtectNZ leader, might have been involved in his own shooting.' In answer to Marla's expression, she added, 'You know, like a crazy PR stunt. But risking pain or death if it went wrong for a higher profile?'

After a period of silence, Marla said, 'Nobody volunteers to be shot, but what if Ball didn't volunteer?'

'Sorry?'

'Ball's personal popularity has benefited, but ProtectNZ is the major beneficiary.'

Grace sat up straight. 'JP's hint was cryptic. I agree, I can't imagine anyone putting their hand up to take a bullet but, if the stunt was organised by ProtectNZ without telling Ball, that's different.'

'I've heard of crazier stunts,' said Marla. 'And there sure are some crazies in those alt-right circles.'

The conversation stalled. Frustratingly, Grace could see the pieces but not the picture. Marla seemed to be in a similar mental position as she drank the last of her coffee, her face creased in concentration.

'Thoughts?' asked Grace.

'If I'd known this was going to be bigger than rounding up a few rednecks, I would've played Western differently. Anyway, spilt milk and all that. Apart from Western, the only link we have to who's behind this – alt-right, ProtectNZ, or both – is who Western is meeting.'

'I can't imagine he'd live in Feilding,' said Grace. 'Too far from the action.'

'That means the location of their meeting could be anywhere, but I doubt it's hours away. The logistics wouldn't make sense. He's involved because he's close to the action.'

'Wellington,' said Grace. 'The dealership that owns the ute is in Wellington.'

'Wellington makes sense, but if we're going to follow Western to this meeting, we need to bug his car before tomorrow.' Marla thought for a minute. 'What would you do, Grace, if you were Western and your world was going pear-shaped?'

'I don't know what I'd do, but Western will get drunk.'

CHAPTER 22

Marla pointed at the left fork of a driveway. 'Drive behind the church.'

They arrived in Feilding at 5.15pm, giving them fifteen minutes until the car dealership where Western worked closed. Marla directed Grace to the secluded location behind the church bordering Victoria Park where she had launched her drone to monitor the attempted ambush.

'We're quite a way from where Western works,' said Grace.

'The drone has a range of ten kilometres, Feilding can't be more than five kilometres wide.'

'It's that small?'

'Urban areas seem bigger because you drive around them slowly. The drone's camera can cover the whole of Feilding if I send it high enough, though the detail suffers. What's the time?'

'Ten minutes until they close. The light's fading, will that be a problem?'

'No, towns are lit up like Christmas trees,' said Marla as she lovingly took her drone out, taking off the cover that protected the camera lens. After attaching the propellors, she slotted in a fully charged battery and turned on the controller.

'It looks like you're getting ready to play a video game,' said Grace.

'Video games are behind some of the sharpest new technology. Did you know the US navy ditched their ten-thousand-dollar submarine periscope controllers for thirty-dollar Xbox controllers because the crew knew how to use them?'

'Jesus,' said Grace. 'Gates would've creamed himself when he heard that.'

'Creamed himself?'

'You know, made a mess in his pants.'

'Gross,' said Marla. 'Though, to be fair, he always looks a bit like that.'

'It's thinking about all his money,' said Grace. 'It's a rich male git thing. Musk, Branson, and Bezos all sport the same post-toss, pie-faced grin.'

Marla shook the images out of her head as she powered on the drone and its controller. 'It's time for take-off.'

'It's bloody noisy,' said Grace. 'Won't he hear it?'

'What?' said Marla, cupping her hand over her ear. She winked. 'Just wait.'

Putting on the goggles, Marla commanded the drone to ascend, setting it to hover at a hundred metres. Grace could faintly hear the drone but, that apart, the church grounds were silent. Once it had established its position, she zoomed the camera in on the car yard.

'Want to look?'

'You bet,' said Grace.

She took off the goggles and handed them to Grace then took out her iPhone and launched the app that allowed her to see what Grace was seeing.

'Jesus, it's like I'm flying. Which one's Western's car?'

'It's a … it's the red one out the back.'

'Got it. You're talking my language.'

Marla zoomed in on the car yard.

'Shit, we're too close,' said a panicky Grace.

Laughing, Marla said, 'I zoomed in, the drone hasn't moved. Try not to *wet* your pants.'

Grace mumbled two words that she didn't catch.

'It's like I'm hovering right above their shitty lot,' said Grace.

'Tell me when you see Western,' said Marla. 'The view on the phone isn't as sharp.'

'Sure. This is so cool. I must get one. The police use these, don't they?'

'I hope so. Ordinary crims use them to scope out houses.'

'Really?'

Marla refocused the camera on a random house's backyard. 'If you wanted to burgle this house, you can see whether there are dogs, if anyone's home, if windows are open. You can even spot security cameras.'

'Shit, that's not good.'

Marla refocused on the car yard.

'Everyone's leaving, I can see Western,' said Grace. 'He's locking up the yard.' Stifling a laugh, she added, 'He's developing a bald spot.'

The women watched Western get in his car and stop outside the lot so he could close the security gate. Five minutes later, he was still sitting inside his car outside the locked gates.

'Get a move on, Western,' said Grace. 'Stop dicking around. How long does this thing's battery last?'

'Thing?' huffed Marla. 'About two hours, longer if it's hovering.'

A minute later, Grace said, 'At last, action. He's off.'

Marla rapidly zoomed out.

'Jesus. Can you warn me when you're going to do that, I nearly lost that sausage roll.'

'Keep watching, I'm hoping he stays in Feilding. If he goes further afield, we'll need to follow him in the car.'

They watched the red car drive towards the centre of Feilding.

'He's parked outside a building with a red roof,' said Grace.

Switching to a map application, Marla said, 'It's the Feilding Hotel.'

'I know it. I've been ratted in there myself on the odd occasion.'

'Ratted?'

'Drunk,' said Grace. 'I overused alcohol as a coping mechanism, it made my then husband bearable. Western hasn't gone inside.'

Marla zoomed in, gradually this time.

'This technology is great, how much did this thing cost?'

Pointlessly glaring at Grace, Marla said, 'This *leading-edge, remote-controlled drone* cost two and a half K.'

'Is that all? No wonder crooks like this thing. I feel a story coming on.'

Marla's eyes rolled before she brought their focus back to the task. 'The building Western has gone into is a liquor store. If he's buying alcohol, won't he get *ratted* at home?'

'Go you, but he'll go to the pub first.'

'What's the "pub"?'

'A public house. You know, a boozer. You need to get out more.'

'Whatever. If the Feilding Hotel's a bar, why would he go in if he's buying alcohol?'

'Because the liquor store's a drive-through. He wouldn't have parked outside the pub if he wasn't planning on a couple of quiets.'

'You're doing it on purpose now.'

Grace chuckled.

Marla recalled the drone home. 'If you're right, we need to get moving. This is our chance.'

Taking off the goggles, Grace watched the drone descend noisily. 'That thing is so cool.'

'A person could easily go off you,' said Marla glaring.

'Sorry.' Grace tried, but failed, to look shamefaced. 'What's the plan?'

'We're going to attach a GPS bug under his car.'

The drone landed at Marla's feet like an obedient dog. 'While I put this *thing* away, use street view to see what the windows on the Feilding Hotel look like where he's parked. I want to know if he can see out easily.'

It took Grace a couple of minutes to check. 'It's hard to say. They look mirrored, which means they don't want people looking in, but he'll probably be able to see out. How long will it take you to plant the bug?'

'Not long,' said Marla putting the drone in its case and getting into Grace's car. 'It's best to plant it in a hard-to-find spot; in case they decide to check. It takes a little longer but I'm talking less than a minute.'

'I've an idea,' said Grace as she started the car. 'We'll hide in plain sight.'

Before they reached the Feilding Hotel, Grace pulled into the Mitre 10 hardware store's car park. Five minutes later they were outside but now wearing white hard hats and lime fluro jackets.

'Perfect,' said Marla. 'Nobody takes any notice of people wearing this gear.'

'And all for' – Grace checked the receipt – 'seventy bucks.'

'How long will he stay in the bar?' asked Marla.

Wrinkling her nose, she said, 'He'll have a couple, maybe three and he won't scull them – half an hour, maybe a bit longer.'

'That term I do know. Let's get this done.'

They walked around the corner to where Western had parked his car. Grace stood in the middle of the quiet side road ready to direct traffic while Marla wriggled under Western's car. Finding a nook to plant the GPS bug, within thirty seconds she was again standing with Grace on the road.

'Any interest from inside?' Marla asked as they walked around the corner.

'Only one window was open. All I could see was a table of old men drinking away the evening. No sign of Western, but he'll be in there staring into his beer, looking for answers.'

Taking out her mobile phone, Marla launched the tracking app. She showed it to Grace — a blue locator arrow sat pulsing next to the Feilding Hotel.

Grace grinned. 'We're golden.'

CHAPTER 23

'How did it happen?' demanded Ball.

'Keep your voice down,' hissed Edward Blackwood. 'This conversation does not need to be broadcast to the whole city.'

Sitting inside one of Wellington's numerous upmarket wine bars, at a small table by the front window, Ball was having dinner with Blackwood, the driving force behind the establishment of ProtectNZ. Blackwood, wearing a suit that ironically didn't suit him, looked the type of man who only wore suits at weddings and funerals. A powerfully built man with a farmer's weather-beaten face, his age, in his sixties, meant he blended his strength with a liberal dose of obesity. Ball was pleased Blackwood had arrived minus his prized autographed MAGA hat, although it reflected him perfectly – boorish.

'Sorry Ted,' he said, lowering his voice. 'They could've killed me though. They were meant to threaten me so I could heroically stand up to the would-be attackers – that was the plan. It wasn't meant to be an attempt on my life.'

'Don't be so dramatic. You weren't in any real danger and the injury has played well – your popularity has surged. The injury together with the eloquent speeches you've been making – you're a natural politician.'

Ball ran a hand over his head, a smile breaking over his face. 'It has gone well lately, I'll admit.' He leaned in close. 'But Ted, the police *and* the SIS are poking around.'

'We know, but they're flailing in the dark. And, if everybody stays on script … How is the shoulder?'

Rotating his injured shoulder gently, Ball's face soured. 'Still sore but they say there'll be no lasting damage.'

Blackwood grunted approvingly. 'Keep wearing the sling. It doesn't hurt to remind people what you've been through.'

The server arrived with the wine Blackwood had selected. Although Ball pretended to be knowledgeable about wine, like ninety-nine per cent of people he bought wine solely on price. He had suggested Blackwood choose and, after much muttering, he had selected a white and a red. When he showed him his selections, Ball had complimented him on his choice but the only information he took in was that the bottle of white cost $175, the red $225. As ProtectNZ was paying, he would no doubt have to answer questions from Ms Pilkington.

The server poured them each a glass, Blackwood having waved away an invitation to taste the wine. After taking a sizeable glug, he asked Ball, 'Are you a member of the New Zealand Initiative?'

Ball shook his head. He had considered joining the rebranded Business Roundtable to increase his business and political networks but had baulked at the membership cost. It struck him as one of those pretentious organisations that would say, 'If you need to ask the cost you probably don't belong'.

'No?' said Blackwood, his unkempt eyebrows meeting, forming a small hedge. 'You need to join, code it as an operating expense. You'll rub shoulders with influential people. People like us. People who understand how the economy needs to function for the betterment of New Zealand.'

'I'll organise it. But I was a bit put off,' he lied, 'by their editor who ran a far-right extremist blog, and nobody noticed until the media outed him.'

'He seemed such a sound chap too.' Blackwood's frown was forcing his eyebrows to join again. After he had drunk more of his wine, his smug look returned. 'Anyway, the next few months are critical for us.'

'They are,' agreed Ball. 'We're getting loads of media attention—'

'And scrutiny,' interrupted Blackwood. 'Now we're a registered political party, our finances need to be squeaky clean and open for inspection. Many of our opponents, and the media of course, want to identify our financial backers, so now the money needs to come from the grassroots.'

'I've checked the rules,' said Ball. 'They're trying to crack down on donations.'

'The rules are the rules and' – Blackwood's face hardened – 'they're made to be taken advantage of. The limits on spending are only for the three months before the election, what they call the "regulated period". Before that, it's open slather *and* it doesn't count money spent offshore.'

'Really?'

'Well, not if they can't find it. Our organisation has attracted the interest and support of powerful international ... personalities. They're keen to support us and our work by providing "marketing assistance" outside of New Zealand.' In answer to Ball's confused look, he added, 'Social media campaigns, blogging, online marketing. We can get associates to run those from outside the country with no provable connection to us.'

'Got you,' he said. 'It won't count towards our expenditure.'

'You're onto it, but don't worry, you don't have to learn the intricacies. You're best out in front, leading the party. We've three top-notch advisers lined up.'

'Excellent.' Blackwood was right; by the time he understood the rules and worked out how to play the game, the election would be over. All the same, he should have a say in these decisions. Blackwood and his cronies might be bankrolling the party, but he was the party's leader.

'The plan is,' continued Blackwood, 'to dominate the political airwaves before the three-month period starts. By then, ProtectNZ should be a major political force. The other parties, who are currently pretending we don't exist, will be calling and wanting to take you to dinner.'

'Sounds great. Who developed the strategy?'

Blackwood eased himself backwards. 'We've created an advisory board to guide the party's development. The stakes are high; our backers want assurance their investment is well managed. We don't want to see our money, and theirs, go up in smoke now do we?'

Without drinking, Ball gulped. 'Advisory board?'

'Through me, you'll receive the board's vision and direction for how we expect the organisation to run. You, as the leader of ProtectNZ, operationalise that direction. Think of it like a private company, the board sets the pathway, the CEO delivers. Can you deliver for us, Seb?'

Blackwood picked up his wine and drained his glass without taking his eyes off Ball.

'I can Ted, but—'

Ball was grateful the server arrived with their food and the second bottle of wine. It gave him the time he needed to get his thoughts in order. Blackwood was painting a picture that, while it sounded attractive superficially, was decidedly unattractive. It portrayed Blackwood, this board, and no doubt the international backers as running the organisation. They expected him to do as they instructed – effectively to do as he was told.

They ate in silence; attacking his rare steak caused his shoulder to throb. That was another aggravation Blackwood had glossed over, it seems they had decided to have him shot. Blackwood alone, or with this board's blessing, had decided a politically motivated attack would play better to the masses if they left him bleeding on the ground. He hadn't signed up for that.

Blackwood finished his mouthful. 'You said "but"?'

'I was about to say I'll need …' He paused. If he was honest, he didn't know what he needed. Before dinner it was funding, but now what he wanted to say was autonomy. But he didn't say autonomy, he knew now wasn't the time for that battle. 'Funding to dominate the airwaves.'

Blackwood's glower turned to a grin. 'Money? You'll have no trouble with funding. I mean, our international backers could fund this themselves, they have so far. Now we need donations from "ordinary New Zealanders", as well as rich ones,' he added with a wink.

'As I understand it,' said Ball, 'grassroots donations will help build local champions and support. We'll build a broad base of supporters who have a vested interest in success.'

'Exactly. Those advisers I mentioned, one's a marketing genius. He used to work for Air New Zealand. Christ, he made the CEO sound smart, that's how good he is. At the moment he's cooling his heels babysitting a couple of government departments. He's lining up a range of local campaigns but also planning several "cash for access" events for the high rollers.'

'Paying to talk to politicians?' Ball offered tentatively.

'That's it,' said Blackwood, between enormous mouthfuls. 'National called it the "Cabinet Club", Labour ran "Business Conferences". Pay enough money and the punters get to rub shoulders with politicians, even the PM, so they can badger them about their pet topics. They'll be keen to talk to you and your future parliamentary colleagues, especially once the polls show we're going to be a significant political force.'

Ball had hardly touched his meal, while Blackwood was demolishing his. After a series of rapid mouthfuls and a sip of wine to catch up a little, Ball said, 'The other urgent task is candidate selection.'

'You don't like the wine?' asked Blackwood.

Glancing at his nearly full glass, he said, 'No, it's excellent. I was listening. You said we should discuss possible candidates to run in the election.'

'I did,' said Blackwood. 'You'll be pleased to know the advisory board has been considering candidates for ... well, before you even came on board.'

Reaching for his wine, Ball listened with growing concern.

'Apart from shoulder tapping you, we've talked to a range of people about their interest and availability. At first, people expressed reluctance to commit to a political party that didn't exist, but as we've gained momentum and public appeal ...' Blackwood took out a folded piece of A4 paper from the jacket he had hung on his chair, sliding it across the table.

'What's this?' Ball asked, suspecting he already knew.

'It's our list of candidates for the election complete with shadow cabinet positions.'

Opening the page, he stared at the list of names, shaking his head. 'There are solid people here, Ted, but some, well, they're involved with organisations like Hobson's Pledge and the Free Speech Union.'

'And?'

'The other parties and' – he twitched as Marks' face came into his mind – 'the media will have a field day.'

'Let them try,' interrupted Blackwood. 'That's why we've hired marketing talent, to turn the tables on them. The world's changed, Ball. The "lamestream" media have had their volume turned right down.'

'Journalists like Marks' – Ball clenched his buttocks to avoid twitching – 'will tear into us. She's already written damaging stories.'

Blackwood's face soured. 'I'm not worried about what she's written so far, but she's also been poking her nose into our financial affairs – our backers have expressed concern. Colleagues of ours have tried to reign her in but she's being difficult. We'll clip her wings soon enough.' Before he returned to his meal, he added, 'I had hoped letting her interview you might get her onside but she's one of those annoying skirts on a power trip. Announcing our candidates will give her a different bone to chew on, hopefully she'll drop her other investigations – her and whoever she has working for her.'

Ball shook his head, not following Blackwood. He took in a deep breath. 'Ted, I think I need to be intimately involved in the selection of our team. I need confidence our candidates are … okay.'

'Okay?'

'You know, not, well, *just* okay.'

Blackwood finished his mouthful. 'All these people are not *just* okay. They're talented and capable, they'll appeal to ordinary New Zealanders, and they have the right' – he raised his eyebrows for emphasis – 'political views. We know they're okay.'

His appetite gone; Ball stared at the list of names. 'There are hardly any women or …' He searched for the right term. 'Non-Europeans.'

'There are enough to keep the media off our backs. Besides, it's the advisory board's view that ordinary New Zealanders prefer typical Kiwi male leaders.'

Ball snorted. 'Ordinary New Zealand *men* might, at least they did in the eighties, but times have changed, Ted. This approach will put people off.' Refolding the list, he put it in his jacket pocket. 'Leave it to me, Ted. I'll work with this as a draft and develop a list that will build the party's popular support base.' He delivered the last sentence with a confidence he didn't feel.

Refilling his glass and holding it up as though he was inspecting the wine, Blackwood said, 'It's not up for debate, Seb. That's our party's candidate list. The advisory board has signed it off. We've confirmed each name, you get to announce it to the media in your inimitable style.'

Ball stared at him, unable to work out what to say or how to argue the point.

After he drank half his wine, Blackwood put his glass down deliberately. 'Look, Ball. Your role is to front the party with style and energy. You get to become a famous politician who, from the obscurity of selling shitty, overpriced, poorly built houses, will rise to what? Maybe prime minister one day. Think of that. And we're paying you handsomely in addition to your MP's salary.' He moved in close, menacing not warm. 'You need to stick to your role, leave the rest to us.'

'Ted, I respect the effort you and this advisory board have put in, but surely you appointed me to run the party. It seems you want me to be a puppet, controlled by you and the board.'

Blackwood sat back. 'Don't be silly. Not a puppet, the leader. The CEO if you like. Implementing the board's vision and direction.'

He went to protest, but Blackwood raised his large farmer's hand. 'And that's what you're going to do. Unless you want us to replace you – or worse.'

Ball's eyes widened. 'What?'

Draining the rest of his wine, Blackwood huffed out a heavy, alcoholic breath. 'I had hoped we wouldn't need to get to this point. If you resign, we have recorded conversations of you helping to coordinate the attack on yourself at the Michael Fowler Centre.' He picked up his phone. 'Would you like me to play one of them for you?'

He stared at Blackwood. Even though the position he was in was abundantly clear, he hoped he had misunderstood.

Blackwood's face grew sterner. 'The police would be interested in those, as would the media. And before you start thinking you'd take us down with you – don't. We are very cautious about what's provable and what's hearsay. Besides, our international backers are, how can I say this, committed. For them, there's not much difference between saying "shoot him in the shoulder" than there is to say … "shoot him in the head."'

Ball's mouth fell open.

'But Seb,' said a now-smiling Blackwood, 'we don't need any of that unpleasantness. ProtectNZ and your own political career are on the verge of greatness. Together we'll do extraordinary things, mark my words. In fact, you should start attending the advisory board meetings. I'll have a word with the directors, clear the way.'

Blackwood stood, his size making it an ungainly operation. Putting on his jacket, he unsuccessfully tried to smooth the creases out of his sleeves. 'I'm glad we've had this little chat, thanks for picking up the tab. I look forward to hearing progress reports and I'll be keeping an eye on developments.' His gaze hardened. 'A close eye.'

Stunned, Ball watched him awkwardly navigate his bulk through the restaurant and out the door. When the man was gone the air rushed out of him like a pricked balloon. Putting his head in his hands, choking back the swear words his faith didn't like him uttering, he said quietly, 'What have I got myself into?'

'Have you finished, sir?'

The server jolted him back to the present. 'Yes, thank you.'

The server started clearing the table. When he made to take away the half-full bottles of wine, Ball said, 'Leave the wine, it's too expensive to waste.'

'Very good, sir. Did you enjoy the wine? The vintage—'

Cutting him off, Ball shook his head and spoke matter-of-factly. 'I'm sorry, it tasted like wine. You know, plonk.'

The server drew himself to his maximum height. These weren't the usual lies he heard from people who also couldn't taste the difference.

'I'll bring the bill,' he said frostily. 'Shall I re-cork the wine so you can take it with you?'

'That won't be necessary.'

When the server had gone, Ball looked around the cosy room. The other diners seemed to be having a great time, engrossed in conversations. No one was taking any notice of him. Picking up the half-full $175 bottle of white wine, he drained it straight from the bottle. By the time the server returned with the bill and an EFT-POS machine, both bottles were empty.

The server's mouth fell open when he realised what Ball must have done. Using his credit card, Ball paid the bill without looking at the server or the amount.

Handing him the receipt, the server said, 'I hope the rest of your evening gets better.' He hurried away before Ball could answer.

Standing unsteadily, the wine having an instant impact, he picked his way through the restaurant, concentrating on appearing sober. Outside, the cool evening air hit him physically, like a punch. He tried to walk normally but the task was now beyond him, and he staggered around the corner into a dark deserted alley. Behind a stairway, he vomited. Not knowing whether to laugh or cry, he watched steam rise off the expensive contents of his stomach as they trickled into a brick drain.

CHAPTER 24

Marla and Grace were eating Vietnamese takeout as they waited in Grace's car. It had started raining around lunchtime and, at 6.00pm when they had parked on the edge of town to eat, it was still raining. As they enjoyed dinner, they kept an eye on the blue locator arrow pulsing on Western's house – he hadn't left yet.

'What did you tell your children?' asked Marla. Damien had become accustomed to her odd hours and didn't ask any awkward questions when she told him she was "on duty" tonight.

'I told them I had a work dinner,' said Grace. 'They'll get takeaways, but I insisted they go out to get them. I have an irrational loathing of having takeaways delivered.'

'What about in a pandemic?'

Grace shrugged. 'It's passable in a pandemic, or if it's hard for people to get out, but teenagers lounging around tracking their food on an app? No thank you.'

'He's off,' said Marla.

As they watched, the blue locator was moving through Feilding's streets. As expected, he was heading towards Wellington, which meant they had picked the right place to wait. They had a ten-minute head start on him allowing them to finish their dinner.

'It's quarter past six,' said Marla between mouthfuls. 'Assuming he's given himself leeway for the weather and traffic, how far can he get by eight?'

Grace put her food on the dash and worked on her laptop. 'Google reckons it would take him an hour thirty-three to get to Paraparaumu, so no further than that.'

Marla pointed at the map. 'How long to Ōtaki?'

'*Or taki*,' Grace pronounced the name deliberately. 'An hour twenty.'

'*Oh taki*.' Marla tried out the name. 'I'm going to need lessons. Anyway, it's too close. The location must be somewhere in here.' She circled a part of the map with her finger.

Grace packed away her laptop while she threw the containers into a rubbish bag.

Looking out the front windscreen at the rain and fading light, Marla said, 'I was hoping we could get near enough to launch the drone, but it's no use in rain or bad light.'

'Does it play cricket?'

'What?'

Giving Marla a friendly eyebrow raise, she asked, 'What's the plan?'

'No plan, we'll be winging it. When we know where they're meeting, we can work on a plan. Until then, we'll make it up as we go.'

'What would your old employer expect you to do?'

Marla bit her lower lip. 'It would be a fifty-fifty call, but he's our only ticket into the dance so we need to try. These operations can be like walking in fog. At the start you can't see anything but, as you keep walking, the fog thins, and you start to make out objects. Eventually the fog disappears, and the picture becomes crystal clear.'

'Speaking of going, we better hit the road ourselves. Where's Western?'

Checking her phone, Marla said, 'He's nearing ... *Kai ranga?*'

'Not bad, lessons will help.'

Marla shrugged. 'We want to stay as close as possible without giving him any chance of making us.'

Starting the car, Grace said, 'That should be easy in this weather. All he'll see is headlights.'

'True, but whoever he's meeting stressed, "Make sure you're not followed". He'll stop to check at some stage and, as he knows your car, we'll need to stop too. As we get near the location, we can close to within a minute. If I was him, I'd want to be in and out fast. It's not a social catch-up.'

'Shit, that makes it tight.'

'The movies make it look too easy,' said Marla. 'I'll keep an eye on the app, so follow my instructions. Let's see if we can ID this fucker.'

For the next hour they followed Western, who kept to the 100 kph speed limit. The tracking app allowed them to stay a comfortable four minutes behind. In Shannon, after he had taken the left-hand turn in the middle of town, he pulled over for two minutes, ironically stopping outside the police station. As they were discussing where to stop, he recommenced his journey. Grace paralleled his car along a back street until they were sure he was heading out of town.

Western tried a similar move before he turned onto Kimberley Road, near Levin, forcing them to wait on the shoulder of the road. If he turned towards them, Marla warned Grace she may need to do a U-turn to maintain their distance. He didn't.

When they neared Ōtaki, traffic slowed to a crawl, making Marla feel uncomfortable. 'When the traffic starts flowing again, let's close the gap. Timewise we're in the neighbourhood.'

After they left Ōtaki, and the traffic was able to flow, Grace accelerated, closing in on Western. It was 7.30pm, though the weather made it feel like the middle of the night. Marla was impressed by how Grace overtook three cars to position them perfectly, about 200 metres behind Western.

'He's turning off,' said Marla. 'Heading towards Pekapeka Road.'

'I don't know it.'

'Shit,' said Marla.

'Do we follow him?'

Marla stayed quiet, her eyes darting over the map.

Grace turned on her indicator light and moved into the turning lane. As the car slowed, Marla said, 'No, turn left.'

Grace switched her indicator and turned in the opposite direction to Western. 'Done. Where to?'

'Keep going, I'll work out a route.' The metronomic sound of the windscreen wipers accompanied her planning. 'He's on a loop road. We'd have driven right up his arse if we'd followed him. We would've stood out like—'

'Dog's balls?' cut in Grace.

Ignoring both the comment and Grace's smirk, she said, 'We need to get to the far end of the loop, that way we won't stand out like a sore thumb.'

Grace giggled as Marla plotted a route. 'He's driven past Pekapeka

Beach. That looked a likely location, so we've still got time. It's' – she checked the time on her wristwatch which she wore on operations – 'eight minutes until their meet, it must be close. We'll make it where we need to be.'

She studied the map while Grace drove. 'Keep on this road, take the turn-off to Waikanae Beach.'

'Got it.'

'According to Google, it's a nine-minute drive to where we can park and monitor traffic.'

'Cool. What's Western doing?'

'He's still driving. No, he's stopped!' Marla zoomed in on the blue locator beacon. 'At Pharazyn Reserve, it's a playground.'

'Odd time for a swing,' said Grace.

Both women laughed. It released the tension that had been building.

After Grace began heading towards Waikanae Beach, Marla said, 'Keep on this road, in about six minutes there's a block of public toilets.'

'Nice. Are you busting?'

'Cars blend in around toilets.'

'Good to know.'

Marla kept an eye on Western's car. As soon as it moved, whoever he was meeting should pass by them four minutes later. At the toilets she made Grace drive around a gravel path to park facing away from where their target would come from.

After Grace parked, Marla jumped into the back seat and set up one of her burner phones so it was recording in high definition out the back window of the car.

'What now?' asked Grace.

'Now we wait. If we're right, the person meeting Western drove past here not long ago and, when they're done, they'll drive past here four minutes after Western heads home.'

'Smart. When did he stop at the playground?'

Marla wrinkled her nose. 'About five to eight.'

'If we assume our target's right on time, or maybe a couple of minutes late, they've talked for' – Grace checked her phone – 'four minutes.'

'Western's still there, we were here in time.'

Time crawled by as they sat quietly in the dark. Marla used a phone to check the surrounding environment where Western was parked as four minutes turned to eight; eight minutes turned to sixteen. They stared at another of Marla's phones, watching the blue locator beacon pulse over Pharazyn Reserve. In that time, cars, vans, and motorcycles had gone past – but no large black ute.

Grace broke the silence. 'Thoughts?'

'Western hasn't moved, at least the bug hasn't moved. They could've found it, tossed it in the rubbish.'

'In this weather?' said Grace. 'And in the dark?'

'Good point,' said Marla. 'Western's waiting. There's been a delay.'

'How long would you wait?'

'At the location? Seconds, maybe minutes. I can always come back, but sitting there exposed, not an approach I'd favour.'

'Western isn't you.'

'True.'

They watched a series of random vehicles drive past as nineteen minutes ticked by. The blue locator pulsed over Pharazyn Reserve.

'If they were delayed,' said Grace, 'they would've driven past here, wouldn't they?'

Marla nodded. 'I doubt they'd make us here, we're all but invisible and that means they'll appear twice on the video.'

Twenty-three minutes ticked past. The blue locator remained stubbornly over the playground. Grace drew in a long breath. 'Are you thinking what I'm thinking?'

'For the last ten minutes.'

'Shit,' said Grace. 'He could be in a different car. I mean, if he's connected to a car dealer, he could grab any car on the lot.'

'It's more likely they are in a different car, but no matter what they're driving, when Western's car moves, they should pass by here four minutes later. But Western's car hasn't moved.'

'What are our options?' asked Grace.

'If we check out the scene, and Western's still waiting, our plan is blown. But given what's going on, it doesn't look like he's going to lead us anywhere.'

'And if he's there but, you know, something bad has happened?'

'That's the worst-case scenario. You'll need to call the police. I can't be there but it's miles from anywhere. The best option is for you to drop me at this bar' – she showed Grace its location – 'and then drive back to the park. It'll take thirty minutes, then call the police.'

'If it's the worst-case scenario,' said Grace, 'I'll be there, or at the police station, for hours. What'll you do?'

'Don't worry about me. I can Uber to another town, back to Palmerston North if necessary.'

'That sounds dodgy. What if the driver is suspicious?'

'Remember, I don't exist. Any trail they'll find is cold before they start.' Marla frowned, adding, 'I'm not worried for myself, I can disappear in a heartbeat. But if it is the worst-case scenario, I think you'll *need* my help, at least for a while.'

'What do I tell the police?'

'The truth, it's easiest to remember. But erase my involvement – you've acted alone. But first things first, we don't know what's happened yet. And, as Western still hasn't moved, it's time we found out.'

CHAPTER 25

'Don't get too close, but park with your headlights on Western's car,' said Marla.

As she had calculated, it was a four-minute drive to Pharazyn Reserve from where they had been waiting. It was raining and pitch-black; no street lights illuminated the playground. Grace turned in, her lights splashing over Western's red car parked against a low wooden barrier. It sat alone.

She stopped thirty metres away, leaving the car running.

They sat watching for signs of movement but saw none. The car looked unoccupied.

Taking out her Glock and checking it, Marla said, 'Let's check it out. Leave the car running, just in case.'

'I hope that's just in case too,' said Grace.

Dropping the gun in her pocket, Marla said, 'In my game, being caught by surprise is inexcusable – usually fatal.'

They got out of the car in unison. It was only raining lightly, the drops highlighted in the car's headlights.

'I'll check it out, you stay here,' said Marla.

'Why?'

'Because your story, and any footprints, have to be that you approached the car by yourself, not with a friend.'

'It's lucky you're here,' said Grace.

Marla approached the vehicle from the rear and to the right. Taking a wide berth, keeping herself out of the headlights, she cautiously approached the driver's door. If anyone tried to burst out, a kick to the door would thwart their plans. As she neared, Grace's car's headlights allowed her to confirm no one was in the car – alive or dead.

'Well?' called out Grace.

'He's not here.'

Peering in the rear windows, the car was immaculate with no sign anyone had ever sat in the back even though he had three children. He must get the dealership cleaners to clean the car, no doubt for free. She rolled up her sleeve and, trying to stay dry with difficulty, felt under the car for the GPS bug. Once she had confirmed it was in place, she pulled her sleeve over her hand and tried the door – it was locked. After studying the interior, she retraced her steps to where Grace was watching.

'Nothing?' Grace asked.

'No sign of Western, though the car's locked which means he took the keys with him.'

'A car's coming,' said Grace, pointing to the road where they could see headlights racing along.

Marla watched for a few seconds. 'It's not coming here, it's not slowing.'

They watched the lights fly by.

Grace exhaled quietly while Marla inspected their surroundings although she could make out little except what the car's headlights illuminated. To their left was the desolate-looking playground and, in the distance, a line of trees that bordered a small lake. To the far right she could see the faint lights of a house.

'What now?' asked Grace.

'He took the keys and locked the car,' said Marla, her thoughts developing. 'He'd only do that if he expected to return. It's possible they met Western here and drove him to a second location. If he's picked up a tail or his car's bugged, the trail stops at the playground.'

'Got ya. He knew what the plan was, so he locked the car and went with whoever turned up.'

'That feels logical,' said Marla. 'Assuming the meeting's closer to Wellington, they must drive past where we were waiting four times, twice each way. We'll have captured them once so far and, when they drop Western back at his car, we'll get them twice more.'

Grace blew out a long breath. 'Back to where we were then?'

Marla nodded.

Parking in the same place, facing away from the playground, Marla set up a burner phone to record. They recommenced their vigil, in the dark watching the tracking app on another of Marla's phones. Once again, time crawled by. Four minutes turned to eight; eight minutes turned to sixteen.

'Do you think you'll ever get back to America?' asked Grace.

'Hmmm ... no. I can't see the world changing enough to tip the men running the world off their throne.'

Grace sighed. 'It's unlikely. All this new technology is making them richer and more powerful.'

'Can you see what they like to call a soft landing?'

'For capitalism?' said Grace. 'God no. I heard it likened to a skyrocket, the Earth's resources, including people, are the fuel.'

'Ouch,' said Marla. 'It flies higher and higher until it explodes.'

'Exactly, leaving blackness and debris.'

A short laugh escaped Marla. 'Have you read *The Road*?'

'Cormac McCarthy, sure. Bleak as fuck but we're heading that way. Dystopia and reality merging.' Grace made a short orgasmic sound. 'That would make a great story, maybe a novel.'

As they chatted, eight minutes turned to sixteen, sixteen minutes turned to twenty-four. The blue locator beacon pulsed steadily over the playground.

'What should we do?' asked Grace. 'It's past nine.'

Marla thought through their options. Grace waited patiently.

'It feels wrong,' said Marla. 'Something's gone down. If you went back, assuming the scene at the playground is still Western's car and no Western, what would you do if you were doing this by yourself? You know, if you were by yourself chasing the story.'

Grace's face creased in concentration. 'People leave cars in strange places for a myriad of reasons, but if I suspected foul play, I'd definitely call the police.'

'And wait?'

'Nah, I doubt they'd turn up. I'd be reporting an abandoned car, maybe my suspicions, but it's Friday night.'

The American blew a long breath out her nose. 'We're going to need to tread carefully. First, let me find a suitable place.' She sensed Grace's impatience while she searched the area. 'This'll do, drop me at the

Pinetree Arms – it doesn't close until one in the morning. You head to the playground. If the scene's the same, call the police.'

'You want me to go on my own?' asked Grace.

'I can't be there if the police might turn up. I doubt the scene will have changed.'

'And if it has?'

Marla pouted. 'You'll have to wing it.'

CHAPTER 26

It was 9.30pm when Grace approached the playground for the second time that night, this time alone. With Marla it had been an adventure, alone it felt perilous.

No other traffic was on the road as she slowed near the entrance. Her heart pounding, she drove in at toddler crawling-pace. Her headlights illuminated Western's car, parked by itself in the same spot, looking abandoned. It was raining again, making the parts of the playground not illuminated by her headlights inky and foreboding. Taking a wide berth, she parked further away from the car than previously. Leaving the engine running, she let a long, slow breath escape.

'I'm not sure I'm made for this shit.'

While she let the tension drain away, she looked around, but she could see little except Western's car and creepy-looking parts of the playground distorted in her car's headlights. When she felt confident the other car remained unoccupied, she switched off her engine and lights. The sound of light rain accompanied the metallic tinging of cooling metal as she waited for her eyes to adjust to the gloom.

Leaving her coat because it was only drizzling, she ventured out of her car. Looking around, she saw nothing concerning although the bleak scene was far from reassuring. And what had happened to Western? She would check his car, retrieve Marla's GPS bug then ring the police. The police wouldn't attend a call this minor on a Friday night, but if they did send a car, she would have to wait. She shivered at the thought that Western could reappear – or that he was already here.

Giving herself a lets-go-team mental pep talk, she stalked towards Western's car. The car still looked abandoned, but she was ready. What she would do if someone sprang out, apart from shitting herself, was unclear. Thankfully she didn't have to find out, the car remained unoccupied. Alongside the feeling of relief was the question, where the fuck was Western? He had driven here from his house in Feilding, that they knew. He had locked his car, taken the keys, and disappeared. If they hadn't picked him up, where was he?

Contemplating these questions, she took out her phone to call Marla. Before she could, headlights on the road caught her attention. She watched with increasing alarm as the lights slowed as they neared the turn-off to the playground.

'Fuck. Fuck.'

There is a moment when panic hits that makes you want to run around in a circle screaming. Grace could physically hear blood pumping in her ears as the lights almost stopped before the vehicle turned, predator-like, towards her. She remembered a piece of advice from a first aid training session a decade earlier. The instructor, an overweight, sweating man who looked as if he would soon need the very training he was delivering, told them, 'If you're first at an accident scene, the first pulse you need to take is your own.'

Taking a moment to consider her options, she sprinted towards the children's playground, the only hiding place she could reach in time. As the vehicle's lights lit up the car park she slipped into the middle of a children's fort. From her position, underneath a slide, she was both hidden and had a clear view of what was happening, which wasn't much. The headlights of what she recognised as a flatbed tow truck had stopped, illuminating both cars.

She considered texting Marla, but her phone would light up like a Christmas tree. Besides, she had no idea who was in the truck – and what could Marla do? It could be Western and his boss, although arriving in a tow truck made it unlikely. It could simply be a tired traveller pulling in for a rest or to have a coffee. That also seemed unlikely. The truck showed no signs of leaving.

As the adrenalin wore off, the cold started to bite. She had planned to be out of her car for only a few minutes and hadn't put on her jacket. After what felt like hours, the doors opened and two figures in beanies, overalls, and high-viz gear got out and moved to the front of the truck. They were tow-truck operators – towies.

The closest towie, who was easily a foot taller than his mate, said,

'The instructions were to retrieve an abandoned vehicle. They didn't say two vehicles.'

'But which vehicle?' asked the shorter towie, her voice surprising Grace, who had assumed they were both men. 'They don't look abandoned, just parked up, bro.'

'I don't know. Maybe they met for a sly fuck?'

'Eww,' Grace whispered. Western and her, what a cringeworthy thought.

'In this weather? Where would they go?'

The male towie pointed. 'The toilets over there.'

'What? And they're still banging away even though our lights have made it like daylight? Jeez, you're a queer rooster, I'm glad you're not my boyfriend. Besides, that Mitsi looks brand new. Anyone driving that can afford a room.'

'It must be the Mondeo we're meant to tow,' he said. 'It's seen better days.'

Grace shook her head. These fuckers had dissed her car and now they planned to tow it instead of Western's car. There were plenty of unknowns, but what she did know was these two towies were not the people they were chasing. Fixing her jaw, she broke from her cover and walked towards them. She wasn't sure what she was going to do but she realised that she needed to do it now.

'Oi,' she called out. 'What are you two clowns doing?'

'Jesus Christ,' said the male towie. 'Who the fuck are you?'

Closing in on them, she said, 'Mind your language, eh, you're not in the rugby clubrooms now.' In situations like this, it paid to assert control.

They shuffled their feet but stayed quiet as Grace joined them, staying outside the headlight beams. 'Now, what are you doing? You're interrupting my investigation.'

The woman towie answered. 'What does it look like? We're towing the battered Mondeo.'

Before she could defend her car's honour, the male towie said, 'Investigation? Are you a cop?'

Grace hoped her use of the word would lead them to that conclusion. 'Close enough. Who ordered you to pick up an abandoned vehicle?'

'How the …' The male towie checked his language. 'Listen, lady, they tell us to tow a car and that's what we're doing. And what do you mean "close enough"? Let's see your ID.'

'All in good time, and that' – Grace pointed to Western's car – 'is the abandoned car.'

They looked at the gleaming red sedan, then at Grace's tired Ford before focusing back on her.

'What sort of cop drives an old dunger like that?'

'An undercover cop.' Her answer was a question made to sound like a statement.

The towies exchanged a glance before reluctantly nodding.

Grace's journalistic antennae told her it was time to push. 'You have no idea who called this in?'

They exchanged a glance and shook their heads.

'I'm calling in my colleagues,' said Grace.

'Why?' they said in unison.

'Because bad shit is going down.'

'Well,' said the male towie, 'we're towing the car right now unless you have ID. We don't get paid if we don't tow the car.'

The scene couldn't have been stranger. A standoff between two tow-truck operators and Grace, pretending she was an undercover police officer; at night in a wet playground; in the middle of nowhere; the near-new car of a missing alt-right car dealer about to be towed.

Grace first rang the police, who took the details but to her relief their enthusiasm told her they wouldn't be making it a priority. While she did this, the tow truck reversed up to Western's car and they started winching it onto the truck.

She rang Marla next, filling her in on events.

'Sounds like you've handled it great,' said Marla. 'And no sign of Western?'

'The scene hadn't changed,' said Grace, 'so who organised to tow his car? And why?'

Grace waited for Marla to chew over the information.

'We can go over what we know on the way back.' Over the sound of a muffled horse racing commentator, Marla asked, 'What's the tow truck doing?'

'It's about to take Western's car. I can't stop them without the police.'

'Did you remember the bug?'

'It's in my pocket.'

'How far away are you?'

'Twenty minutes, max. How's your evening going?'

'Fantastic,' she said flatly. 'Had I known I was coming here I would've dressed differently. I stand out like, what was it, dog's balls.'

'You may get lucky.'

'Thanks for that. I've had a few approaches, male *and* female. See you soon. Text me when you get here, and I'll meet you outside.'

With a final clang, the towies secured Western's car in place. Grace watched them drive off, Western's abandoned car bouncing on the tow truck. Pitched back into total darkness, she hurried to her car.

It was almost 10.30pm when Grace arrived at the Pinetree Arms to rescue Marla. Rather than texting, sensing a little fun, she went inside. Marla was sitting at a leaner with a man who looked like a long-retired accountant. She was looking bored as the man, oddly dressed for the location in a suit, beamed as he chatted to her.

As she walked over, Marla saw her, checked her phone, and gave her a steely look.

Grace had to semi-shout to make herself heard over an animated race commentator. 'I thought I'd find you here – *again*.'

Finishing her drink, Marla said, '*You're* always working late.'

The man's face beamed. 'Another lovely lady, what'll you have?'

Turning to the man, Grace said, 'And who might you be?'

'Derek,' he said, 'at your service. What would you like to drink?'

'Sorry Derek, it'll have to be another time.' She turned to Marla. 'Come on you, it's past your bedtime.'

Derek's eyes widened but they were out the door before he could work out what to say. They were still giggling when they were in Grace's car.

'He was harmless,' said Marla. 'He was explaining how he made money betting on dog races. It helped pass the time and he kept worse elements from trying their luck. Fucking boring though. It was like sitting in an army bar in the bad old days.'

'Did he win any money?'

She gave Grace an are-you-serious look. 'What do you think?'

Grace navigated through the suburban streets to the highway heading to Palmerston North. 'What a surreal night. And we're no closer to finding out who's behind whatever's going on.'

'We've a few avenues to follow, but we'll need your SIS contact to follow them up.'

'JP will help, if it helps the SIS or the police.'

'It will. Between politely putting off drunk admirers and dog racing, after you told me about the tow truck, I couldn't come up with a scenario that leaves Western alive.'

'Really?'

'Think about it. He drives to the playground, parks, and locks his car. The next event we know about is a tow truck turning up to pick up his car. I doubt he'd willingly abandon his work car.'

Grace bounced the logic around while she drove. 'You're right. If Western had a choice, he wouldn't have done it that way. What do you think's happened? This is your field, not mine.'

'Unless they've pulled off an elaborate deception on the off chance he was followed … he's still at the park.'

Groaning, Grace didn't need Marla to complete the logic.

Marla continued. 'They arrived at the appointed time or, more likely, they were waiting. We'll have them on the video, but only once so they'll be hard to spot because we have no idea what time they left.'

'I called the police, but if they turn up now his car's gone. They'll assume he picked it up himself.'

'That's why we need to involve your SIS contact. Something bad is happening but I can't work out what all the fuss is about. It can't just be your alt-right stories, they're not worth killing someone over, but someone's worried.'

'If it's not the alt-right, it involves ProtectNZ. I'll call JP, it's past eleven but she's a public servant,' said Grace, smirking. 'First, though, let's get my story straight if I've been acting solo.'

They spent five minutes running through events, massaging them so it sounded like she was acting alone in her capacity as an investigative journalist. When they were happy her story sounded solid, Grace found a quiet place to park and called SIS agent Jenna Parata, putting the call on speaker phone.

'Who's this?' a groggy voice asked.

'JP, it's Grace Marks. Sorry it's late. I hope I haven't interrupted um … anything.'

'Ace?' After an extended silence, Parata said, 'I forgot I gave you my number. Jesus, this better be important.'

'It's about the alt-right, and maybe ProtectNZ. I think the person who put the hate mail in my letterbox has gone missing, in a bad way.'

After a long, tired sigh, Parata said, 'Start at the beginning.'

As rehearsed, she took the SIS agent through the events that led to the abandoned car and missing alt-right car dealer. Parata interrupted with the odd question, 'Why didn't you call the police?' and 'How did you track him?'

'There's nothing I can do now,' said the agent. 'Without a body or stronger evidence, I can't get the police involved until the morning. Can you meet me at the playground tomorrow at ten?'

'Sure.'

'If this is a wild goose chase, I'll change my number and have you thrown in jail.' Parata terminated the call.

'I'm one of her favourites,' said Grace.

CHAPTER 27

Grace had expected a typical morning-at-the-park scene when she arrived at Pharazyn Reserve. Children yahooing over the playground while rugged-up mums and dads sat around drinking coffee. But what she saw was a lot of police cars and emergency tape. The playground was a crime scene.

The day had dawned clear but cold, the weather system that battered them the previous night having blown itself out. Grace, in tartan tights, black skirt, a fashionable dark-blue hoodie, scarf, and sunglasses, had allowed plenty of time for the drive back to the playground to meet the SIS agent. Edging her car up to the emergency tape, she buzzed down her window. The police officer gave her a hard stare before ambling over to her open window. 'Sorry, the park's out of action today.'

'I can see that. I'm here about whatever's happened. I'm meeting JP.'

The police officer narrowed her eyes. 'Who?'

'Agent Parata, she's with the SIS.'

'One moment.'

The officer stepped away from Grace's car to talk into the radio microphone on her shoulder. After a rapid exchange, incoherent to Grace, she leaned over. 'You need to park along the road. The techs are still at work. Follow the path between the tape, I'll let them know you're coming.'

Grace followed the instructions and was soon walking towards a scene containing uniformed police officers, what looked like plain clothes detectives and, in the distance working in the scrub, techs in hazmat suits. Agent Parata peeled away from a group in conversation to intercept her.

'For once I can honestly say it's great to see you, Ace.'

Forcing a smile, she said, 'What's going on.'

'I'll get to that later.' Grace opened her mouth to protest but Parata held up a hand. 'If I told you now, it'd muddy your recollections. We need to hear what happened to you yesterday before I can fill in any blanks.'

'That makes sense.'

Parata signalled over to the group she had just left and a man in plain clothes headed their way. Grace instantly recognised Detective Fergusson from the time he had interviewed her in a murder case, the murder the police believed Marla committed. He had taken the role of bad cop bordering on arsehole cop, a part he played too well and seemed to enjoy too much.

'Detective Fergusson,' said Grace, 'you haven't changed a bit.'

'I didn't think you'd remember me.'

'Oh, you made quite an impression.'

'Enough banter,' said Parata. 'Can we record this, Ace?'

'It's off the record,' said Fergusson, 'but it'll make our life easier.'

'Sure, I have nothing to hide.'

'Thanks,' said Parata. 'You rang me last night because you were concerned about a missing person.'

'That's right and I also rang the police.'

'What time?' asked Fergusson.

Grace's face scrunched. 'I rang the police first, that must have been around ten. They didn't seem interested, but it was Friday night.'

'Take us through what happened,' said the detective.

They stayed silent, allowing her to walk them through the Grace-on-her-own edited version of the night's events. It was the truth less Marla enabling her to deliver it confidently. As Marla and Grace had agreed, she omitted using a drone to stake out their attempted ambush at The Lookout. Trying to pretend she did when she didn't own a drone would stretch her credibility. She knew she was on thin journalistic ground as she told them of staking out her own house, seeing the person post the note and following him to his car to get his number plate through to bugging Western's car to see if he would lead her to bigger fish.

They listened without asking any questions, waiting for her to finish. She didn't detect any sign that they were suspicious.

'And you called me on your way home,' said Parata.

'The more I dwelt on it, the more it felt off. I mean, where was Western?'

The SIS agent's gaze intensified. 'What sort of bug did you use?'

Marla warned they would be interested in the bug; Grace had an answer ready. 'A cheap GPS one. I figured out a while ago if I can't beat you, JP, I can join you.'

For the first time, Parata didn't look convinced. 'Is it still on the car?'

Taking the bug out of her pocket, she tossed it in the air. 'No. The car was heading to a car yard. I'd never see it again.'

Fergusson asked, 'Were you the last person to leave the park?'

'Totally. I left a minute after the tow truck. It was pitch-black. I wasn't hanging around.'

'Why did you hide from the tow truck?' asked Parata.

Grace, feeling tag-teamed, tried to suppress her annoyance. 'Because I didn't know it was a tow truck. I expected it was going to be Western and whoever he had met.'

'But your car was in the car park,' said Fergusson.

'I may have panicked a little. I don't normally do this shit.'

'Why were you doing this shit?' he asked.

'Because something is rotten in the state of Denmark, and I write stories about that stuff. It involves the alt-right and maybe ProtectNZ, but I haven't connected the dots, not yet.'

Parata nodded. 'Interesting. Anyway Ace, I'm happy to feed you enough for a story, but you'll need to leave parts out.'

'I saw a few familiar faces parked along the road. When can you let me in on what happened?'

'When we're done here.' Parata looked at Fergusson, who nodded. 'But we need to find out what you know first.'

They took turns asking more questions, which she answered carefully. They had no idea of her movements last night, her appearance at the Pinetree Arms and the time gaps in her story that would stand out exactly like a dog's balls. Not that she had any involvement in what she assumed was now a murder inquiry. Equally, she didn't want them thinking she was holding back information as that would make them suspicious. If she did stumble, her fallback position was that she was protecting a source, which was true – sort of.

'Thanks, Ace,' said Fergusson switching off the recorder on his phone. 'We'll need to interview you again, officially. Any problem with that?'

Grace shook her head.

'Great. I'll keep plodding away and let JP give you as much as she can.'

Fergusson jumped into a conveniently parked car and drove away, lights flashing.

Having to look up at the tall SIS agent, Grace said, 'I assume you've found Regan Western's body?'

Shaking her head, the agent said, 'There's a body all right, but it's not Regan Western.'

A range of expressions crossed Grace's face before it settled on confusion. 'Who then?'

'His brother, Geoffrey Western.'

Grace watched Marla enter the café, look around casually but carefully before sauntering over to where Grace was sitting at a table near the back.

After sending Marla a heads-up message about what she had learnt from Agent Parata, she spent an hour in the café writing a story. She took her time, wanting to include all the information that would become public but also hold back information pointing to a bigger story. Why give other media outlets a sniff? Her story would become breaking news, containing details rival outlets couldn't know but would eventually copy.

Parata had told her she couldn't name the victim; they wanted to keep that out of the public domain to see if they could use it to generate leads. Grace was also careful not to include information that would alert the police or the SIS she knew more than she had told them – it was a balancing act.

'I ordered smoothies,' said Grace.

'Perfect,' said Marla as she joined her. 'So, Geoffrey, not Regan.'

'I know, that floored me. They were still searching the scene, but JP said as the weather overnight was bad, they didn't expect to find more evidence.'

Marla pursed her lips. 'Western was scared, he sends his more violent brother in his place. Whoever met him didn't know one Western from the other, or the meeting went bad. Both scenarios sound plausible. Where did they find the body?'

'In the bushes near the water. JP said he'd been shot, and his body dumped far enough in so it wouldn't be easy to find.'

'Did she say who found it?'

'An early-morning walker whose dog wouldn't come when she called. They found drug paraphernalia on his body, but JP said the scene techs thought it looked dodgy. The killers might have planted it to make it look like a drug deal gone wrong.'

'Killers?' Marla frowned. 'Plural?'

'That's what JP said.'

Marla grunted.

'What?'

'It's like we're in amateur hour,' said Marla, 'A dead body. Western's car will be in a tow-truck yard. All easily traceable and yet there's no link to the killers.'

'But if we hadn't bugged his car, which they didn't expect, nobody would've known he ever went to the playground – apart from his dead body of course.'

'Exactly. That's what I mean about amateur hour. It looks like they've been lucky, but in this game it's never luck.'

The smoothies arrived, the interruption giving them a moment to reflect.

'Is it like how you've hidden from the authorities?' said Grace. 'They're confident any evidence they leave behind will result in a dead end. They must have figured Western's disappearance, no matter which brother it was, would eventually create a search. His body would turn up or the plates of the car run, but they don't care. They're confident the trail's stone cold.'

'Except the trail's not stone cold.'

Grace tilted her head.

'It would be if it was Regan Western who was dead, he was their weak link. They must know they killed the wrong Western; they chucked his body in the bushes.' Marla stirred her smoothie. 'They know Regan Western's alive; the police now know he was the target; and he knows he should be dead. What they won't know, unless they have an informer inside the police, is that you were there – that's handy. But what's their next move? And what's Western going to do?'

'The police have him,' said Grace. 'JP said when they realised it was his brother, the police *detained* Regan Western.'

'He'll be shitting himself,' said Marla. 'And he got his brother killed.'

'Will he talk?'

Marla shrugged. 'It doesn't matter. Even if he doesn't, it will look like he has. It's a common police tactic. The act of bringing the person in for questioning makes them look like a snitch.'

'I doubt he'll give them the names of those at the top,' said Grace.

'I doubt he knows them, he's hardly likely to be in their inner circle. An alt-right car dealer living in a small town?' She shook her head.

Grace harrumphed. 'The SIS have a lead, Western, but we're back to square one. There's dodgy dealing going on and I'm sure it links the alt-right with ProtectNZ.'

'You're probably right, but at least you're safe now.'

'Am I?' said Grace, her nostrils flaring. 'For how long? Whatever's going on, whoever's controlling this, they think murdering people who get in the way is reasonable. The only way I'll be safe is if I drop investigating their activities.'

After a suitable period of silence, Marla said, 'You could drop it,' adding as Grace's eyes flared joining her nostrils, 'or you could fan the flames.'

'I can't drop it.'

'I know,' said Marla. 'I had to say it for completeness, it *is* an option. Leave it to the police and the SIS, maybe they'll work out who's at the top of the pyramid.'

Grace scoffed.

'I agree. Whoever Western gives up, if he gives up anyone, will have a cast-iron alibi ready to roll out.' Marla picked up her phone, tapped briefly, and slid it across the table.

Scrutinising the blurry image of a motorcycle, Grace asked, 'What's this?'

'I went through the footage again. None of the cars looked right, but this motorcycle … I dismissed it the first time because I was looking for a car or van.'

'The two who shot Ball wore black motorcycle gear,' said Grace, staring at the image.

'I know. Flick to the next image.'

It showed the motorcycle on a forty-five-degree angle as it approached their position outside the public toilets. 'There are two of them,' said Grace. 'It's blurry, but there's a passenger.'

'If it *is* them, it explains a lot. JP mentioned killers, plural. Western's brother wasn't a saint, he wouldn't have turned up unprepared. Hard for one person to take him by surprise, easier for two. Even easier if they're professionals.'

'It's also easier for two people to carry a body and dump it halfway into scrub,' said Grace, her eyes lighting up. 'This is excellent, we've a lead.'

Marla put a finger to her lips and Grace realised she had been almost shouting.

'Sorry, it's the excitement.' She continued, leaning closer and whispering. 'We've captured them on film. You can run the number plate before we give the information to JP.'

'I hate to burst your bubble,' said Marla who leaned closer and mimicked Grace's whisper. 'Have another look at the images.'

After she had flicked through the images on the phone, she returned Marla's phone. Speaking in her normal voice, she said, 'They've taken the plates off.'

Marla shook her head. 'Motorcycles carry a single plate. Even if they weren't using a fake, which they would've, we captured them front on – riding away from the playground.'

'What about when they arrived? They would've ridden past us the other way.'

'If it was them, they were at the playground before we had parked. If they planned to take him out, or even just lean on him, getting there early gave them options. It's what I would've done.'

'Fuck, another dead end.'

'It looks that way,' said Marla.

'Are we any closer than we were when you first nailed Western?'

'Regan Western has information, but the police have him. Even when they let him go, I doubt he'll talk to either of us.'

Grace groaned. 'He won't.'

'On the positive side, whoever's behind this is desperate to keep a low profile,' said Marla. 'They won't risk trying to intimidate you. Their main concern will be keeping Western quiet.'

'They're too late, aren't they?'

'It depends if he plays ball. If he keeps quiet …'

'The police can't hold him,' said Grace. 'Not if he hasn't committed a crime.'

'We can't even prove it was him posting the hate mail.'

Grace finished her smoothie with a loud slurp. 'Well, I don't intend to sit on my hands. I need to get more material to bend ProtectNZ and the alt-right over the table. What are you going to do?'

'Bend them over the table; colourful,' said Marla, shaking her head. She drank the last of her smoothie. 'I'm not sure. I'll hang around for a few more days, see what happens with Western. If you get any news, fire it through our secure comms.'

'Sounds like a plan.'

'How bad do you think this is?' asked Marla. 'I mean really?'

Her nose wrinkling, Grace said, 'I'm a journalist looking for a story, so I'm biased as hell. If the same people were behind Ball's shooting, there's an alt-right ProtectNZ connection. And if Ball's shooting was someone's fucked-up idea of a publicity stunt, they're trying to manipulate New Zealanders and change the trajectory of our politics, of our society. This may sound OTT, but they're trying to pervert New Zealand's political system, our democracy – that's pretty big.'

Marla pursed her lips. 'It doesn't take much. Add a few smart geeks to a bunch of rich, corrupt, power-hungry men and you end up with Cambridge Analytica treating democratic elections as their plaything. The two on the motorcycle, they must be pros and that means they're not cheap. There's money sloshing around, lots of it.'

Grace stayed quiet.

'The assignments I was given, I did them because the money was great, but it also meant the world was a better place because we fucked over power-hungry, greedy arseholes who wanted to control the world.'

'As long as they weren't power-hungry, greedy arseholes aligned to the US,' said Grace.

'There was that,' agreed Marla.

After a lengthy pause, Grace asked, 'And?'

'And … I don't like power-hungry, greedy arseholes who think they can do what they like. I'm working on a plan.'

Agent Parata hadn't bothered to take off her sunglasses even though the police interview room was windowless. Located in the bowels of the Palmerston North Police Station, the room was tiny, containing a small round table with three uncomfortable schoolroom chairs. She was here in her official SIS domestic terrorism capacity, but they had agreed that Fergusson, as lead detective, would ask the questions.

'Sorry to keep you waiting Regan,' said Detective Fergusson. 'Did they give you something to eat and drink?'

Western, eyes down and looking miserable, nodded.

'I'm sorry about your brother. It must be a shock.'

Western nodded again.

'This is an official interview, Regan, as part of our homicide investigation into the murder of Geoffrey "Hans" Western. We're recording the interview.'

Western flinched at the mention of his brother but kept looking at the table.

Fergusson stated the date, time and who was present for the interview. 'Regan, take us through the events that led to your brother borrowing your car on Friday night and driving to Pharazyn Reserve. Take your time and give us the whole story, don't leave anything out.'

Scrutinising him, after two sentences she knew he was giving a dubious, pre-prepared account. Western told them his brother, who he called Geoff, had asked to borrow the car to "pop down to Wellington". He had no idea where his brother was going or who he was meeting. Fergusson played his part well, looking attentive, letting Western do the talking.

Like most liars, Western would gain confidence if he thought his audience believed his bullshit. So, as he talked, he relaxed. His problems increased when his growing confidence allowed him to add embellishments in his attempt to make his story sound more concrete.

When he had finished, Fergusson quietly took his time looking through the notes he had taken. Eventually, he asked, 'Does your company let you lend lot cars to family members?'

Western shifted in his chair. 'No. But, well … you know.'

'Know what?'

'Everyone does it. Geoff often borrowed my car.' Western smiled weakly, evidently happy he had knocked the question out of the park.

Fergusson stared at Western for an uncomfortable length of time before returning to his notes. 'When did you say your brother picked up the car?'

Parata watched the strain on Western's face as he tried to remember the story he had told.

'Around five, I can't remember exactly.'

Fergusson made a note before asking, 'Does your company track its fleet?'

'What do you mean?' Western looked like he had smelt dogshit on his shoe.

'Use GPS tracking so if a car's stolen it can be tracked down.'

'No.'

Fergusson made a face. 'Interesting.'

'Why is that interesting?'

'The information I was given is that your car was being tracked with a GPS bug.'

Fergusson had chosen his words carefully to avoid entrapping Western with a lie. Western's face creased as his mind raced to work out what that small piece of information did to his story. He knew the dealership hadn't bugged his car leaving a range of scenarios, none of them good. They knew the bug belonged to Grace, at least that was her story, though it didn't fit with the journalist Parata knew. She had let it slide at the time but now, as she considered it again, it sounded dodgy.

'If not your company, who put it there?' asked the detective.

Western shrugged, kicking for touch. 'Maybe they've started and haven't told us.'

Fergusson made an are-you-serious face before leafing through his notes. 'What did you do Friday evening, Regan? After your brother had taken your car.'

'Stayed home. Drank too much and watched the rugby.'

'Anyone with you?'

Western shook his head. 'My ex had the children.'

The detective kept asking a range of unconnected questions. This ploy made storytelling harder. To keep his story from disintegrating, Western had to keep adding small pieces of information. Fergusson was giving him time to stumble and second-guess himself.

'You said your brother often borrowed your car. How often?'

Western shifted uneasily, it was exactly what he said. 'It wasn't that often. Maybe once a month.'

'To go to Wellington?'

'Usually.'

'Did your brother carry a mobile phone?'

Western stared at the detective. 'Everyone does.'

'Do they? We didn't find one on him … or in your car.'

Western, playing his cards terribly, blew out a shallow breath before he caught himself.

'We obtained his mobile number from his partner and dragged his phone records,' said Fergusson, sliding a piece of paper towards Western. 'The number highlighted in yellow, that is your number, isn't it?'

Western reluctantly dragged the page over. 'Yes.'

'You called him nine times but' – unhurriedly, Fergusson turned over multiple pages of his notes – 'you didn't text him. Why?'

Parata nodded imperceptibly at the line of questioning. Phone companies didn't record voice calls, much to the annoyance of the SIS. The amount and cost of the storage required would have been astronomical. Some companies kept text messages for a few months so people with secrets, criminals mainly, didn't text. It wasn't proof, but it was indicative.

Western stared at the page.

'You don't strike me as the worrying kind, Regan, especially if you were drinking. What was going on?'

'I was worried about the car. Getting into trouble at work.'

'Did you call or text anyone else?'

'I can't remember. I told you; I'd been drinking.'

'Check your phone. Take it out, have a look.'

His hand moved towards his back pocket but he stopped, placing his hand on the table. 'No, it's … personal.'

Fergusson stared at him. 'What are you hiding, Regan?'

'Nothing. I don't want you looking at my personal information, that's all.'

'Okay, Regan. We can revisit that later.' Fergusson lazily flicked through his notes. 'Ah yes, were you planning to meet someone on Friday?'

They had no evidence to back up the question, it was another piece of information that had come from Grace who had been vague about how she uncovered their meeting plan. Now, as the question hung in the room, Parata wondered how the hell she had found out. That was closer to spying than investigative journalism.

Western's eyes flicked around the room. 'No.'

'Oh,' said Fergusson. 'I was under the impression you had a meeting at eight o'clock, around the time your brother was killed.'

His entire concocted story rested on the fact that, apart from those he was meant to be meeting, nobody else knew he should have been at the fatal meeting. Now, as she watched him squirm, it was the pivotal moment of the interview. Would he stick to his story, or would the truth come gushing out?

After a long moment, he said, 'No. Who told you that?'

'I'm not able to disclose that information.'

Parata watched the detective change gears from naïve inquirer to inquisitor, his voice rising.

'Come on, Regan, don't play games. We can't protect you if you don't tell us who you – not your brother who went in your place and who's now dead – who you were meant to meet at eight o'clock on Friday.'

Western's head dropped. They leaned closer.

'I want to leave now,' he said, not looking up. 'I know my rights.'

Fergusson sat back, licking his lips. 'If you want to leave, you're free to do so.' Western made to stand, but Fergusson slapped his hand on the table with an open palm, causing him to flinch. Western eased back into his chair, staring at the table. 'A word of advice, *Regan* – be very careful. The world is soon going to know, if they don't know already, it's *Geoff*, not you, lying in the morgue. If the story you've given us is true, and we both know it's total bollocks, you've nothing to worry about.'

'Can I go now?' Western asked, without looking up.

Fergusson glared at him before glancing towards her. Parata shrugged. They had to arrest him or let him go, and he hadn't committed a crime.

Fergusson noisily pushed his chair back, stood, and opened the door. As Western passed him, Fergusson said quietly, 'I doubt they'll make the same mistake again. Call us, we're here to help.'

They listened to his footsteps fade as he made his way to the front desk.

Fergusson slumped into a chair. 'Fuck, I thought I had him.'

'I thought you did too. You played it well. Hopefully it'll dawn on him that he's fucked and we're his only way out of this … alive.'

'Have you put a tail on him?' asked Fergusson.

The agent raised her eyebrows. 'I'm tying this case to Ball's shooting, so it falls within my orbit.'

'With Ball's shooting?'

'Call it a hunch, but I think there's a connection.'

The detective frowned.

'Marks was there when Ball was shot,' said the agent. 'She was in the vicinity when Western was shot. And she knows more than she's letting on.'

'Really?'

'She's not involved, but I know Ace, I know her limitations. She's had help. I'm curious to know who it is and why she's keeping it a secret. I've put eyes on her too and, on my way back to Wellington, I'm going to pay her a surprise visit.'

CHAPTER 30

'Mum, there's a tall woman at the door.'

Grace's daughter came into the room Grace used as an office. She was working on yet another story featuring ProtectNZ, her working title was, 'ProtectNZ: the alt-right connection'. The method she followed was to write the story she wanted before rewriting the parts where she didn't have evidence to support her assertions. In this case, she had little evidence to support any of them.

She stopped typing and turned to her daughter. 'What? How tall?'

'Very. And she's familiar, I think I've met her before.'

Grace smiled. If it was agent Jenna Parata her daughter had indeed met her, though thankfully she hadn't joined the dots. Parata had once been part of an SIS team that had come to Grace's house to arrest her. Her daughter had stood in their way, and she was giving them a right gob-full, as only teenagers can, when the team leader, not Parata, punched her in the stomach, flattening her. Her daughter was still dark about the incident as, in her daughter's charming words, 'the police had not yet publicly hung, drawn and shat on the perp'.

'Thanks, sweetheart,' said Grace, shaking herself back to the present. If Parata was indeed at the door, she needed to make a quick check of the lounge to make sure there was no sign of Marla's visits – there wasn't.

When she went to the front door, she found Parata sitting on a bench on the front porch looking like she always did: her hair in a tight ponytail, sunglasses, white shirt, black jacket, black pants and black shoes.

Standing, Parata asked, 'Hidden your secret radio and all the other items you don't want me to find?'

Ignoring her observation, Grace countered with, 'Do you only have one set of clothes?'

The agent walked over, pushing her sunglasses onto the top of her head, stopping a few feet away. Because she towered over her, Grace felt, as she always did when face-to-chest with Parata, that she was in trouble with the school principal.

'Do you have time for a quick chat?' asked the agent.

'Sure, JP, come in. We can sit at the dining room table, I'm sure you remember the way.'

She walked past Grace smiling slyly. 'Touché.'

After Grace had introduced her daughter and organised coffee, the two women sat opposite each other across the dining table.

Without waiting for Parata, Grace snuck in the first question. 'Did Western talk?'

Leaning forward, putting her elbows on the table, Parata said, 'The problem I have is that you're a journalist.'

'And the problem *I*' – Grace widened her eyes for emphasis – 'have is that the SIS are a law unto themselves.'

Parata smirked. 'What I meant was, I have information which if I shared and you printed, I would get into a world of trouble. I'm sure you realise my superiors don't think we need a relationship with the media, let alone with you. Anne, not her real name and my boss, would have an apoplectic fit if she knew I was here.'

'Yeah, I get that. But we *are* on the same side, at least on this one, aren't we? Ball's shooting, that's domestic terrorism. I want to expose the people calling the shots, you want to catch them. Sounds like win-win to me.'

'If we can help each other – under the radar – I agree.'

'Great. So did Western talk?'

'Whoa,' said the agent. 'Before we get to that, you need to come clean. Take me through the events before the murder, all the events. The police may have bought your story, but personally I doubt it. It looks like Swiss cheese from where I'm sitting.'

'What?' Grace tried to look shocked.

'You staked out your own house; saw Western post a note; you tracked him to his car; traced the plate; bugged his car then followed it to a playground where his brother was murdered. And you did all this by yourself, that's your story, right?'

Grace shrugged. 'More or less.' When Parata put it like that, it sounded as dodgy as it was.

'How did you trace the number plate, Ace?'

'Through contacts. They looked up the plates on Motochek.'

'Very clever. Do they work for a car dealer?'

Hoping her face wasn't giving her away, Grace raced to remember how Marla had looked up the number plates. 'I think so.'

'Who do they work for?'

'Ah, I … I don't know.'

'Not a close friend?'

'They're a contact,' snapped Grace, annoyed Parata was grilling her.

Parata appeared calm, cocky even. 'According to the Motochek logs – I figured I should look – the only person in the last month, apart from me' – she raised her eyebrows – 'who's looked up the number plate of the car Regan Western drove worked for Vehicle Direct … in Otahuhu.'

'That could be right, for all I know,' said Grace, sipping her coffee. She felt like a mouse that a large, hungry cat was delightedly playing with.

'Otahuhu's a long way from Feilding. *He* looked up two more plates during the same session, guess whose they were?'

'All right, all right,' said Grace. 'I need time to think.'

'Think about what?'

The patronising tone annoyed Grace. 'Don't get all fucking SIS on me, JP. I was investigating a story.'

'Your contact looked up Geoffrey Western's car. Why? I'm sure the police would be interested.'

Grace glared.

'Listen,' said Parata, her voice lowering. 'I have discretion over what information I give the police and when I give it to them. We call it "incidentally obtained information". But I need to be on solid ground. You've told me part of the story, but you've left out important bits. I know you're not involved in the murder, but I need to be certain you've told me everything you know. Do not try and mug me off, Ace.'

Biting her lip, Grace knew Parata was right. She could hardly hold back information, not now her story didn't hold water. 'Let me make sure my daughter can't hear.'

The agent's stare was almost physical as she left the room.

She didn't need to check, like most teenagers her daughter had little interest in what her mum was doing, what she needed was two minutes to work out what she was going to say. Under no circumstances could she divulge Marla's involvement. When she returned, Parata had resumed her slouched position and was checking her phone. When Grace sat down, she eased herself up, putting her phone onto the table.

'I'll tell you exactly what happened, but I need to protect my source.'

Parata nodded once but didn't speak.

'I didn't stake out my house, my contact did. And he' – she was happy to keep her contact's sex as male – 'caught Western in the act. That's how he found out Western's identity.'

'Don't journalist's contacts just provide information?'

'He's sort of a friend too.'

'Is he?'

'It's the truth,' Grace protested.

'Why the three plates?'

'I'm getting to that,' said Grace. 'Western, as you know, is a bit player. I wanted to know who was in charge, so my contact set up a sting. In return for not making his involvement public, Western agreed to pass over the names of his superiors. That way I get the arseholes off my back *and* a big story to go chasing. But Western, with the help of his friends, tried to pull off his own sting. Western's brother was there, armed and waiting along with one other person who was driving the ute – the third number plate my contact checked. That's who we think knows who and what is behind this.'

'We? Were you there?'

Grace shook her head. 'I found this out after the fact.'

Parata's eyes narrowed.

'True story,' she insisted.

'Go on.'

'That's when he recorded the three number plates, they were all involved in what was an attempted ambush. It was *his* contact who looked them up.'

Staring for a long moment, Parata said, 'The third plate number, that car was there as well as the two Westerns?'

Grace nodded. 'It was a dead end. It's owned by a dealership in Wellington.'

'I know. I assume it was your' – Parata licked her lips – '*contact* who bugged Western's car and you both followed him, at least you followed his brother to the playground.'

'That's right. My story was accurate except there were two of us in the car. My contact remains anonymous, but I'll hand over what we have to you and the police.'

'I'd get on to it sharpish unless you want Fergusson breathing down your neck. What *do* you have?'

'We staked out the playground from a distance, recorded vehicles coming and going. We didn't notice it at the time, but a motorcycle with a passenger appeared on the video. They could be connected, but ...' She shrugged.

'A motorcycle with a passenger,' said Parata, frowning. 'How soon can you get the information to me?'

'After you leave, I'll drag it together and send it to you and Fergusson.'

'Do yourself, and me, a favour. Write a detailed list of what happened, and when. You've one chance to get your story straight so you don't look guilty as hell. I'd hate to watch Fergusson interrogate you – again.'

'Liar, you'd love it.'

Parata went to stand.

'Hang on,' said Grace. 'You haven't told me anything yet.'

Frowning, Parata slid back onto her chair. 'Western kept his mouth shut. And because we couldn't charge him, the police had to let him go. We've put eyes on him.'

'Isn't he in danger?'

'A shitload I'd say.' Parata appeared to consider what to say before adding, 'And we found Western's car.'

'In a tow-truck yard?'

Parata shook her head. 'Abandoned near Ōtaki Beach.' Grace frowned as she listened to her fill in the details. 'It looks like they wanted to add to the drug-deal-gone-bad scenario. It doesn't feel planned, more like they were scrambling to create a story – they obviously didn't know you and your contact had tracked the car. The car keys weren't on Western's body, so why they had it towed rather than driving it is a mystery. But if the killers rode a motorcycle …'

Grace went to ask a question, but Parata carried on speaking.

'Before you ask any more questions, as I said I can't give you much without climbing out onto a fucking shaky limb. What I *can* give you, *if* it never happened, is the name of the person driving the car a week ago.'

Grace's eyes widened.

'Can I have a pen and paper?'

Leaping up, she retrieved the items from her office. Parata wrote the details on the paper, folded it in half, and slid it to Grace.

'It's the CEO of the dealership who owns the car – he was ticketed for speeding. Whatever you find, you share – deal?'

'Deal.'

'In return, I'll share what I can, but on the down-low. Whoever was behind the wheel of the ute in Feilding, we need to talk to them.'

Standing, putting her sunglasses on, she pointed to the paper in Grace's hand. 'As you can imagine, we're going to pop in and introduce ourselves, but it wouldn't hurt having a journalist poking around at the same time.'

'I see,' said Grace. 'You're using me.'

'And you're not using me? Isn't another term for win-win, use-use?'

'I suppose it is if you're a glass-half-empty sort.'

Almost through the door, Parata turned around. 'Your contact's talented. To do all that and keep in the shadows, I'd like to meet them. Possible?'

'Ahhh … maybe.'

'Good. I'd like to have a chat' – Parata's eyes narrowed – 'with her.'

Marla held two fingers to her face, imitating the pose she had seen on many images of people taking selfies. She stood with one foot on her hired e-scooter, the other foot on the pavement, pretending to take a selfie. It was such a common sight that you could photograph people and scenes in front of you while everyone thought you were in love with your own reflection. The scene she was capturing was on the street where Grace lived, her focus was a plain white car and the sunglass-wearing woman behind the wheel.

Spy agencies such as New Zealand's SIS used a wide range of vehicles to blend into the scenery. But no matter the make and model they chose, they stood out like dog's balls – as Grace was fond of saying – though she wanted to make sure.

After scootering around the corner, out of sight of the spy car to limit the chance the agent might take an interest in her, she sent Grace a text from a burner phone. *Can you visit the supermarket? I think you've picked up a tail.*

She had been on her way to visit Grace after she had messaged about Parata's unexpected visit and that Parata had passed over a lead in identifying the man in the ute. Grace's children were out, and Sean was busy, so she was alone. Although Marla was keen for an update, it always paid to ensure the location hadn't been compromised.

While she waited for a reply, she rode around the block so she could approach Grace's house from the opposite end of the street. Halfway around she stopped to read Grace's reply – *Sure*. While still out of sight, she ended her e-scooter ride, put on a cap, took off her sunglasses, put on a set of headphones, and strolled around the corner.

A minute later, Grace's radiant-red Ford Mondeo trundled towards her. If she recognised Marla, her face didn't give it away. As Grace stopped at the intersection, she crossed the road in front of the plain white car. The driver took no notice of her as she performed a slow U-turn and cruised after Grace.

Using her phone, Marla located a replacement e-scooter, one in the opposite direction of the supermarket. Grace's tail wasn't interested in where Grace was going, she wanted to know who Grace might meet. That meant she would follow her into the supermarket in case there was a brush-contact exchange of information. She was now free to head, unobserved, to Grace's house, but Parata turning up unannounced together with the tail made it feel risky.

In a second text, she wrote – *White car, woman in sunglasses. Must be SIS.* She stopped typing – must it? Could she be part of the alt-right? Or the killers? She thought hard before concluding, no. The alt-right didn't use women and it wasn't the killer's MO. It was, on the other hand, the SIS's modus operandi to a tee. She finished the message – *I'll contact you later, no need for alarm. They're looking for me* – adding a smiley face emoji.

As she unlocked an e-scooter her phone pinged.

Cool. Pity, I'm buying South Island wine. Grace added an emoji with sunglasses.

Were they becoming friends? With a smiling shake of her head, Marla dismissed the idea and headed to Damien's house.

When she arrived, Damien was asleep on the couch, the strange game he liked to watch which took forever was on TV, her dog Indy was curled up with Damien like best friends forever. She wasn't surprised. He was so kind to Indy, giving her food off his plate and encouraging her to sleep on the bed. Those were two habits she had worked diligently to train out of her. Indy opened one eye but remained curled up. Marla mouthed 'traitor' – Indy closed her eye.

Taking a can of beer from the fridge, she sat on the outdoor settee in the last of the afternoon sun. After a long drink from the can, she closed her eyes. This assignment wasn't running as she expected, nor as she had wanted. She had envisioned being in and out in a few days, back to her life in Parapara. On the surface it was a straightforward identify-and-neutralise assignment, but it had become so layered.

The murder at the playground, the leader of ProtectNZ shot, and two killers riding around like phantoms all added to the situation's complexity. Professional killers aren't cheap. And then there was why? Most alt-right groups, to her mind, consisted mainly of involuntary celibates poncing around in Nazi gear and pumping iron because they couldn't get a date. She couldn't begin to understand the mentality of Nazis, or incels for that matter. It clearly wasn't just the sex they wanted; an entire industry had existed for centuries catering to that need. What these men wanted, seemingly craved, was power over women.

Drinking the cool beer from the can, she decided to contact Grace later in the evening, and get the name of the man who was involved. It might be the lead they needed but, given events, it was doubtful. It could send them on another wild goose chase, and the geese were ready for them now. She would need all her skills to stay in front of this operation.

'I thought I heard you,' Damien called from the house. 'I wonder why Indy didn't wake up?'

'Because she's your dog now. She loves you. I can see it in her eyes.'

He chuckled as Indy sprinted towards Marla, jumping into her lap and staring up at her. Marla instantly forgave her as Damien joined them, bringing out two more cans.

'Cheers,' he said as they clunked rather than clinked cans. 'How's the scumbag hunt going?'

Marla wrinkled her nose. 'It feels like we're chasing our tails.' She had kept Damien informed about progress although she had omitted salient details that might allow him to link what she was doing with the story about Grace which had been in the news.

'Has the harassment stopped?'

'For now. But unless we can find out what's going on, it'll start again.'

'Hmmm,' he said, sipping his beer. 'Time for leapfrog philosophy.'

Marla tilted her head.

'We contracted a consultant who used to work for the local university to do some leadership training. He was ... different, looked like a forestry worker, not an academic. Wore a "Pink Freud" T-shirt, can you imagine?'

'Academics can be odd,' said Marla.

'I know. When he turned up, I thought what the fuck have we here? Anyway, he was great. Attacked what he called "leadershit", talked about focusing on the people not spreadsheets. He made sense and he used that term, leapfrog philosophy.'

'I can guess,' she said. 'Don't follow the leader, leap over them.'

'Exactly. Bloody simple, but it changed the way we went about gaining business. Don't worry about what everyone else is doing. What do we need to do differently to get to the front of the pack?'

'I like it,' said Marla after sipping from her can. 'I mean, if we keep doing what we're doing, we're sure to stay a step behind.'

Damien patted Indy while her mind revisited an assignment in South America. She had flown in to provide technical support for an agent who had honey-trapped a target. In less than an hour she had sucked a treasure trove of files off the victim's laptop while he or she slept off the excesses of sex, alcohol, and whatever drug the agent had employed. The files, and the fact the target didn't know they had been compromised, had let them get way ahead.

After a long pause, he said, 'You have an idea, don't you?'

Marla leaned across the table and kissed Damien on the cheek. 'I love the concept. And yes, if I can "leapfrog" who we're chasing, it would help to expose these people and what they're doing.'

'What's your plan?'

She couldn't tell Damien about the honey-trap plan forming in her mind. She didn't even know who the target was – yet. But after she had talked to Grace, she would examine ProtectNZ and develop a list of potential targets.

'I'm still formulating it, I'll get there. I'll need to head home for a while.'

Damien's face fell.

'Not for too long,' she said, putting a hand on his arm. 'Maybe a week. I need to make sure my world is still spinning, that's all.'

Shaking his head, he said, 'Sorry, I know this isn't a forever arrangement, I just ... I like your company. And Indy's a pleasure to have around.'

'I'll bet she is.' Standing, causing Indy to spring from her lap, she grabbed their half-finished drinks. 'Let's finish these in the bedroom.'

CHAPTER 32

Agent Parata took in the unremarkable office. It could have been the office of any New Zealand CEO – car dealer, government agency or insurance company. The minimalistic furniture, fake plants, obligatory leather sofa, the technology of the office warrior, the masturbatory leadership images on the walls and, the *pièce de résistance*, the company values, as fake as the pot plants, framed on the wall – *Integrity, Communication, Respect* and *Excellence*.

She was again sitting in with Detective Fergusson, this time for the interview of Dawid Styles, CEO of the same nationwide car dealership that Regan Western worked for in their Feilding office. After introductions and handshakes, Styles offered hot drinks.

'We're fine, David,' said Fergusson, glancing at the SIS agent for confirmation.

'It's "Dawid", not David.' His chair protested as he settled himself behind his desk. 'How can I help the police?'

The man was, as Parata suspected, a stereotype of the majority of New Zealand CEOs – older, overweight, jowly, white, greying, presumably rich, confident and, it almost went without saying, male. Sporting an upmarket suit, white shirt, and green and white striped tie, she took an irrational instant dislike to him.

'My mistake … *Dawid*,' said the detective. 'We're investigating the murder of Geoffrey Western, whose body was found at the Pharazyn Reserve.'

'I expected a visit. I've already had the media trying to get hold of me because one of our cars was involved. I'd like to know who leaked that information to the media.'

'Shocking,' said Parata. 'Did you talk to them?'

'God no,' he said. 'It was the socialist rabble-rouser Marks. Female journalists are always the pushiest. I told her to go away, but not politely.'

Parata suppressed a smile.

Fergusson put on the perfect I'm-confused look. 'You knew the victim was Geoffrey Western?'

Following up before Styles could answer, Parata asked, 'How did you find out?'

His mouth dropped open. 'I've had all manner of people call me; word gets out. They say New Zealand is like a big village when there's gossip.'

'Is it?' said the detective. 'Can you remember who told you who the victim was?'

Styles shook his head, his jowls swaying under his chin. 'It sounded like common knowledge.'

Fergusson stared hard for a moment. 'How well did you know the deceased?'

Styles took his time before answering. 'Not well. He helped when we needed cars moved around the country. I've met him a few times when I've been around the dealerships and at work functions.'

'You didn't spend time with him socially?'

Styles shook his head, looking like he viewed the idea as preposterous.

'When were you last in Feilding?'

Parata watched the man's face and body language for signs he was lying. Not able to instantly recall, he checked his diary on his computer. It didn't look like an act; he genuinely couldn't remember.

'Here we are, three months ago. Do you want the exact date and time?'

'Not at the present,' said Fergusson. 'What car do you drive?'

'A Mitsubishi Outlander P-H-E-V. It's a hybrid, great for the planet.'

'It uses tyres, a lithium battery, and drives on asphalt,' she said. 'That means it's shit for the planet.'

They both stared at her.

Shrugging, she said, 'Just saying.'

Styles sniggered. 'Are you one of those green nutters who believe the planet's doomed?'

'No, but I'm not one of those gits who thinks there's no price to pay for raping the planet.'

A flash of anger crossed Styles' face.

Fergusson intervened. 'Righto, we're not here to solve the world's problems.'

Styles' face returned to what Parata considered his resting-pig face. The flash of anger she witnessed indicated to her he didn't like his views challenged – possibly because she was a woman. He fitted the entitled arsehole category of man who liked to throw his weight around whenever he could. Today he couldn't. She let it go, for now.

Fergusson flashed her a look before returning his focus to Styles. 'Do you drive cars off the lot?'

'Not often. It's usually when my wife wants to impress her friends at the golf club and is driving the Outlander.'

'And what's the protocol?'

Styles raised a bushy eyebrow.

The detective added, 'For when you, or anyone, takes a car off the lot.'

The second bushy eyebrow lifted. 'Ah, I understand. Well, for staff there's an online logbook they're supposed to fill in, but we're relaxed about it. I trust my staff to not rip off the system.'

'And you?'

'I should fill it in too but …' Styles shrugged to finish his sentence.

'I need to know the history of the orange ute parked out the back, out of sight. Have you sold it?'

'No.' Styles moved uneasily in his seat. 'It's been valeted.' Adding quickly, 'We valet the cars on a rotation, keep them spic and span for the punters. That wasn't the car involved in the incident though.'

'Wasn't it?'

'It can't have been,' said Styles. 'It's been here all weekend.'

'Has it?' asked Parata.

Styles nodded vigorously.

The detective said, 'I want a list of everyone who's driven it in the last month.'

Styles shrugged as he picked up his desk phone, stabbing the base with a pudgy finger. 'Peach, can you print out the driver logbook for the orange ute.' He listened to the reply. 'I know, print out what's there.'

After he had hung up, Parata asked, 'Is Peach her real name?'

Styles shook his head, his jowls following. 'No, it's an office nickname.'

'Lovely,' said Parata flatly, mentally adding misogynist to Styles list of human shortcomings.

A minute later an attractive woman with a curvy figure – presumably how she earned her nickname – came in and gave a single piece of paper to Styles. Thanking her, he inspected it then slid it across his desk, facing it towards them. 'Five test drives and AJ, he's in our sales team, took it home three weeks ago.'

They glanced at the page.

'No trip to and from Feilding on Wednesday the twentieth,' said Fergusson.

Parata added, 'And no Dawid Styles who was caught speeding in it ten days ago.'

'Can't hide anything from you two.' Styles shrugged. 'Eight k's over in a fifty-k zone. Arsehole policewoman didn't have a sense of humour.'

'I can imagine your sense of humour wouldn't impress everyone,' she said.

'You're right there,' he said chuckling, his face wobbling.

Parata took in a calming breath.

After he was sure Parata had finished, Fergusson took a picture from one of the folders he had brought. 'This image is from Feilding on the Wednesday I mentioned. The number plate matches, so someone took it to Feilding – who?'

The image was grainy, but it clearly showed the car and number plate but not the driver. Parata expected Styles to squirm, but he stayed relaxed, untroubled. She could tell he felt on safe ground. Before they arrived, she thought he might have been behind the wheel of the ute. Now he was a longshot and drifting. Added to that, he didn't look the type to get his hands dirty, he would have sent hired muscle.

He sat back smugly. 'Maybe the Feilding dealership had a client who wanted to take it for a test drive. I'll get Peach to ask around' – he grinned – 'get her to do *your* job.'

Like a cat who has been surprised by a dog, Parata felt her hackles rise. 'Do you own a Nazi uniform?'

If Styles had been drinking his coffee, he would have showered it over them, such was the shock of the question.

'What? How dare—'

Parata cut in. 'It's a simple yes or no question.'

'I don't have to sit here and be subjected—'

Holding up a hand, the detective said, 'Let's each take a breath.' He stared at her, but she knew it was a performance for Styles' benefit. 'My colleague asked because Geoffrey Western was a known member of an alt-right, white supremacist group.'

'Was he?' Styles spat.

'He was. You might have known him by his preferred name, "Hans".'

Styles shook his head briskly. 'As I said, he helped from time to time when we needed cars moved around the country. I really didn't know him.'

Fergusson pushed. 'You see, Geoffrey was also at Victoria Park on that Wednesday.' Taking out a second image he slid it towards Styles. 'And so was Regan Western.' He slid over a third image, lining them neatly on Styles' desk.

Styles stared at the images intently. 'I don't see what any of this has to do with me. It's terrible Regan's brother – Geoffrey – was murdered, but I don't see how I can help.'

The detective leaned closer. 'We want to know who was driving the ute. Our information suggests three people, the brothers Western and the driver of the ute – your company's ute – were working together to intimidate a person they expected to meet. Incidentally, where were you on Wednesday at 7.30pm?'

'I beg your pardon? Am I a suspect?'

'Everyone's a suspect at this stage, Dawid.'

'If you must know, I was at the movies with my wife.'

'What did you see?' Fergusson snapped out the question to cut down Styles' thinking time.

Styles didn't hesitate. 'Oh, a biopic about Anthony Bourdain. My wife liked it, but I fell asleep.'

Again, she watched for signs he was lying; she didn't see any, but it sounded like a well-rehearsed story. Most people need time to remember where and what they were doing days ago. Besides, it was an easy story to check. If he was lying, he was an absolute muppet.

'We'll check that out,' said Fergusson, adding, 'for verification,' heading off any protest. 'The immediate problem is the ute. I'll need a list of the people who could've been driving it.'

'It'll be long, but I'll get Peach on to it.'

'Send it through to me' – he handed Styles a business card – 'when it's collated.' Fergusson looked at her, his eyebrows raised. 'JP?'

She took her time before shaking her head slowly. 'We'll need to cross-check the information with what Regan Western told us. That'll highlight possible avenues of inquiry.'

Styles smiled at her, a shit-eating grin on his face, which caused her to clench her buttocks tight.

Outside the dealership, Fergusson turned to her. 'What do you reckon?'

Drawing in a deep breath, Parata said, 'Ace might have mentioned to Styles who the victim was, but I doubt it. She knew not to, and it wasn't in her story.'

'He would've heard through the criminal grapevine,' he said. 'He's dodgy as fuck.'

'Him knowing is suggestive, but it's no smoking gun.'

'If he knows,' said Fergusson, 'it's what he said, common knowledge among those involved. My read is that not only did he know Regan Western is alive, he knew he kept his mouth shut. He knew we were fishing.'

Nodding, she said, 'The most obvious information source is the killers themselves, but Styles would've heard it second-hand.'

'If Styles' alibi stands up, it eliminates him as the ute driver.'

'It'll stand up,' said Parata. 'And the list, that'll be a dead end too. Anyone with access could've taken the keys and handed them over to a third party. The list becomes ten, twenty times longer. Do you think he's involved?'

Fergusson scratched at his stubble. 'He sure fits the bill to be an alt-right devotee. Male, misogynistic, white, rich arsehole, but that's a decent chunk of society. Could you picture Styles dressed as a Nazi?'

'Totally,' she said.

The detective's laugh turned into a long sigh. 'You know, I assumed this one was going to fall over like dominoes, but they're super-glued in place. Are you, the SIS that is, still looking at this as domestic terrorism?'

Parata's face puckered. 'At the moment, but unless I can find a material link to the Ball shooting, I'll get pressure to leave it to you and yours. And if there is a link, does that mean domestic terrorism is now part of mainstream politics?'

CHAPTER 33

The noise of the front door opening and Roxy moaning with excitement made Grace jump up, wide awake. Holding up her hands as if in surrender, she recognised she was at Sean's house. She looked around the room, the fog of sleep starting to clear. The game show she fell asleep watching was reaching a squawking climax.

'You okay?' Sean asked, dropping his massive lawyer's briefcase, and patting an excited Roxy.

Grace stretched and yawned. 'I lay on the couch. It was only for a minute, but Roxy joined me and the two of us must have drifted off.'

Sean kissed her on the cheek, located the remote and muted the excitable host.

'They should prescribe game shows for insomniacs,' she said. 'How was your day?'

They caught up with each other's day as Sean attended to all the usual tasks that greet a parent when they arrive home, though both their sets of children were away so they had a rare "adults only" evening. Usually, when these opportunities occurred, they were both too tired to make the evening anything other than a PG.

While Sean put on a load of washing, Grace watched the news. When he joined her on the couch with a beer, she had paused the TV on a story that covered the latest political opinion poll.

Pointing at the screen, she asked, 'How is it possible?'

Sean raised his eyebrows. 'It's happened fast. When you first poked around ProtectNZ they were a rabble of a lobby group.'

'I know. Now, if you believe the polls, they'll easily get over the five per cent threshold. That would get them six MPs into parliament. Ball could become kingmaker, and he's loving the role too. For a while, after the shooting, he looked different. Quieter. Almost haunted.'

'Have you dug up any links to the alt-right or questionable groups?' he asked.

Grace shook her head. 'They're involved with the alt-right – somehow.

Their paths are merging but there isn't any evidence. And they seem to be playing by the political rules, but …'

Sean waited.

'It feels wrong. It's like they're twisting democracy, gaming the system to advance their own interests and those of their backers. All in plain sight and, at the moment, they're winning.'

Sean blew out a long breath. 'I know what you're saying, kind of. But if enough people in New Zealand think they're the party they want to represent them, that's democracy in action, isn't it? That's why Winston was able to cling on for so many years. You could argue he gamed the system too.'

'He did, but this is different,' she said, 'This is darker. It feels like they're tampering with the process of free will.'

'Whoa, that's a big claim,' said Sean. 'People's free will tampered with? Now that sounds like a conspiracy theory.'

'I know, maybe it's not free will. I haven't nailed the phrase right for my story. Here's my logic though. What percentage of the voting population are interested in politics?'

'I have no idea, twenty per cent?'

'Nobody actually knows, but let's take your figure, which feels way too high – if twenty per cent are interested in politics, what do the rest use to work out which way to vote?'

Sean's face creased in concentration, but he stayed quiet.

Grace waited before continuing. 'Exactly, there's an ocean of *swayable* people. And, if you know which buttons to push … Look at the so-called "freedom" protests, our version of the Canadian trucker convoy. Target the disenfranchised, sow discontent and you can even get millionaire morons, who have lived their entire lives with a silver spoon up their arse, feeling the government's wronged them.'

'I'll bet you don't get that sentence past your editor,' said Sean. 'You're right, though. People with their buttons pushed are far more likely to get off their arse and vote.'

'People's views can be moulded by vapid, self-titled social media influencers, marketing campaigns and evil algorithms. "Protecting the lifestyles of ordinary New Zealanders", that's evocative, but they're protecting their own lifestyles because climate change, like the pandemic, recessions, inflation, and every war ever fought, smashes the poor and gives the rich a free pass.'

Sipping his beer, he said, 'It's still democracy though. The majority deciding who best represents their collective interests.'

'It is,' she said. 'Otherwise, it's a minority deciding.'

'History tells us that doesn't lead anywhere positive,' he said.

Sitting up, eyes wide, she said, 'But it *is* a minority deciding, don't you see? By financing political parties, owning and controlling parts of the media, that's where the gaming occurs.

'You think the wealthy have learnt to rig democracy?'

'Maybe they've always rigged democracy,' said Grace. 'I'm sure Roman senators knew which civic buttons to push to get citizens excited before they headed to the polls.'

'Maybe. But, as you love to ask, so what?'

'I'm not sure,' she said, her face pinched. 'The definition of corruption is the use of public office for private gain, but there's no way to prove that's the reason they're trying to win seats in parliament.'

'Their pitch is that they represent ordinary New Zealanders,' he said. 'If they benefit as well, that's what, incidental?'

Grace snorted. 'Incidental. But you're right. Private gain used to mean embezzlement, giving contracts to your brother-in-law, getting the keys to a new BMW in return for granting planning permission for a casino, that sort of stuff. But if you and your chums get richer through the general implementation of government policy, what's that?'

'Politics?' he said. 'You could argue every time the Nats play the only card they ever play – tax cuts – they and all their mates personally gain.'

'So, if an individual lies, cheats or steals, the consequence is shame and jail time. But if it's done on a national scale, that's politics, there are zero consequences, and you get your name on the New Year's Honours list. It is so fucking bollocks.'

Sean laughed.

'What?'

'It's the similarities this has with your battle to get the rich to pay their fair share of tax. Then they had loopholes to cheat the tax system. This time they're gaming the political system to achieve the same result.'

Grace shook her head angrily. 'I guess they're called the "stinking rich" for a reason. But I reckon there's a trail that leads to ProtectNZ, a trail they'll want to bury. If it's criminal, the police can arrest them. If they've stayed within the law but if it's unethical, maybe immoral, when the public find out they'll abandon them – hopefully.'

'Will they? When Trump talked about "grabbing pussy" or the long list of horrible, ridiculous stuff he did, everyone waited for *consequences* which never came.'

'It's like Stockholm Syndrome at a population level,' said Grace.

His eyes widened. 'I'd write that down. That's clever.'

They stared at each other before Sean broke the silence. 'Say it, I know you're thinking it because I'm thinking it.'

'Sure,' said Grace, putting on a shocked look. 'It couldn't happen in New Zealand.'

CHAPTER 34

'Norma, I was hoping you could make it,' said a tall, impeccably dressed man. He was wearing a tailored coal-black suit, a stylish red-plaid business shirt, but was minus the black tie he had worn all day at the ProtectNZ conference.

'Brian,' said Marla, who was attending the conference under her Norma Smith identity, 'I was about to seek you out, now I have a well-deserved wine. Cheers.'

The hotel reception room was steadily filling with delegates, candidates, party faithful and hangers-on. They clinked glasses.

'Have you found the day useful?' he asked.

Using her full American accent, she said, 'Very.'

In truth, the day was a strong contender for the dullest-day-of-her-life title. Sitting, pretending to listen to an endless parade of would-be ProtectNZ politicians outline their vapid plans for what they were calling *New Zealand's Great Reset*. The only exciting part of the day had been lining up Brian Henderson, her chosen target.

A wealthy horse breeder, Henderson was the party's spokesperson for horse racing and climate change – seemingly in that order. With his dark hair flecked with grey and a real estate agent's grin, he was undeniably handsome, a fact he appeared to know too well. Her cover was as an independent reporter covering the rise of ProtectNZ for Breitbart, the dog-whistling American alt-right media rag. To make sure Henderson, who despite being married had a playboy's reputation, noticed her, she had worn a tight-fitting black business outfit with a slitted skirt. With her hair in a severe ponytail, red lipstick, and black mascara, she had created a mix of business dominatrix meets ravenous cougar – it wasn't hard to play to men's fantasies.

'It's make-or-break time for your party, Brian,' she said. Many of the ProtectNZ tragics had used that line over the course of the day, she thought it sounded insightful yet vague. If he pressed her on New Zealand politics, she would be on shaky ground, but she counted on him being more interested in her body than her mind.

Stepping well into her personal space, his voice low, he said, 'It sure is. I didn't ask you at lunch, are you based in New Zealand or just visiting?'

It was in the lunch queue that she had injected herself into his world. Lining up behind him, she had introduced herself. Over lunch they had chatted, allowing her to flirt. He left lunch early – he was second speaker in the afternoon parade – but she had given him a come-on line to dwell on, 'I hope we can catch up at the networking event, I'd like to know what makes you tick.' It was sickeningly obvious but, as with most men, subtlety was lost on him.

'It was meant to be a visit,' she said, 'but, what with Covid and the fact I fell in love with New Zealand, I'm here for a while. I was lucky Breitbart wanted overseas reporters, including here.'

'How did you get involved with Breitbart?'

'Brian, great stuff today,' interrupted the unmistakable figure of Seb Ball. 'I hate to drag you away from this attractive lady, but you need to meet Trish, she's a top-notch pollster. I won't keep him long …' He raised his eyebrows as an invitation for Marla to introduce herself.

'Norma, reporter with Breitbart.'

'Seb Ball,' he said unnecessarily, holding out his hand. 'Breitbart. Interesting.' His tone sounded simultaneously impressed and concerned.

The next hour became a test of her staying power as she talked with a range of people about ProtectNZ, their policies and vision for the future. Playing the role of a reporter allowed her a measure of safety in that she could ask more questions than she had to answer. She kept an eye on Henderson, who was networking his way around the room. She knew he wouldn't leave without her. When she talked to him at lunch, he had been wearing a wedding ring – he wasn't wearing it now.

As the event concluded and numbers thinned, she went and stood at the window and pretended to check her messages. In the window's reflection she watched Henderson shake hands with another of the seemingly endless parade of identical, suited, tieless, white male candidates, excuse himself and walk towards her.

As he approached, she turned around and gave him a welcoming smile.

'I'm sorry,' he said. 'We've hardly exchanged two sentences. You must let me buy you dinner if you haven't any plans.'

'No plans and that would be delightful.'

As they left the function, she laced her arm through his and talked about how friendly she found New Zealanders. Ball, who was farewelling the last of the guests, winked and said, 'Be careful Brian, she's a reporter.'

Everyone laughed.

After dinner, and more red wine than she needed in the small Italian restaurant off Courtenay Place, they strolled towards Brian's hotel. He asked where she was staying, and she answered honestly; that she hadn't booked a room as she hadn't intended on staying the night.

'What were you going to do?'

'I wasn't planning on attending the networking event,' she lied. 'I was going to get a rental car after the conference finished.'

'It's too late now and besides, you'll be over the limit to drive.'

'I am. I suppose I'll get a room.'

Putting his arm around her waist, he said, 'You could share my room.'

She put on her best sultry look. 'Now there's a thought.' It was a standard tactic, make the target think that it's their idea, not yours.

In the mirrored entrance to the hotel, she took the opportunity to scrutinise him. He was handsome all right and, in her alcohol-induced relaxed state, she felt aroused. Normally looks alone didn't do much for her. She preferred intelligent and thoughtful partners like Lucas, the civics teacher in the US she had been dating until her life flip-flopped and she needed to go to ground in New Zealand. As the elevator doors closed, she made up her mind, she would drug him after they had made love.

Alone in the elevator, she turned to him. 'Tired?'

'Uh-uh.'

Shutting the room door behind him, he asked, 'Another drink?'

Unbuttoning her jacket, she said, 'After.' Stepping towards him, she let her jacket slide off her shoulders and onto the floor.

Over the years Marla had enjoyed what she considered an appropriate number of eclectic sexual encounters. Henderson, like most practised playboys, was a sensitive, considerate lover. She hadn't climaxed, she seldom did with new partners, but she faked it well enough to get him over the line in a timely manner. As they lay on top of the bed, and he was recovering, she flicked into agent mode.

'I haven't been fucked like that in ages,' she said with a long, exaggerated sigh.

Henderson blew out a long breath. 'It was as great as I've been imagining all day.'

'Wine,' she announced. 'Not too much, I do have work tomorrow, but a little celebratory drink won't hurt.'

He padded to the minibar, bending over to look in the fridge. 'There's white, red, or bubbles.'

She looked away, admiring the view from the window. Naked men bending over was not an image that did it for her. 'Definitely bubbles.'

Opening the bottle, he poured two glasses before going to the bathroom, shutting the door. When he had finished, she was sitting up in bed, the sheet pulled over her waist leaving her breasts exposed. She held her glass. His glass, which contained a dose of zopiclone, she left next to the TV. They chatted amiably until the drug kicked in and he lolled towards her. She plucked the glass from his hand before it slid from his grasp.

Making sure he was out to it, but comfortable and in no danger, she poured his spiked drink into the toilet. It was a mistake an agent in Europe had once made; she had taken an absent-minded drink from the wrong glass and woken up in time to be detained.

From her bag, Marla took out her portable boot drive. Ten minutes later, while she copied his laptop's hard drive to her portable drive, she was busy installing software on his phone. Technically malware, the software operated in a similar way to the Pegasus spyware developed by the Israelis. It allowed her to capture keystrokes, intercept communications, track the device, and use the camera and microphone. She wasn't sure if she would need to use it, but it didn't hurt to have options.

She felt a little guilty honey-trapping him in this way, but the fact he was married and should have rejected her obvious advances assuaged her guilt. She would make sure, as far as she could, that any information she used wouldn't expose his involvement.

When he woke in the morning, his possessions would be exactly where he had left them, looking unmolested. He would have a hangover which he would put down to the wine – she had also tipped most of the bottle into the toilet to make it look as if they had drunk more than they had. His technology would appear untouched, and, the final touch, she left a note saying how much she enjoyed their encounter and looked forward to "bumping into him again" as the campaign continued. She doubted she would ever see him again, but who knew? The only way he would find out that she had played him would be if he contacted Breitbart.

A last check of the hotel room confirmed she was leaving no incriminating evidence behind. She would appear on numerous surveillance feeds but, as no crime had been committed, no obvious crime, no one would review them. And even if they did, she wasn't staying in the hotel – the trail would run cold.

The time had ticked past midnight when she gave him a kiss on the cheek, she wasn't sure why, before heading to Courtenay Place to find a late-night coffee. Before she recovered her car from the Clifton Terrace car park and drove to the ferry terminal, she needed to sober up.

CHAPTER 35

The information on Henderson's laptop revealed little Marla didn't already know. He was, as she should have expected, having multiple affairs – she was thankful she had made him use a condom. She discovered the information any ProtectNZ political candidate would have, but it didn't appear that he was inside the party's inner sanctum as she had hoped.

It was in among his emails that she found the lead she was hoping for. Dawid Styles, the car dealer they suspected was involved with the alt-right, and a man called Ted Blackwood had been exchanging views on whether Seb Ball should attend the upcoming ProtectNZ Advisory Board meeting scheduled for the following Friday in Wellington. Styles had then forwarded the email, and its lengthy thread, to someone he called "Peach", who forwarded it to Henderson asking him to increase the booking size to eight. It was a common enough mistake but a rookie error.

The ProtectNZ website made no mention of this advisory board, nor was it in any of their promotional material. An internet search revealed Google didn't know an advisory board existed – that had made her eyebrows rise. You need to be bloody secretive for Darth Google not to know you exist. Google had information on America's Special Collection Service, a shadowy part of the American intelligence community that the American Government denied existed. The real question was – why did ProtectNZ need that level of secrecy?

The meeting was scheduled for 6pm. Putting two and two together from information in the email, it would be at the airport. It made sense. Attendees fly in, have their meeting without having to leave the airport and fly out the following morning. All out of sight of the public and, importantly, the media.

The only option for a venue and accommodation was Rydges Wellington Airport Hotel. In her former life as a US-sponsored agent, she'd had access to the complete range of cloak-and-dagger resources needed to bug meeting rooms, if that's what it took. She had lost her ability to tap into that technology, but low-tech approaches could be as effective.

She spent the week before the meeting at home in Parapara with Indy who seemed to be pining for Damien. Grace had sent a message saying *Fuck nothing was happening* and she was working on other stories. Marla replied advising patience. *Something is always around the corner, and you still haven't told me the "fuck nothing" story.*

On the day of the board meeting, leaving Indy with her elderly neighbour who loved looking after her, Marla drove to Picton, parking on a busy suburban street with free parking, close to the ferry terminal. The Cook Strait crossing was the roughest she had experienced. She had never seen so many people vomiting in one place in peacetime. Even she felt rough and spent much of the journey on deck, pleased to step onto solid North Island soil.

After a short, ugly walk to the bus station, she caught the number two bus that dropped economy-focused travellers near the airport, checking into the Rydges Hotel under the name Norma Smith. When they asked for a credit card, as hotels invariably did to ensure you couldn't skip without paying, she employed her thickest American accent. 'I'm paying in cash' – she pointedly looked at the man's name tag and smiled broadly – 'Terry.'

'Oh,' said Terry, thrown by this. 'We still need a credit card, we won't use it to charge you, it's hotel policy.' He finished the sentence with an equally broad smile, seemingly happy with his explanation.

Playing a semi-obnoxious American traveller, she said, 'I don't *own* a credit card, darling. It's the credit card companies that end up owning you.'

Marla enjoyed these exchanges, but they did make for a memorable interaction which wasn't ideal. The goal was to keep them short, but out-of-the-ordinary issues related to money usually involved what happened next.

'I need to talk to my manager.' Before Marla could answer, he disappeared through a door behind him.

Marla leaned against the desk, no one else was waiting. Her Norma Smith identity, even though it might trigger alerts in the States, was solid in New Zealand and a dead end. There was no link between Norma Smith and Alice Green, that was the discipline.

A minute later a woman in a similar uniform to Terry emerged, Terry following behind. Marla knew the manager would now explain why they needed to take a credit card impression because she assumed Marla was either mad or lying because she didn't want her sociopathic husband or partner to see the transaction. This was the response she received universally.

Marla didn't give her the chance. 'I don't have a credit card so there's no point in repeating your hotel's policy. I strike this everywhere I go. It's so frustrating that credit card companies dictate your hotel's processes, but let's not go there.' Taking an envelope out of her bag, she said, 'I'm staying for one night. This envelope contains five hundred of your New Zealand dollars. You put it in the safe and we'll settle in the morning. Unless, of course, you think I've come all the way from the USA to demo the minibar and skip town.'

The manager had listened, her mouth pursed. She surprised Marla by saying, 'That's perfectly acceptable. Terry, please print out a receipt for' – she checked the computer screen – 'Ms Smith.'

'A receipt for the cash?' said a confused Terry. 'But how do we put it in the system?'

The manager smiled apologetically. 'We don't do this often. I'll get the receipt sent up to your room.'

'That'll be just fine.' With a beaming a smile she took the card key and headed to the elevator.

As expected, her room was the dimensions of a large shoebox, though it did have a view of the airport that would appeal to plane spotters. It was 4.05pm, plenty of time to recon the hotel and adapt aspects of her plan to suit the environment.

Walking casually along the hallway to the elevator, she took note of the security cameras. Hotels teemed with cheap high-definition security cameras. Without significant IT help it wasn't possible to tap into the camera feeds or secretly bug a meeting room, even if you knew which room to bug. Besides, these people were ultra-careful, they might decide to sweep the room for listening devices. If they found one, not only would that ruin her evening's plan, but they would know their secret board wasn't so secret. As with Henderson, she needed to get information about the board without them knowing they had been compromised.

The meeting rooms came off a long corridor interestingly decorated with tall, black, friendly humanoid figures. Acting as though she was checking out the venue for suitability, she looked inside each meeting room. Only one was set up for a meeting – eight places set for eight people. Marla allowed herself a moment of professional satisfaction before shutting the door and heading towards the restaurant and bar.

'A whiskey sour, thanks.' One never hurt.

As the bartender made her drink, Marla asked, 'Do I need to book for the restaurant tonight?'

The bartender made a face. 'Probably not, Fridays are quiet.'

'No big groups of generously tipping business people?' she said with an eyebrow raise. The possibility existed that they would dine in the meeting room, but the room hadn't been set up to cater for dinner. They were cautious, but they were also rich entitled men which meant they would be over-confident to the point of arrogant. They would view drinking to excess in the bar and dining lavishly in the restaurant with ProtectNZ picking up the tab as their due. She was hoping the bartender would confirm this.

'I wish,' he said, pouring her drink. 'There's a group of businessmen in tonight but they've never tipped before.'

'Typical. I guess that's how they stay rich. What time do I need to be gone to avoid them?'

The bartender tapped his computer. 'They're booked in for seven thirty, so before that.'

Smiling, she handed him a fifty dollar note. 'Keep the change,' she said with a sly wink.

'Thanks,' he stammered.

The confirmation of when and where they would be dining was worth every cent. She also learnt he would be working tonight, which may come in handy.

After a slow lap of the restaurant pretending to admire the décor and views, she sat at a corner table near the windows overlooking the tarmac. From this position she could monitor the bar and most of the restaurant. It was a large space, but a party of eight should make spotting ProtectNZ's advisory board simple.

The plan she was running, if she was successful, would provide a solid insight into the existence and make-up of the secret board. She wasn't going to find out their darkest secrets, but once she passed the information over, Grace would attack them like a Rottweiler. Besides, you don't always need people's darkest secrets – you just need them to think you have them.

CHAPTER 36

Outside the meeting room door, Ball drew in a deep breath. When he heard Blackwood's voice from inside the room, 'New Zealand is facing its gravest threat since Europeans first tamed this land', a fight or flight response surged through him. Exhaling, he fought it down.

'Feel the fear and do it anyway,' he whispered.

He politely knocked on the door and waited. Blackwood stopped talking and Ball heard shuffling before the door opened and he came face to face with Blackwood wearing his favourite bright red "Make America Great Again" cap. Autographed by Donald Trump, the cap had cost him several thousand dollars from an online auction. They stared at each other for a long moment before Blackwood stepped back.

In a jovial voice, Blackwood said, 'Ah, come in, Ball. I was about to tell the board you'd been caught up in traffic.'

Ball walked in, smiling hard. 'Gentlemen,' he said with forced confidence.

Around the table sat six middle-aged, stocky, white men. He recognised three of them, though apart from Styles he wasn't sure he could name them. They wore expensive suits, with unfashionably wide lapels, ranging in colour from grey to navy. Although they could afford crisp white shirts, they seldom invested in items without four wheels and consequently, their shirts were various hues of white due to the shirt's age and the individual's propensity to sweat. Their ties differed but were all variations of old-boy school ties. With their grey hair receding or cut short, they looked like every 1970s New Zealand board of directors, a homogenous group of stale human peas in a pod. Was he one of them too? It was an uncomfortable question.

Blackwood placed his MAGA cap on the table like a police officer. 'Now the action's heating up it makes sense to have Ball attend so he can hear the board's thinking for himself. We in turn can ask him for the latest updates from the field. Most of you will have met him, we'll do informal introductions after the meeting … over a beer.' Indicating Ball, he added, 'It can be his shout for being late.'

Ball's what-can-you-do gesture brought smiles all around.

Blackwood went efficiently through the agenda, getting Ball to provide an update on operational progress. After they had completed the standard items, Blackwood set aside his handwritten agenda. 'Now we come to the meat. The election is four months away. If we're to build on the work we've done to date, we need a clear, focused strategy.'

'I hope it's cleverer than handing over money,' a board member said. 'We've given thousands over the years to political parties, hundreds of thousands, and it hasn't helped. As soon as they get in all they try and do is stay in power. Any party we align with will ignore us the minute they park their arse in the Beehive.'

'How many politicians have reached out to you, Seb?' asked another man.

'Plenty of desperate ones who want to join now we've hit the five per cent threshold. But none from the major parties.'

The group nodded solemnly.

Blackwood chuckled. 'The game's changed, gentleman. The battleground is no longer in the corridors of Parliament, trying to get MPs to earn their salary. The battle's gone online; the world's gone cyber. We aren't going to achieve our goals if we follow the tired political ruts. We need to become popular with the people, not the other parties.'

The solemn nodding continued, although the looks hinted at confusion.

'Think about it gentleman, how did America end up with Donald as president?' Blackwood left the questioning hanging.

'Trump appealed to ordinary Americans,' said a board member.

'That's right, he focused on ordinary Americans – Republicans and Democrats. We may not have a personality like Donald driving political change, yet' – smiling, he looked at Ball – 'but we need to tear a leaf out of his playbook.'

'What are you proposing, Ted?'

'I'm saying we need to operate in the twenty-first century,' said Blackwood. 'Unless we do, we'll be walking around shaking hands with our own voters or driving a bus with Ball's face plastered on it, what use is that? That wasn't edgy in the seventies. At best we'd scrape into parliament with five per cent and, as you say, we'd be ignored. It's all Donald might have done too, but those who pulled his political strings knew better. They understood how to create a surge of popular support that swept him into power.'

It was obvious where Blackwood was leading the board, at least to Ball, though judging by the faces of the board, they were less sure. He spoke quietly but firmly. 'What Ted's saying is we need to be a political force that appeals to both the left and the right. To gain enough support so the other parties *can't* ignore us. To force politicians to act and introduce the policies demanded by the ordinary people who put them there.'

Blackwood stared at him, a look between pleased and concerned. Ball had noticed Blackwood glancing at him, presumably looking for signs he wasn't on board with the direction. Since their exchange at dinner, Blackwood had taken a greater interest in the day-to-day running of the organisation. Ball realised, in the position he now found himself, he needed to box clever to avoid being knocked out – or taken out.

'Well put, Seb,' said Blackwood. He looked back to the board.

'Populism, that's the game now. I'll explain it as our backers explained it to me. New Zealand has been slow on the uptake, we still believe politics is about policies. Using a populist playbook, we need to first focus on becoming the party of the people. Secondly, make ProtectNZ a party railing against the elite. Thirdly, identify an enemy ordinary New Zealanders can focus on. It's that simple. I've had discussions with like-minded people from across the globe. They say the trick is to change the mindset of people so they're fed up with *all* the parties, left, right, centre, whatever. We want them hungry to embrace a new political force unencumbered with the old labels – ProtectNZ.'

Blackwood looked from face to face as the board collectively digested the information.

'What we need is a campaign that erodes confidence in both the government *and* the opposition.' Blackwood smiled broadly. 'Think of it like political climate change.'

Most of the board were clearly baffled.

A board member offered, 'But, haven't the opposition been trying to erode confidence in the government for years … unsuccessfully? And why erode confidence in the opposition? Where the fuck does that leave us?'

'That leaves us with real political change,' said Blackwood. 'Look, our previous tactic of trying to get a government in power that's most likely to listen to us has failed. As you said, we've given them thousands to convince voters they're the best party to lead New Zealand. The problem is, as we're all too bloody aware, they never are. We always end up with a hapless centrist government with minor parties as dags. That's what ProtectNZ would become too, a boil on a right-wing government's arse. We need to change that. We need people to see there's a different way, one focused on their best interests. One that takes support from the left and the right.'

From where Ball was sitting, the board's collective thinking had advanced to between confused and captivated. Blackwood ploughed ahead.

'The debate we want the country to focus on is this: what the government is planning to do, no matter which way they lean, will be the death of the Kiwi way of life. For the decent, ordinary, hard-working New Zealanders we need to keep the economy strong. It's okay for the rich greenies, driving their Teslas and drinking chardonnay, while the workers and small business owners of New Zealand lose their jobs and struggle to put food on the table. China, America, and Australia are laughing at us while they burn coal, import oil, drive cars, and live the life of Reilly.'

Ball saw a collective light go on for the board. They finally understood the strategy.

'If we're successful' – Blackwood again turned towards him – 'and under Ball's leadership we will be, we will keep the New Zealand we all know and love.'

CHAPTER 37

Timing her entrance into the hotel restaurant was vital. Marla didn't want to arrive at the same time as the advisory board or to sit waiting for them any longer than necessary. She passed the time in her room reading and dozing. At 6.30pm her alarm spurred her into action. She changed, dressing as a do-not-fuck-with-me, ladder-climbing businesswoman. The last thing she needed, or wanted, was to draw the attention of any sad, lonely men who fancied taking a Friday night chance.

Part of her plan had been to sit at a table bathed in sunlight which would allow her to wear sunglasses without drawing attention. As it was winter, however, the sun had already set but sunglasses wouldn't look out of place given the severe style she had adopted. Her sunglasses were the most important part of her outfit.

Taking them out of their case, she gave the two miniature lenses a careful polish. If you looked closely, the cameras mounted on each side of the frame were noticeable, so the trick was to make sure nobody got close or took any notice of her. She had long ago disabled the small LED light designed to alert people you were photographing or recording them. Alongside these special sunglasses, she placed an identical pair of normal sunglasses. Needing to wear the special sunglasses only when she was photographing the advisory board, she would swap them as required.

The restaurant was busy but a long way from full when she sauntered in at 7.20pm wearing her normal sunglasses. Eating dinner wearing sunglasses would look odd, so her plan was to appear to be having a pre-dinner drink. Putting her bag on the table where she wanted to sit, she went to the bar where the same bartender was working, though much harder.

Not recognising her, he said, 'I'll be there in a minute.'

Marla pushed her sunglasses onto the top of her head, raised her eyebrows in acknowledgement then looked around. It was difficult to know how the action would play out. She normally needed to have rough plans for three or four scenarios but tonight she was in luck. A reserved sign sat prominently on a table set for eight. From where she would be sitting, she had a clear line of sight.

The bartender came over. 'Are you here for dinner?'

Nodding, she pointed. 'I'm at that table.'

'I'll send a server over.'

Settling herself in, she scanned the menu before taking out her phone in readiness. She ordered a glass of wine, telling the server she wouldn't be ready to order dinner for a while. Ten minutes after her wine arrived, she heard the confident clamour of a rabble of men marching towards the restaurant. They acted as if discretion wasn't required, laughing raucously and not seeming to care that they were drawing attention to themselves. The tall, black, friendly humanoid figures in the corridor seemed to be laughing at the squat, white, trollesque figures walking past them.

As they neared the entrance to the restaurant, Marla was right in their eyeline. Without fuss, she held up her phone so it obscured the lower part of her face. She left on her normal sunglasses; it was too risky to take photos while they were looking in her direction, no doubt giving her the once-over as men like this invariably did. They filed into the restaurant in twos, surrounding the two bar leaners closest to the bar.

Until the last two had entered the restaurant, the only man she recognised was the portly Styles. She knew of his involvement because of the email thread sent to Henderson. Last into the restaurant was Seb Ball, walking alongside a large, confidently strutting man in an ill-fitting suit. What made Ball's companion stand out was his 'Make America Great Again' hat. An odd choice in New Zealand, she thought. His voice cut through the low restaurant chatter. 'We're on the verge of greatness, Seb. You're going to be the one history will say saved our way of life.' Ball nodded seriously.

When they were busy drinking and talking, she subtly swapped sunglasses by pretending to clean them. To anyone glancing her way, she was trying to look cool while reading and replying to messages on her phone. What she was doing was taking photos of the men, the images sent to her phone via Bluetooth. The cameras had limited ability to zoom in, so she took dozens of photos to help with identification. When she had completed her task, she put both pairs of sunglasses away, caught the attention of a server and ordered dinner.

When the men finished their drinks, they filed past within a metre of her as they waddled to their table. She kept eating her fish and chips, not looking up. It was a dish she had acquired a taste for on her South Island travels. She glanced over at the men from time to time as the loud, obnoxious group drank, ate, and added to their already considerable joint gravitas. In among the general revelry, Ball stood out. He looked guarded, not quite belonging, like the awkward kid in the class.

The odd snippet of conversation was discernible, but it always revolved around rugby. After she had finished eating, she headed to her room as their mains arrived. Before she left, it occurred to her they might have left intelligence behind in the meeting room. After making sure nobody was taking an interest in her, she strolled into the now-empty meeting room, leaving the door open. Security cameras recorded her actions but, unless they received a complaint, the footage would remain unviewed, stored on a remote server farm until the world of capitalism ended.

The only items on the table were half-filled water glasses and empty mint wrappers. She checked the hotel pads to see if anyone had used one and left an impression on the page underneath. No. As she went to leave, she glanced in the rubbish bin. It contained a single piece of screwed-up paper. Picking it out, she smoothed it to reveal a handwritten list. At the top of the page was an underlined word – Agenda.

CHAPTER 38

Grace wasn't sure if she still had an SIS tail. But if she did, the agent would be bored out of their tree. Literally nothing of consequence had happened over the past fortnight apart from the mundane tasks that confronted every parent of teenage children. She kept in touch with Marla over their encrypted channel, but their communication had become spasmodic since she had headed back to the South Island. Marla said she was working on a plan and, although Grace hadn't heard from her, Marla never struck her as the giving-up sort.

Grace was right, she wasn't.

Whatever plan she had developed, Marla had struck gold. She had sent through a series of photos of what she called the ProtectNZ Advisory Board – Grace had never heard of them. They were, in Marla's words, *drinking up large at Wellington's Rydges Hotel after a board meeting* and that they *stood out like dog's balls*. Grace laughed out loud when she read that.

Along with the captivating images, Marla had included an image of a handwritten agenda for the meeting.

Grace had previously written several critical stories on ProtectNZ, but until now she had little to use other than her own research and their PR material. The uncovering of a ProtectNZ Advisory Board made up of well-known right-wing zealots was journalistic gold, if not platinum.

It hadn't taken her long to identify each board member. They were either prominent, wealthy, tax-avoiding businessmen or well past their best-before-date politicians. To her delight, Dawid Styles was on the board. When she had rung him about his involvement with the Westerns, he had vented a string of misogynistic expletives down the line. *Payback time, arsehole.*

Unsurprisingly, Ball, as leader of the party, was there. But the image that was the cherry on the cake was of Edward Blackwood wearing a Make America Great Again cap. To the media, he was like a cross between a young Bob Jones and a Rottweiler – arrogant, openly hostile, and dangerous to approach. Grace and Blackwood's paths had never crossed, until now, and she relished the chance to put him and his ultra-conservative views into the spotlight.

Her reply to Marla read: *Outstanding! I need to use the images in my story, will that compromise you? I'd like to send them to JP as a courtesy before I publish. Keep her onside … G.*

Getting comfortable, Grace started writing a fresh story. The angle she was taking was an exposé of who was behind ProtectNZ, and why it was important the public knew. First, she identified them individually and provided a brief resume of their careers. She wrote each bio as a balanced snapshot; it wasn't her fault their main activities centred around making money and right-wing elitism.

Saving Blackwood for last, she clipped a photo of him wearing the tasteless, infamous cap. He had stood for the National Party decades before, losing heavily, though he was contesting what at the time was a safe Labour seat. After his defeat he had focused his energy on amassing a fortune by accumulating property as though he was playing Monopoly.

A loud critic of the wave of regulations to improve the standard of rental accommodation, "the market", he argued vociferously, "would eventually drive out shoddy landlords. The legislation was another example of the government crucifying the entrepreneurial spirit."

A virulent climate change denier, he appeared occasionally on vapid, self-important, right-wing media platforms – both in New Zealand and overseas. The moves to legislate farming's environmental impact, he argued, was "a move towards a Marxist state". Grace couldn't imagine Blackwood had the faintest notion about Marxism. People like him used the term as a dog whistle, designed to needle the public's irrational fears and excite alt-right trolls.

Liquidating his property portfolio in 2015, he had abandoned the real estate industry and returned to his farming roots, his media appearances dwindling. That was how it looked his story was destined to end, until now. No matter how sympathetic an angle she took, the man came out looking like what he was – wealthy, arrogant, egocentric, and dim.

Grace titled her story, *Playing with democracy: The wealthy puppet masters behind ProtectNZ.* The handwritten agenda also asked many difficult questions. The first items were standard – *Minutes, Poll results, Operations report,* and *Finance report.* But after that it became murky – *Election strategy, US funding issues, Deplatforming the media* and *Offshore payments for SM.* Not your typical political party agenda.

To give ProtectNZ the opportunity to put their side of the story, she emailed both Blackwood and Ball for comment, following up with a phone call. Ms Pilkington declined on behalf of Ball with barely controlled outrage. Blackwood's reply was unprintable. In the story, she said both declined to comment.

It took her two hours in a café to bash the story into a final draft. In that time Marla had replied: *No issue with the images or sending them to JP. Go hard.* She had added an emoji with sunglasses.

Grinning, she filed the story adding a note to her editor: *This should put the cat among the pigeons!*

CHAPTER 39

Ball read the story in disbelief, even though he knew it was coming. Ms Pilkington saw it first and charged into his office, interrupting his preparation for the speech he was giving at the upcoming Federated Farmers annual conference. She stood over his shoulder as he read, tutting and making comments like 'that horrible woman' and 'she should be arrested'. When she had enquired quietly if it was true, he had politely told her that he needed space to digest the story.

It was, of course, all true. They, especially Blackwood, were puppet masters, his masters. They had pulled the strings and he had danced on stage. Marks didn't know the position he was in, how could she? She had included him as part of the all-singing, dancing and drinking board, unaware his arm was being significantly twisted behind his back.

He massaged his temples. Was he their *unwilling* leader? When he had searched his soul, it wasn't true. He loved the attention, the limelight. The party's values were roughly aligned with his own and they would make a splash on the political scene worthy of international headlines. If it wasn't for Blackwood holding the sword of Damocles over his head, his world would be perfect. If he could change that …

It was coming up 3.30pm. Marks had published her story in time for the TV media to pick it up; they would be calling for comment any minute. He stood up, still massaging his temples, and looked out the window. The blustery, threatening day made Murphy Street look desolate, the odd pedestrian struggling by oblivious to the political storm brewing. Even if they did know, most "ordinary New Zealanders" wouldn't care, they had their own lives and worries. Ordinary New Zealanders might not believe it either, such was the job they and others had done discrediting mainstream media over the years. Politics, as he was fast discovering, wasn't about winning people's hearts and minds; it was about shepherding them along the drafting race that led to your voting pen.

Leaning out of his office, he caught Ms Pilkington's willing eye. 'Can you let Colin know I need to see him urgently?'

Colin Cromarty was the marketing "guru" that Blackwood had hired and, as much as it irked Ball to admit it, Cromarty was talented. He had orchestrated a series of campaigns that had them constantly riding the crest of a wave. As soon as one issue lost steam, he engineered – that was the only word for it – another issue to sweep them onwards.

The communication strategy Cromarty developed, he had told Ball, was based on Frank Luntz's work with Israel. Luntz helped them develop media spin designed to misdirect and win international favour. Using it as a template, Cromarty had developed three core phrases for Ball to employ to focus or deflect attention. "In all we do, we seek the best outcomes for ordinary New Zealanders." "That is a tomorrow issue, we need to solve today's issues." "If you saw your fellow Kiwis going under, what would you do?"

The media saw through these messages, but Cromarty hadn't designed them for the media. He designed them for the public to hear through the media so, like red wine spilt on artic white carpet, they could seep in and irreversibly stain the public's conscience. If the media tried to tear apart the messages, as they liked to do, they had to deliver them first – which played into their hands. Smiling in his tailored suits, Cromarty liked to rhyme, 'We have them in a catch-twenty-two and there's nothing they can do.'

Standing at the window, Ball recognised a journalist walking towards their offices. Well, Marks has done something about it, let's see how the guru turns this one around. The first shark was arriving.

'Come in,' said Ball in answer to a polite knock.

Cromarty walked in looking as he always did – immaculate. After he had joined ProtectNZ, Ball had noticed how the office had collectively upped their attire game in an attempt to match him. Encouraged by Cromarty, he did too. 'Seb,' Cromarty would say in his manufactured accent, 'if you want to be the prime minister, you must look prime ministerial. They might want you to be "one of the people", but members of the public don't want their leader to look like a member of the public.'

'Well,' said Ball turning to face Cromarty. 'Have you read it?'

'Of course,' said Cromarty lounging on Ball's couch.

'And?'

He shrugged. 'Marks is always attacking us, but she's writing for a different audience.'

'I'm not sure you understand. What about the public fallout?'

An unflustered Cromarty said, 'Which we'll manage. You told me it was coming; we're prepared to counter.'

Returning to his desk, Ball said, 'What about the shit that's going to land from above, namely from Blackwood? Marks has made him look like a Trump moron.'

Cromarty shrugged again. 'From what Marks wrote, he *is* a Trump moron. I can work miracles, but I can't polish turds.'

Ball stared at him, sprawled on his couch, oozing confidence. The difference between the two men was that he, Cromarty, could walk away in a heartbeat, get another job where he could trowel on his flavour of business bullshit at two thousand dollars a day. He, Ball, couldn't.

'How did she find out?' asked Cromarty. 'It looks as if she sat in the bar, and you all posed for her. Wasn't the board determined to stay anonymous?'

It was a good question: how did she find out? How did she know where and when the meeting was? Was she there? He would have recognised her, surely. And what else did she know? It was clear she had seen the meeting's agenda but, from what she had written, she didn't have an in-depth knowledge of their discussion which meant the room wasn't bugged. It was as if she obtained a copy of the agenda but nothing more.

'They, we,' Ball corrected himself, 'assumed we were in the shadows.'

'Who knew about the meetings?'

'Apart from the board and myself, only a handful of our candidates marked for shadow cabinet positions.'

'Well, what's done is done and can't be undone. It's what we do next that's important.'

It annoyed Ball that Cromarty spoke in the same cliches he peddled. They weren't truisms, they were worn-out management bullshit. He was about to reply when Ms Pilkington came in after the briefest of knocks.

'Sorry to interrupt Sebastian, I've Mr Blackwood on the line. He said it's important.'

'Put him through.' Looking at Cromarty, he said, 'I'll put him on speakerphone.'

A stab of anger hit Ball at Cromarty's dismissive shrug as though the phone call was of little consequence.

'Ted, I have Colin with me. We can discuss what action to take.'

'Hi Ted, how's the farm?' asked Cromarty calmly.

To Ball's surprise, Blackwood wasn't livid, he sounded calm.

'Seb, Colin, and the farm's great, thanks. Pity I'm stuck in Wellington at a mate's place, but it shouldn't be for long.' Before either could speak, he carried on. 'About Marks' story; she's becoming an absolute pain in the arse. I had hoped letting her interview you, Seb, would've kept her quiet but it's had the opposite effect.'

'How did she know when the board was meeting?' asked Ball.

Blackwood spoke after an uneasy silence. 'I've people looking into that. For now, we need to focus on turning around the bad publicity.'

'There's no such thing as bad publicity, Ted,' said Cromarty.

Ball winced. It was a trite observation likely to enrage Blackwood, but he was wrong.

'You're dead right, Colin. How do we turn this to our advantage?'

'I've brainstormed with the team,' said Cromarty. 'The media are attacking us, it's time we counter-attacked. Invasion of privacy, dirty tactics, trying to undermine the will of the people – that sort of stuff.'

'Trying to undermine the will of the people,' said Blackwood thoughtfully. 'I like that, excellent thinking. The media trying to influence the election. Other thoughts, Colin?'

'We're going to focus directly on Marks. It's best to target an individual, people can get outraged at a person, it's hard to get angry at a concept, like "the media". It was a tactic Key loved. Play the man, or woman in this case, not the ball. Excuse the pun.'

Blackwood chortled.

'We need to be careful,' said Ball, ignoring Cromarty's cleverness and mindful he would be fronting the response. 'After the attempt on my life the environment is … volatile.'

'Volatility's what we want,' said Blackwood. 'We must go hard. We want our supporters outraged, venting on social media, marching in the streets demanding the media are reined in, that Marks is reined in. She needs to know there are consequences for her actions. I'll leave the media in your capable hands. I'll focus on turning down Marks' volume. And use the internet trolls, Colin, they're expert at piling on the shit.'

Blackwood terminated the call, and they sat in silence for a long moment.

'We're drafting up a response plan and press release.' Cromarty glanced at his expensive watch. 'It's four, I'll let the media know you're going to make a statement at five. When it's ready, I'll send it to the TV news outlets, embargoed until then.'

Ball nodded. 'What trolls?'

'We use a company in the Philippines to help with our social media activities.'

'How long have we been doing that?'

'Since I came on board.' Standing, Cromarty finished the sentence with an annoying wink. 'I'll be back to brief you when we're ready.'

Ball watched him leave – confident, well paid and carefree. He, on the other hand, felt sick. It was his role to appear in front of the cameras outraged that the media had invaded the privacy of ProtectNZ and, in effect, ordinary New Zealand citizens. To whip up their supporters to demand – what? That was the insane beauty of the misdirection, they wanted people outraged at a corrupt system that wasn't corrupt. If anything, they themselves were corrupting it, turning democracy against itself. He could see it, but he had a privileged seat at the magic show where he could see the rabbit up the magician's sleeve.

Rubbing his temples hard, Ball groaned. He was in deep, too deep to get out. But when the opportunity presented itself, he would be ready.

CHAPTER 40

It was the sound of a strident, distorted voice on a megaphone that first alerted Grace to the situation brewing outside her house. When she went out onto her front porch to investigate, she saw four people on the street outside her gate, one with a megaphone, another with a placard claiming *The Media Lies*.

Her story had hit New Zealand's political scene like a small thermonuclear device. The unfortunate side effect of her professionalism in seeking Ball and Blackwood's input had been to give them a heads-up on what they would be facing. They were more than ready.

Since Ball's retaliatory press conference the previous evening, the amount of hate mail arriving in her inbox and posted online had increased to an insane level. Many of the accounts hurling abuse were obviously "bots", programmed en masse to make the outcry seem widespread, encouraging others to join the mudslinging. Ball had called her story an attack on democracy, before rabidly attacking the media and her. It was "Ace Marks and the media" this, "Ace Marks and the media" that. He had made sure everyone knew who ProtectNZ blamed for what he called "an attack on the foundations and fabric of our democracy".

She had watched his performance with interest if not mild amusement. What she hadn't expected was a small group of protesters descending on her house. Thirty minutes after the first protesters had arrived, she found the mob had grown to around twenty people. Among the various unflattering placards were the standard anti-media messages, including the concerning and unrelated image of post-Second World War hangings in Kiev. When she went out to look, they yelled moronic, misogynistic abuse, forcing her inside. She called the police, rang her children, telling them to stay with friends, called Sean to let him know what was happening and sent Marla a message.

Around four in the afternoon, two police cars arrived. One parked several houses away, seemingly to keep a watch on the crowd, the other parked opposite her house, nudging the disgruntled mob out of the way. Two identical-looking police officers pushed their way through the swelling, mainly male crowd and onto her property. When she opened the door, the noise quadrupled in intensity and hatred.

'Come in,' she said, with an eyebrow raise.

'Thanks Ms Marks.' The police officer had a cheery voice as though he was there to rescue a cat stuck in a tree.

They introduced themselves, but Grace's mind was elsewhere, the names didn't stick. After they refused the offer of a hot drink, she asked, 'What can I do? What are my options?'

It was only when they took their hats off that she could tell them apart. The officer with short cropped red hair spoke. 'Well, as you know, not too much unless they break the law.'

'Fuck,' she said. 'Hoist with my own petard.'

The officers exchanged a confused glance.

'*Hamlet*?' she said.

They shook their heads.

'It means a mob of alt-righters can do what I encouraged the public to do to politicians a year or two ago.' To demonstrate the power of surveillance, she had called on the public to follow politicians legally, to give them a taste of 24/7 surveillance. The same laws that protected activists following politicians protected the mob outside.

'I think I get you,' said the red-haired officer, his voice indicating he didn't.

The officer with dark hair surveyed the crowd through a window. 'More are joining, I guess the word has gone out on social media. There's an element drawn to protests like flies to a long drop.'

Grace looked at the young officer, surprised at the analogy.

'Grew up on a farm,' he said grinning. 'Half of this lot won't have a clue why they're here. They're hoping for free food, drugs, and a chance to get on TV.'

'What do you think I should do? I've let my children know not to come home.'

In unison, they scratched their heads – not a positive sign.

'We could give you a lift to a friend's house. If you stay here, we'll keep a visible presence until they go home. Make sure they know we're watching.'

'What if they don't go home? At what point can you *disperse* them?'

The red-headed officer pursed his lips. 'If we consider they're endangering life or property, we'd consider that breaching the peace and we'll intervene. But it's getting dark and cold, that usually makes most of them piss off.'

Grace's face scrunched. 'I'll stay, at least for now. If they come on to my property?'

'We'll act immediately. We can, to prevent crimes from occurring.'

They gave her a mobile number to ring if she needed help. From her office she watched them close her gate and string do-not-cross tape on it before edging their car through the protesters and parking behind their colleagues.

She took several photos of the protesters from her office window; she planned to use them in upcoming stories. Several local reporters, who she recognised, were standing near the police cars. For the second time in a matter of weeks she had gone from covering the news to becoming the news.

The crowd continued to swell. The confined space in the street outside her house made them appear more numerous, and she sensed they were growing a mob's confidence. As the evening drew in, there were roughly fifty of them, mainly white, mainly men, wielding placards and chanting stupid slogans. It reminded Grace of the anti-mandate protests when Covid had been circulating dangerously. This crowd would have devoured all the conspiracy theories doing the rounds, including that the media were paid government stooges. They were so far down rabbit holes she decided in future stories to borrow the SIS's collective noun "warren" to describe them.

What was happening to the New Zealand media, and her, was a replica of the tactics used by populist right-wing groups the world over. They used social media channels and mainstream echo chambers to paint the media as liars, government puppets and enemies of the people, "ordinary New Zealanders" in this case. A decade ago, it would have been laughable.

The media's role has always been to provide the same ordinary New Zealanders with information to keep them informed. Today, fuelled by a need for survival and profits, many media organisations seemed to be abandoning balance and openly promoting a distinct political view. Maybe it had always been this way and it was just more blatant. Eventually, she hoped, Murdoch's legacy would be as a figure of derision, like Trump.

Adding to the farce, it seemed social media was now accepted as a legitimate media channel, mixing news, opinion, belief and conjecture until the terms real and fake became meaningless. Social media companies didn't give a shit what people slapped online – although the companies proclaimed they did – as long as it circulated virulently, making money. Weird conspiracy theorists, deluded fringe political parties, quack clinicians, climate change deniers, misogynistic criminals, and even the alt-right, Nazis, and white supremacists found that relatively mainstream platforms were happy to broadcast their grotesque beliefs. If these groups were honest, even they must have been surprised they were welcomed back with open arms.

The unruly mob outside her house kept swelling until by early evening the chanting, unkempt protesters blocked the street. Most of her neighbours would be frightened, unable to leave their homes. The protesters had even forced her neighbour Carl, who liked to stand in the middle of the road forcing boy racers to stop for a defensive-driving chat, to retreat into his house after confronting them. His strategy of telling them to 'Fuck off home and get a job' hadn't gone down well. He had sent her a text telling her if she needed help to text him and he would 'hop over the fence'. Carl was a rare breed of neighbour.

The protesters hadn't done any physical damage, yet. But anger and volatility hung ominously in the air. One spark and who knew what might happen? The scenes of brick-throwing protesters from the occupation at Parliament were fresh in her and society's memory.

Night had fallen and it was drizzling when the required spark ignited the crowd.

Watching nervously from the office, Grace recognised the change in the crowd's behaviour. Like a swarm of the walking dead, the majority surged away from her house and headed towards the police. The last she saw of the police was when the protesters mobbed them on all sides – they took shelter in their cars. The last she saw of the journalists was them wisely beating a jogging retreat. Now the police couldn't see her house because the swarm of protesters meant she couldn't see the police cars.

As she watched, four darkly dressed figures wearing motorcycle helmets jumped over her gate. They stalked towards her front door as a fifth person followed them over. Aware this was a possibility, her plan was to head into her backyard, jump the fence between her and Carl's house and seek shelter.

Dashing out of the office, she heard a crash as the first attacker thudded into and through the front door. She swore because, having anticipated the front door would slow them, she had locked the French doors in case they tried to sneak around the back. Now she couldn't escape – she had trapped herself.

Her back to the French doors, she turned around as the four black-clad figures stalked into the lounge, two were carrying baseball bats. They spread out, making a wall four metres in front of her. Too late she saw her defence canister sitting on the mantelpiece behind them.

'Stop,' she yelled, holding her hands up to show she wasn't armed. 'You'll go to jail if you don't get the fuck out of my house.'

One of the four took a step towards Grace. With sunglasses on, the open-faced helmet he was wearing revealed a dirty, straggly beard, giving away his sex and the fact he was white, but that was all.

'Listen, you bitch,' he hissed. 'If you don't shut the fuck up—'

Moving into a karate sparring stance, she was ready to fight for her life when his sentence was abruptly curtailed. He lunged clumsily forward, and she readied to kick him squarely in the balls. But instead of attacking her, he made a noise as if he was vomiting and landed prone at her feet.

All eyes turned towards the newcomer; a small woman protester dressed as if she had ridden in on a Harley-Davidson. From her posture it was clear she had landed a flying kick in the middle of the attacker's back. Even though their helmets and clothes hid their body language, it was obvious Marla had taken everyone by surprise.

Before they could react, she grabbed the baseball bat of the nearest attacker, a woman, who didn't want to let it go. Marla swung her through a short arc into the other two attackers who were moving towards her, causing them to fall in a tangled heap. With a ballet dancer's elegance, she moved in front of Grace, brandishing the seized baseball bat.

Without taking her eyes off the attackers, Marla said, 'Get your phone out, Ace. Let's ID these fuckers.'

It took a moment for Grace to compute what Marla had said. Then she snatched her phone from her back pocket. Two of the attackers, wearing full-face helmets, having untangled themselves had sprung up and spread out. They took positions to the left and right of the two women, creating a pincer movement.

The man on the left rhythmically swung a baseball bat as he edged to their right. Pausing, he pointed at the injured man still spluttering on the floor. 'Get him out of here,' he said in a hard-to-place European accent.

The remaining attacker dragged the groaning shape on the floor to his feet.

From her position behind Marla, she took photos as the attackers corralled them into the corner of the room. She hoped Marla had a trick up her sleeve. Although it was two on two, these two looked as if they knew how to handle themselves. And she hadn't been near a dojo in a decade.

'Fucking bitch, you'll get yours, Marks,' spluttered the injured man as he was half-carried, half-dragged from the room.

'Get ready for jail, dickhead,' shouted Grace as she photographed their retreat. When she focused back on their current predicament, the two attackers had stopped their advance and were now retreating slowly towards the door.

Their change of tactics coincided with Marla dropping the baseball bat and pointing a gun at them.

Speaking evenly, Marla said, 'If you're still here in two seconds, you're going to be bleeding on the ground … waiting for the police.'

The attackers exchanged a glance and a nod as they continued to back away. When they reached the door, they turned and ran. Following them, Grace photographed their retreating backs. At the front door, she switched to movie mode and recorded the scene unfolding in the street. Until America had become a world-leading exporter of hate and idiocy, this was a scene most people in New Zealand saw only on the international news.

She couldn't see any of the home-invader crew; in the dark and the chaos they had disappeared into the crowd. The police, who had their hands full dealing with the protesters, were now on the street with reinforcements. The mob was melting back towards her house, and with the police pushing they were dispersing.

No one took any notice of her as she filmed. Surprisingly, they had done little damage. They had broken a few fence pickets and, she shivered when she noticed, they had decapitated her letterbox. It could have been worse.

The red-headed police officer jogged towards her.

'Are you okay? What happened?'

Grace took him through the attack, again improvising to take credit for Marla's handiwork.

'You kicked him in the balls?'

'I used to do karate. I know how to do a mae geri. I grabbed his baseball bat and yelled "You're going to jail". Well, that was the polite version. They took off and I tried to photograph them.'

'Any luck?'

'I doubt it,' she said, shaking her head. 'It was dark. I'll check, but I think it'll be mainly their backs.'

'Bugger. It looks like they're clearing out, we'll keep a car here until they've gone. We'll tell them we'll arrest anyone who remains, that usually makes them fuck off home. Are you going to be okay tonight?'

'Yeah, now they're gone. I'll head to my partner's, make sure nobody follows me.'

The officer nodded. 'Once I've filled out the paperwork' – he closed his eyes and groaned – 'we'll get you to come to the station, see if we can find out who it was. Home invasion, that's bloody serious.'

'It bloody well felt serious.'

Back inside, she inspected her front door. The door was undamaged, but the wood around the lock had splintered easily. No doubt the repairs would cost a dollar less than her insurance excess. Like banks, insurance was a miserable industry that tried, but failed, to portray itself as a corporate version of Mother Teresa.

In the lounge, you wouldn't have known she had hosted four home invaders. The sofa was askew from when Marla piled the three attackers onto it and a baseball bat was on the table with an empty wine glass. Under the glass was a note.

Picking it up, Grace read it aloud. 'I came to check out the mob, it looked like you needed a hand. I would've waited, but you might have brought a boy in blue home. The two I drew on looked handy. The motorcycling duo? Stay safe.' She had signed the note *M*.

The French doors were still closed but they were now unlocked. In the darkness Grace could imagine Marla merging into the crowd and slipping away quietly, unnoticed.

Overfilling a glass of wine, she sat wearily at the table. What would have happened if Marla hadn't turned up? It sounded as if they were only going to threaten her – but the baseball bats? Marla had rightly not given him time to finish his speech. Threatening journalists, or worse, a home invasion – that was a massive increase in the anti-media flames fanned by Ball and the ProtectNZ machine.

Where does it stop? Journalists are murdered all over the world for doing their job; nobody expects it will happen in New Zealand. Equally, nobody expected massacres in mosques or mobs camped outside Parliament declaring they wanted to execute politicians and the media.

Her phone rang, it was RNZ's political editor. She simultaneously laughed and sighed. Of course, this was breaking news that needed reporting and she was the closest journalist to the action by a country mile. She clicked accept.

CHAPTER 41

Adorned with his MAGA cap, Blackwood stared at his computer screen. The security camera image he was studying was from the restaurant where the board had dined. The woman resembled Marks – but it wasn't Marks. Who was she? From the information he had received, she was also the one who had ambushed Regan Western, which culminated in his brother's death and almost exposed Styles' involvement. Worse, she had discovered where they were meeting, photographed them, and handed the information over to Marks. Now she had intervened when they were going to teach Marks a well-deserved lesson and take her out of the game – at least for a spell.

'Was it her?' he asked without looking up.

A man and a woman, both dressed in expensive smart-casual clothes and sunglasses, nodded. The man answered in a difficult-to-place Eastern European accent. 'She was staying in the hotel under the name Norma Smith.'

'And she must have been in the crowd outside Marks' house,' the woman added. She too had a hard-to-pin-down accent.

Turning from the screen, Blackwood asked, 'How did she get the jump on you?' He was about to add 'You're meant to know what you're doing', but he thought better of it. The atmosphere in the room was tense.

The man shrugged, looking bored. 'She was armed, we weren't. We don't carry guns for intimidation assignments, especially with the police on the scene.'

Blackwood harrumphed. 'I wanted you to send a message to the media, "Don't fuck with us", and what do we have? The media painting our followers as violent thugs.'

'I'm sure your PR machine can turn it around,' said the woman.

'They're onto it. Ordinary New Zealanders have had enough of media lies – that sort of line. Ball's calling for calm, exhorting our followers to remain peaceful. The mainstream media don't want to, but they're covering it.' Blackwood chuckled to himself. 'They're the cheapest marketing channel we have.'

'Good for you,' said the man flatly. 'Do you want to know about this woman?'

'You know who she is?'

The woman's face screwed up. 'We know who she *was*.'

Blackwood's wildly bushy eyebrows joined.

'We passed the name Norma Smith to our network,' she said. 'We assumed it would be fake, but it set off flashing lights in the US – it was an alias she had used previously. Her real name is Marla Simmons. She was in US Special Ops, then an agent for hire working for parts of the US machine we can't access.'

'What are you telling me?' said Blackwood. 'The US has an agent in New Zealand working against us?'

The man answered. 'She said *was*, she's on her own. She came to New Zealand on an assignment that cratered. They tried to take her out, but she went to ground suspected of murder and leaving two US agents in hospital. According to what we could find, she had disappeared without trace, until now. The US is keen she's a loose end that's taken care of.'

'I don't understand,' said Blackwood. 'What's her interest? I mean, from what you've told me she's not on anyone's payroll. Or is she?'

The man shook his head. 'Marks is the only link.'

'How?'

'From the reports we can access, the two agents she put in hospital were targeting Marks.'

'She's protecting Marks?' said Blackwood, his eyebrows joining.

The woman shrugged exaggeratedly. 'You'd have to ask her. What we're saying is there's a trained agent on the scene. The identity she's using doesn't exist in New Zealand, so we've no idea where to find her. She just keeps turning up uninvited.

'But how did she know what our plans are? Where to be and what we're doing?'

The man answered, still looking bored. 'She infiltrated the crowd outside Marks' house, saw what was happening and followed us in. As for your board meeting' – he made a dismissive gesture with his hands – 'if you leave an agenda for her to find, you're leaving loaves of bread, not breadcrumbs.'

Blackwood opened his mouth to protest, but the man continued.

'We were put at your disposal, told to do what you asked, to not ask questions. You want us to ride shotgun with your crew to beat up a journalist, we do it. And it was lucky we attended, otherwise they would now be in custody, singing their hearts out. You need the man at the playground killed, we do it.'

Blackwood stammered, 'I-I wanted him scared, not – not killed.'

Although the man's look didn't change, his voice became icy. 'The wrong man turned up, armed to the teeth – it was him or us. The right man, his *brother*, is still walking around. He'll be shit-scared and eventually he'll tell everything he knows. That'll lead them closer to you, which will lead them closer to us.'

Staying quiet, and with a dawning realisation, Blackwood understood the dynamics of their relationship. These weren't employees who he could bully in his usual manner. He had assumed they worked for him, that he was in charge. Now he could see the reality of his position.

The man continued. 'The fact there's an ex-agent on the scene, armed, that nobody knew about is fucking concerning. In short, *Ted*, I'm worried you don't have a tight grip on this operation and we're the ones who'll be burnt. The people who financed your project, your pet political party, would like you to know they're watching events with interest, and they expect results. They have enough incriminating evidence to make your life … difficult.'

'That would make *you* a loose end,' the woman added.

As they stood, Blackwood stayed sitting, closing his mouth when he realised it was hanging open.

'We're to be extracted,' said the man. 'You're now on your own. But, before we leave, we're going to do you a favour by tidying away Simmons. Without her, Marks should be easier to neutralise. Besides, Simmons has a useful bounty on her head.'

The woman said, 'If I was you, I'd hope we don't meet again.'

Blackwood watched them leave without saying a word. When they had left, he took off his favourite cap and ran his hands through his grey, thinning hair. Although unused to dealing with people like this, he knew the smart play was to keep quiet.

If they took out this Simmons woman, and left the country, that would buy breathing space for him to smooth over relations with his overseas backers. Besides, if they were successful, nobody would care and whatever evidence they had would never see the light of day.

CHAPTER 42

For the second time Marla's presence caused Regan Western to wet himself. He had swayed unsteadily into his lounge, turned on the light and froze. The box of beer he was carrying slipped from his hands and thudded to the floor as a dark stain zigzagged down the left leg of his pants.

'Not again, Regan.' Marla was standing in her preferred Weaver stance. Her feet positioned like a boxer, toes pointing toward the target, a two-handed hold on her Glock, her arms not fully extended, the gun aimed at Western's centre mass. 'I would say sorry but I'm thinking you might have a bladder problem.'

Not drunk but well on the way, Western stood staring at her gun, the whites of his eyes impossibly large. It was as if he expected to watch the bullet emerge.

'This is how your life is going to end, Regan.' Marla eased into a normal stance, letting the gun drop to her side. 'Just not today.'

Western continued to stare wide-eyed.

'Pick up your beer and sit down, I'll have one with you. You're in no state to try anything, but in case you forget, I won't kill you, but I will shoot you. Maybe in the shoulder, like your friends did to Ball. Or maybe in the leg, that's more dangerous. There are big arteries in your leg, you could bleed out fast. I'll tell you what – I'll surprise you.'

His eyes fixed on her, Western picked up his beer. Looking at the dark stain running down his left leg, he muttered, 'Can I at least change?'

'Sure. Unfortunately for me, I'll have to watch.'

She followed him as he walked awkwardly down the hall in his wet pants. They went past three tidy children's bedrooms to what she assumed was the master bedroom.

'I picked your house to be a tip,' she said. 'Do you use a cleaning service?'

Shaking his head caused him to fall against his bed. The alcohol he had consumed wasn't helping as he struggled to remove his wet pants.

Marla observed he didn't bother with fresh underwear, merely pulled on a pair of track pants.

'Don't feel too bad, it happens,' she said, as they headed back to the lounge. 'Sit over there,' indicating the far end of the couch with her Glock. She pulled over a chair from his dining room table. She doubted he would try to get the better of her, but distance is your friend.

Opening two bottles, he held one up, his face displaying a childish hope-to-please look. Marla stepped over and took the beer in her right hand, the gun staying in her dominant left. Keeping her eyes on him, she sat before having a long draw, putting the bottle and gun on the table within reach.

After a long pause, Western asked, 'Why are you here?'

Marla's top lip curled. 'To give you a chance to live. I wasn't joking, that's how you're going to die. Whether it's here, lying in a pool of your own blood for your children to find; or maybe at work, stuffed into a vehicle inspection pit for your workmates to find. The SIS agent down the street isn't there to protect you.'

'The SIS is watching me?'

Raising her eyebrows, she said, 'You're more like live bait. They're hoping you will lead them to someone more interesting. You see, that's the problem with tails – they're always behind you. You need them checking your front for people like me.'

He gulped before having a long drink, nearly emptying the bottle. 'Who are you?'

'That's a long story, Regan. All you need to know is I'm not with the law. I'm closer to a merc, but a good one. Your so-called friends, the ones who killed your brother, they're mercs too, but they're bad motherfuckers.'

'Mercs?'

'Mercenaries. Like in the movies.'

He gulped. 'What do you want from me?'

'Information,' she said. 'Information that could help save your life. You see, the police and the SIS are at least two steps behind, and they have to stay within the law. Well, the SIS don't, but they try to. Your best chance of surviving this is for me to take your two friends out of the game.'

Western finished his beer and looked hopefully at her.

'Go for it.' She waited while he clumsily opened another bottle.

'Whose idea was it to send your brother to the meet?'

'His. Geoff reckoned they were going to threaten me, he was angry. He reckoned they'd think twice if he turned up' – he fought back tears – 'and not me. He was armed but—'

'He was?' she interrupted. 'The police didn't find a gun at the scene.' And, as she had sent the police his way to confiscate his weapons, she had assumed he went unarmed.

'Geoff had loads of guns, illegally.'

'How did you get involved in this, Regan? You've a family, children, a tolerable job if you like selling cars. Dropping hate mail in journalists' letterboxes? Your organisation is like an evil version of the Boy Scouts.'

Regan's eyes flashed, but briefly. She recognised that underneath whatever mask he was wearing, he was an angry man. Why were so many men angry at the world? Jesus, the last time she looked, it was still a fucking man's world.

'Geoff was involved with a white supremacist group. I went with him a few times. Some of the stuff they believed in was nuts but some of it made sense.'

'Made sense?'

Alcohol fanned his anger. 'Yeah, it did. How the government is undermining our way of life. How there soon wouldn't be a New Zealand, not one we recognised.'

'That "we" would be white folk?'

'Well, yeah. It's not that I don't like Māoris, some of my—'

Marla cut in again. 'Best friends are Māori. I've heard variations of that logic over the years. Let's leave your racist views to one side, they make *me* want to shoot you. You joined and they made you do what?'

'Pledge allegiance, pump iron. We spent weekends in the bush, learnt survival tactics, how to handle guns. That sort of stuff.'

Marla briefly closed her eyes at the image of dumb white men charging around in the bush with guns. 'And threaten journalists?'

'I volunteered. I figured it would up my profile – and I didn't think I'd get caught. Until you showed up.'

'If it's any consolation, I'm good at what I do.'

Western frowned as he drank more beer.

'Who was driving the ute at the ambush?'

'I don't know,' he said, not looking at her.

'Regan, I saw you talk to the driver. Did you have your eyes closed?'

'You can't have.'

She rolled her eyes. 'Was it Styles?'

Western shook his head. 'He's our contact, but he's just a rich crook who lends out cars and fake number plates to other crooks. He's done that for years.'

'Fake plates?'

'Yeah, he has a stack of them hidden in the garage of his Wellington dealership.'

Tucking away that piece of information, she asked, 'What was the plan? It looked like you were setting up a hit.'

Western shook his head seriously. 'No way. Find out who you were and scare the shit out of you. Geoff was going to act the heavy, find out where you live, like you did to me. Maybe give you a few slaps.'

'You're not lying to me, are you?'

'No. Geoff was a nutter, but he'd never hurt a woman … badly.'

'How reassuring.' She stared at him for a long moment. 'I believe you, Regan, but that's what doesn't add up.'

He stared at her.

'In my game, killing is a big step, especially if the body is going to turn up. It's not like the movies where you can run around leaving a trail of corpses and confused cops. Those above you think you have information dangerous to their continued lifestyle. Dangerous enough for them to decide to kill you. And, I hate to tell you this, to them you're still dangerous.'

Western finished his beer and, this time without asking, opened his third.

'Who was in the ute, Regan?'

This time he stared at his beer.

'They'll kill you unless I or the police get to them first. Think of them like Arnie in *The Terminator* … the first one.'

He continued to stare at his bottle.

Marla sensed she was making ground. After giving him time to chew over his situation, she added, 'There's no going back, if that's what you're hoping. They've used you, your brother, and your alt-right friends. To them, you're expendable. Every one of you.'

'They said if I kept my mouth shut it would soon blow over. It would go back to the way it was.'

'The people you're dealing with don't like loose ends. And remember, behind them will be a hoard of rich white men trying to get richer who despise loose ends. If you're not worried for yourself, what about your children?'

His nostrils flared. She had hit the right note.

'If I tell you, can you protect me?'

Marla shook her head. 'The police can. Whatever you tell me, you need to tell them five minutes after I've left. You know they'll find out eventually – the only question is whether you'll be here or in the morgue.'

His voice started to crack. 'Like my brother.'

'You could make it harder for them.'

'How?'

'Like not coming home for a while. Get your ex to look after the children until it's safe. Not going to work, say you've tested positive for Covid, that'll buy you a week. It's not rocket science.'

Western digest her advice, along with yet more beer.

'And don't drink, at least not as much, until this is over. Having your wits about you might mean you keep them in your head.'

'Right.' He took a long look at his bottle before putting it on the floor. 'We know them as Mr and Mrs Smith – The Smiths for short. You know, like the movie and the band?'

'I know of them.'

'They came along to our camps. Taught us how to use weapons and self-defence moves.'

Marla stayed quiet. It was useful information, but it wasn't inflammatory enough to put Western on the liability list.

'I arranged to get them a fake number plate from Styles each time they came up. You know, for speed cameras and security cameras.'

'Did you say plate? Singular?' Marla wanted to make sure the beer wasn't making him stumble over his words.

Western nodded. 'They rode a motorcycle.'

A shot of adrenalin hit her system. 'There were two people in the ute?'

'I told you, Mr and Mrs Smith.'

Marla frowned deeply; this information was material. 'You know them by sight, is that all? That's still not enough to get you killed. Otherwise, they'd have to take out your dickhead mates too.'

Western fidgeted before picking up his beer. 'I know they shot the politician.'

'Ball?'

He nodded. 'They asked Geoff and me to do the job. No shooting, just make it look like he was under attack.'

'Go on,' she said, the dots joining.

'Geoff was keen, but I said no way, we'd get caught, so they used The Smiths. They must have changed the plan, decided it would play better if it looked like an attempted assassination.'

'Who are *they*?' she asked.

Shaking his head, he said, 'I told you; I don't know. I communicate with Styles on an encrypted channel. He's our link to the wider brotherhood.'

'The brotherhood,' she said, briefly laughing. 'I think you're the link, Regan. You know they shot Ball, that they were in Feilding with your brother, and that they murdered your brother. If you talk, they – and whoever is paying them – are in danger.'

'What can I do?'

'If I was you, as I suggested, I'd tell the police. They might catch them in time.'

Western shook his head.

'It's your call.' She left a long pause before adding, 'I'm developing a plan to neutralise them. You might be able to help. Interested?'

'Will I be in danger?'

Picking up her Glock, she said, 'Less danger than coming home.'

CHAPTER 43

'What are you doing?' asked a small but determined voice.

Marla had been so preoccupied setting up her drone she hadn't noticed the approach of two little girls, who she had last seen playing tag on the jungle gym. They now stood in front of her, holding hands.

It was four o'clock. The school playground near Grace's house was almost deserted although after-school activity rang out in the form of music from two schoolrooms. Marla was launching her drone so she could check which actors were watching Grace. She was confident the SIS had eyes on her; what she needed to know was whether the two people Western called The Smiths were also in play. Her bet was yes.

It had been a calculated risk letting Grace use the images. Without them, her story would have been conjecture, if she even had a story. The pictures, along with the agenda, were the smoking gun identifying the men pushing the ProtectNZ agenda on an unsuspecting public. The pictures also pinpointed the time and location when they were taken, it wouldn't take much digging to come up with the name Norma Smith and wherever that led them.

'This is my sister,' said the girl who had asked the question. 'She's still a baby.'

Marla couldn't help but smile. 'It's lovely you're looking after her. Where are your parents?'

The older sister pointed to the block of classrooms where Marla could hear the faint, discordant sounds of a piano. 'My mum's a *pin-nano* teacher.'

Her little sister nodded exaggeratedly, frowning seriously.

Marla gave what she hoped was a friendly smile. 'That's nice. I'm a little busy right at—'

'I *asked* you what you were *doing*?' cut in the little girl.

'That's right, you did.' Marla wasn't adept at handling children, having little to no experience, but she decided to tell the truth. 'I'm about to fly this drone so I can take pictures from way up there.'

The older sister stared up at the sky, then back at Marla, eying her suspiciously. Then her face erupted into a grin. 'Cool.' She dragged her little sister away at a gallop, heading towards the classroom.

Shaking her head, Marla checked the time – 4.07pm. She now had three minutes to get the drone airborne and in position. After she had raced through the pre-flight checks, the drone was soon buzzing its way into the afternoon sky. She decided to use her phone rather than the goggles to watch what her drone was capturing. After all, two small children had just caught her unawares, she wanted to maintain situational awareness. She watched the image of the playground shrink until it nestled into the surrounding leafy suburb.

Hovering the drone at one hundred metres, she adjusted the image so it covered Grace's street and adjacent side streets. At 4.10pm exactly she watched Grace's red Ford reverse onto the street then head towards the nearest supermarket. Marla knew this would happen because it was what they had arranged.

As Grace drove through a kinked intersection, the white SIS car parked nearby moved off in pursuit. The SIS agent tailing Grace was doing just that.

Marla adjusted the image so she could watch the two cars as well as monitor other vehicles. For the second time in days, she tingled with professional satisfaction – she still had her touch. A motorcycle, that must have been waiting nearby, slipped in behind Grace's SIS tail. If it was them, and she was sure it was, they couldn't have seen Grace leave from where they were waiting. They must have either bugged her car, set up a wireless surveillance camera to cover her house or, least likely, bugged the SIS agent's car. They were pros all right.

Zooming in to watch the action, she watched Grace park in the busy supermarket car park and go inside. Her SIS tail parked in the same car park, the agent following her inside at a discreet distance. The motorcycle parked across the road, but neither the rider nor the passenger went into the supermarket, preferring to watch from a distance.

So far so good. Grace wasn't in any danger and both tails were hoping Grace would lead them to her. It was 4.15pm: Grace was going to shop for fifteen minutes, which gave Marla time to get to their agreed rendezvous.

Commanding the drone to return to home base, she started packing up. Twelve minutes later she was sitting in Rosie O'Grady's, a bar on the corner of Fitzherbert Avenue and Fergusson Street. Ordering a ginger beer for her and a glass of wine for Grace, she had selected the bar because of its location, not its ambience. Stereotypical inner-city Irish-themed bars were the same the world over, except in Ireland. Grace arrived right on time, a manilla folder under her arm.

Grace's eyes were gleaming as she sat down across from Marla, claiming the wine. 'Well?'

Looking in the folder which was, as Marla expected, empty, she said, 'Yep, you've two tails. The SIS one we knew about … and the other one.'

'Do you know who the other ones are?'

'Not their real names, but they're on a motorcycle.'

Grace's eyes widened. 'The ones who killed Western and shot Ball?'

'I'd say so, but we don't have any evidence. I'm hoping they do.'

'Am I in danger?' Grace drank a large mouthful of her wine.

Marla shook her head. 'I wouldn't have involved you if you were. When you leave, minus the folder, the SIS tail will follow you home, but I'm positive the motorcycle duo will wait. They'll be hoping I emerge and, when I leave with the folder, they'll follow me.

'Will you be safe?'

'If I lose them, which is what I'm planning to do.'

Grace frowned.

'Don't worry. It's all planned.'

'I do worry, though,' said Grace. 'Then what?'

The American raised her eyebrows. 'We need to end this fast. I don't like having a couple of killers on my tail. We need JP or the police to catch The Smiths and lock them up.'

'The who?'

'That's what Western and his mates call the two on the motorcycle.'

'Like the movie? Lame,' said Grace. 'We also need to make sure they don't catch you, or worse. And we, make that I, need to get the dirt on ProtectNZ.'

'It's great to know you're thinking about me – before your story.'

'Jesus, it's the least I can do,' said Grace, missing Marla's irony.

'I've developed a plan to trap them. The downside is that, because I'm acting as bait, the SIS will trap me too.'

'Go on.'

'I need you to make a deal with the SIS. I'll give them the two killers on a platter, but I get to walk away.'

Grace whistled. 'They might go for it. They *should* go for it. What's your "or else"?'

'I walk away. Head home.'

After a slow, thoughtful sip of wine, Grace said, 'I'll contact JP, see what she says. She'll have to get it cleared, it's bound to be above her pay grade, but you'd want that assurance. They'd be mad not to go for it. I mean, what's the worst that could happen?'

'They double-cross me?'

'There's always that. I'd better get going.' Grace drained her glass. 'Send me a message, I want to know you made it home safely.'

'Yes Mom,' said Marla.

It was 4.45pm when she left. If Marla was right, Grace would be home in five minutes and her SIS tail would be back in position. The motorcycle duo, however, would stay in position watching the bar.

Marla left the bar after five o'clock to make it appear she had been studying the material Grace passed over. Walking casually, sunglasses on in the last of the day's sunshine, she walked up Fitzherbert Avenue towards The Square. The advantage of wearing sunglasses was you could look around without looking like you were looking around.

The motorcycle duo had parked in the shadows outside a restaurant across the street.

She turned left into a lane, out of sight. The colourfully decorated lane led to a large supermarket and its equally large car park where she had parked. In among the noise of the busy street, she heard a motorcycle engine start. She hustled along the lane and into a small satellite car park enclosed by a low, two-foot-high cinder-block wall. While she could, and did, jump it easily, they would beach their motorcycle if they tried to follow.

Parked close by, she drove away before they could follow on foot. Accelerating along planned side streets, she gave them no chance to get on her tail. The only information they gained, or what they thought they had gained, was how she and Grace rendezvoused. The next time they wouldn't follow her into the satellite car park, they would be waiting in the main car park – and she would be ready for them.

CHAPTER 44

Grace sat down next to Agent Parata who had been waiting for her on a park bench as they had arranged. 'Kia ora, JP. I bought coffee.'

The SIS agent accepted the takeaway cup. 'Thanks, e hoa.'

It was a cloudy afternoon, warm for the time of year. Dressed in jeans and her go-to grey hoodie, Grace arrived five minutes early armed with two Americanos, planning to arrive before Parata. But as she walked towards the checkerboard in The Square, a small park in the middle of Palmerston North's city centre, the tall figure of Parata, unnecessarily wearing sunglasses, was already lounging on the park bench. At an adjacent bench sat a homeless man Grace often saw around the town's centre.

'What's with spooks and sunglasses? You lot have seen too many spy movies. Life imitating art and all that.' Grace rummaged in her bag. Taking out a ten-dollar note she walked over to the homeless man, holding out the note. 'We need a bit of privacy.'

Taking the note, his eyes lit up and he stammered a thank you before walking away unsteadily.

Parata shook her head. 'He'll only spend it on alcohol.'

'I didn't expect he'd use it to add to his share portfolio. Besides, do you enjoy a drink, JP?'

'That's not the point.'

'What is the point?'

Rolling her eyes, the agent said, 'Fine. You've thought about it, I haven't. Anyway, how are you after your close encounter with the protesters?'

'I'm okay. It's not comforting knowing so many fuckheads know where I live. I might need to get a big dog.'

'That'd help, though anyone who can *kung-fu* four attackers and send them packing should sleep soundly enough.'

Grace glared. 'It was karate.'

'I'm sure it was. Let's get to the real point. Marla Simmons.'

'Did you know there are two tails on me?'

Parata's eyes narrowed.

'Marla's been watching them both. Your agent and a couple on a motorcycle.'

Anger flashed in the agent's eyes. 'Why didn't you let me know immediately? Fuck, Ace, from what we know they're the killers.'

'I know, I know. Marla told me last night. I'm letting you know now.'

'They'll be watching, we could've set up a trap to catch them.'

'How? Only Marla knows what they look like.' Grace sipped her coffee before adding, 'I think they were two of the attackers who invaded my home.'

'Then how the fuck—'

Interrupting the agent, she said, 'Marla surprised them – and me.'

'I figured she was involved.' Parata's face was stern. 'We know you're working with her; we studied the images you sent through.' Her face softened when she added, 'Thanks for that. It gave me the chance to front foot your story, even impressed my boss – for five minutes.' Her face hardened again. 'Anyway, I pulled the security feeds from the hotel. I doubted you took the photos; they'd have recognised you.'

'I didn't know she was there. I don't even know how she discovered a ProtectNZ board existed let alone when and where they were meeting. She sent me the images. I forwarded them to you.'

'We've done this dance before, Ace. You might not have known what she was doing, but it's obvious you're working with her. Do you know where she is now?'

She turned towards Parata, shaking her head. 'She arrives, she leaves. As you can imagine, she plays her cards close to her chest.'

Parata stayed quiet for a long moment. 'My boss is keen to get her hands on Simmons but, if she can't, she's even keener she stays in the shadows. Politically, she's a fucking nightmare.'

Grace scoffed. 'What do you care about the politics?'

'I don't, but everyone above my pay grade is a political junkie.'

'What's your interest then?'

'Catching the two who shot Ball and murdered Western.'

'And that's it? Isn't that a police matter?'

'Shooting Ball put it in the terrorism class. Nailing those two will play well for the Service.'

Grace gathered her thoughts. 'You're in the domestic terrorism unit, so tell me, is it domestic terrorism if a faction tries to corrupt our democracy?'

Parata closed her eyes and shook her head. Grace gave her space.

'You think ProtectNZ is doing that?' the agent finally asked.

'That's exactly what they're trying to do. Sadly, they've learnt from overseas how to do it legally, how to do it by gaming the system. There's a story of an election in Africa where the government sat soldiers, armed to the teeth, on top of ballot boxes to stop people voting in areas that supported their rivals.'

'That's the state making its wishes known,' said Parata.

'That's an obvious way to rig an election. A subtler way is to use social media, scripted populist messages, marketing, and shitloads of money to convince people their way of life is under threat, that the media are evil and mythical Tesla-driving greenies are the enemy.'

'I get that,' said Parata, 'but that's not illegal. That's – what do you call it in your stories – a contest of ideas.'

'But the contest's rigged, that's the problem.' Grace sighed, putting her coffee between her feet. 'Trump did it in the US, Bolsonaro in Brazil, and dark money helped Brexit over the line. We think domestic terrorism is about nutters shooting up mosques, and it is, but the same twisted alt-right hatred and money is lurking behind ProtectNZ.'

The SIS woman shook her head as though she needed to physically clear it. 'Jesus, Ace. I don't make the law; I just catch bad fuckers. If they're clever enough to operate within the law, and I assume you have no evidence to the contrary otherwise you'd have plastered it all over the news, what do you expect me to do?'

Grace opened her mouth, but Parata carried on.

'Don't answer that. I need to talk to you about Simmons. She's wanted for murder, and' – she held up a hand to stop Grace from interrupting – 'if we catch her, there are parts of the US administration who want her quietly extradited to, ahh … answer questions. We, the SIS, know you're working with her and that puts you in a dodgy position.'

'Dodgy? Piss off. You know they framed her.'

'I, and certainly the police, *know* nothing of the sort.'

'Right. Because they did a bang-up job framing her, I'm supposed to, what? Lead you to her? Set up a sting? Even if I could, which I can't, I wouldn't.'

The women glared at each other. Stalemate.

'Fuck, you're a pain in the arse,' said Parata. 'All right, tell me how she became involved. I mean, what's in it for her?'

Breathing in deeply through her nose, she considered the question's angle. 'Nothing, as far as I know. It's the same situation as when she saved my life from *your* colleagues. I came home one afternoon and she was in my house having a glass of wine. She said she had seen me on the news about the hate mail and had come to lend a hand. She thought it would take a couple of days, not become this involved.'

'She's acting the Good Samaritan? Again?'

Grace rolled her eyes. 'It is possible, you know. Not everybody on the planet has bought into the new religion of "What's in it for me?". I assume she made heaps doing whatever she used to do for the dodgy parts of the US spy machine. I don't think she needs the money, but not everybody wants to retire, waste the planet's resources hacking divots out of golf courses, and star in their own TV series – lifestyles of the rich, selfish, and seriously stupid.'

Suppressing a laugh, Parata said, 'I'm sorry I spoke.'

'I've no time for rich wankers and their tax-avoiding societal parasitism.'

It was Parata's turn to roll her eyes. 'Shall I get you a soapbox?'

Grace's stare turned into a short laugh. 'Fair enough. But I think Marla became involved because someone needed to do something, and that's it.'

'She's helped us out too,' said Parata. 'It's been like having a roving field agent. But …'

'I know, she's wanted for murder.'

Parata bit her lip. 'I know I'm going to regret asking this, but your message said she wants to make a deal.'

'Actually, *we* want to make a deal.' In response to Parata's look, Grace added, 'I have teenagers to feed, you know.' Parata went to speak but she didn't pause. 'I'm not in any danger. They're not after me, they're after Marla.'

Parata re-bit her lip.

'She's developed a plan to catch them using herself as bait, but she wants a guarantee about what happens to her. The deal is – if she delivers you the killers, she's allowed to walk away.' She waited, letting Parata process the request.

As Parata was about to speak, Grace said, 'And I want first bite of whatever you get on ProtectNZ … please.'

'I'm not running the SIS, Ace. I'm a lowly government employee.'

'Don't give me that. I've known you to wangle the system when needed.'

Sipping her coffee, the agent asked, 'If we say no to the deal?'

Shrugging, she said, 'I'll let Marla know. She'll presumably disappear to wherever she's living. Leave you, me, and the police to carry on.'

'I could get you arrested for obstructing a police inquiry.'

Grace's teeth clenched. 'For fuck's sake, JP, I'm not obstructing the police. I'm in the middle, trying to help. My easiest option is to say this shit's between y'all. You talk to Marla if you think she's obstructing their inquiry.'

The agent held up her hands in surrender. 'Part of me gets what you're saying.' She ran her tongue over her teeth. 'I'll have to run this past my boss, I have no idea what she'll say. Her face will turn an interesting shade of red, that I do know.'

'You don't have to answer this, JP, but what do you have now? It was Marla who managed to get ahead of ProtectNZ. And she's ahead of the two who killed Western and shot Ball. They link this all together. Get them and God knows what we have. I mean' – she smiled – 'what you have.'

Parata half-smiled. 'I'll call it in, let you know when I have an answer.

It won't be in writing, obviously, but if we make a deal, I'll do my best to make sure we're solid. How soon can she organise the operation?'

'She wants to do it tomorrow afternoon. She said you'll need a few bodies in place to make sure the two can't get away.'

Parata's face pinched tight.

'You decide whether you're in or out. If you're in, I'll get the details from Marla and send them through.'

The women stood up, Grace coming up to the agent's chest. Parata looked down, not able to suppress her smirk. Stepping back, so she didn't have Parata's chest in her face, Grace was about to head to her car when Parata said, 'Be careful, Ace. You can't have many of your nine lives left … not at your age.'

CHAPTER 45

Sitting opposite Marla, Grace fidgeted with her keys. They were both drinking ginger beer this time as they waited inside Rosie O'Grady's. If the plan was running as Marla anticipated, outside the bar would be an SIS agent ready to follow Grace. Waiting for Marla in the supermarket car park would be the motorcycling Smiths.

'Relax, Ace, it's under control.'

Grace shook her head. 'Most of it's under control. Do you trust the SIS not to shaft you?'

Parata had contacted Grace the previous night with the SIS's best offer. They would hold Marla without bringing in the police. If she could explain to the SIS's satisfaction that she was innocent of the murder the police believed she had committed, they would let her go. There would be no record of the SIS detaining her – it would be as if it had never happened. Grace would get the inside running in terms of information the SIS could release about ProtectNZ's involvement with the killers.

Marla shrugged. 'I've put them in a tricky spot, but I didn't kill anyone. I know exactly how it went down; I'll convince them.'

'If I don't trust them,' said Grace, 'I can't believe you would.'

'Every now and again you need to take a leap of faith. This is a chance for them to close their file, even if the police can't. You never know, they might offer me a job.'

'You're not serious?'

'No,' said Marla, laughing. 'More importantly, is JP set?'

'Yep. I'll be with her and her team at the airport.'

'Great.' Marla checked the time on her watch. 'You leave right on four. It'll take you fifteen minutes to get to the airport. I'll leave at quarter past four. That'll give you fifteen minutes to make sure everything's right.'

'If anything's wrong,' said Grace, 'I'll text you on your burner phone.'

'It doesn't need to be a message; one letter will do. You're the only person who knows the number. If you text, Samuel L Jackson will let me know and I'll drive away.'

'A question,' said Grace. 'What do we do if it goes tits up?'

'Tits up, I know that one too. There's no plan B. I'll be winging it, but so will they. And so will the SIS.'

'That's not comforting. I'm imagining a Keystone Cops chase scene. Will you be packing?'

'"Packing", listen to you. Definitely. Everyone else will be, bar you.'

Checking her watch, Marla said, 'It's time for you to go.'

She went to stand but Grace eased back down. 'Be careful, Marla. You've already saved my life twice. And you're here because you wanted to save me from a group of white Neanderthals.'

Reaching over, Marla gave her hand a squeeze. 'You're right, you owe me shitloads.'

Their laughter broke the tension.

'It's always been my choice, Ace. Besides, democracy needs a helping hand from time to time.'

'It sure does.'

Fifteen minutes later after an uneventful trip, Grace arrived at Palmerston North's airport. Taking a ticket at the secure car park gate, she parked as arranged in the left-hand corner of the car park where the SIS had used a maintenance vehicle to command eight parks. She pulled in next to a white panel van Parata had told her would be there; it was the mobile headquarters for the operation. Seconds later a car reversed into the park next to her. The driver smiled at her as she got out and headed to a different car.

The side door of the van slid open revealing a smiling Agent Parata. The van was kitted out with all manner of screens and electronic panels and resembled a cockpit. An agent wearing headphones sat in front of the dizzying array. It reminded Grace of Dr Who's Tardis, bigger on the inside than it appeared on the outside.

Stepping into the van she stood next to Parata who was also sitting. 'Was that my tail?'

'She's part of the team now. You're free from our protective view.'

'I can think of more appropriate words. Do you have the situation under control?'

'Simmons picked a solid place for an ambush,' said Parata. 'The car park perimeter is surrounded with a security fence, once they're inside, they're a rat in a trap.'

'Where are your team?'

Pointing to a screen, she said, 'Did you see the two gardeners when you arrived?'

'No, I was busy getting a ticket.'

'Exactly, they blend into the scenery. Apart from them, we've two cars in play, one for each escape route out of this part of the car park.' Pointing at a screen displaying a helicopter view of the airport, she said, 'We want to keep them penned in here. We couldn't get them to shut the whole airport, so there's the chance of civilians popping up in other parts. There are no planes due in the next hour, so the airport should be quiet, and we've warned airport staff to keep away. They've also let us put up a drone to watch the red zone. The only unconfirmed aspect of the operation is the car Marla's driving.' She gave Grace a hard stare. 'We've had to trust you on that.'

'It's a silver Honda Fit. I gave you the plate number. Why would she lie?'

'The plate tracks to a phantom living on Waiheke Island. And why? Because she's driving into the same rat trap.'

'But you've given her an assurance.'

Holding up her hands, Parata said, 'We have, but if I was in her shoes, it's not much of an assurance. I'm just saying.'

'Don't you think she'll turn up?'

'No, I think she'll be here. I mean, if she was going to do a runner, she could've done it days ago, not left you hanging out to dry to explain to a very pissed-off team of agents why we wasted time and resources on a knock-on-the-door-and-run-away prank.'

The tech monitoring the screens interrupted their conversation. Without taking his eyes off the screen, he said, 'Grey car, looks like a Honda, has entered the red zone.'

Lowering the microphone on her headset, Parata said, 'We're go. Check in.'

The three teams answered in the affirmative.

'Unless necessary, radio silence from now. I'll keep up a running commentary.'

Grace gave Parata space while making sure she could watch the action across the multiple screens. It all looked as they had agreed; she didn't need to text Marla.

The tech spoke. 'Confirmed, silver Honda, woman with long hair and sunglasses at the wheel, plates are a match.'

Putting her thumb over the microphone, she whispered to Grace, 'I put someone on the corner too.'

'Target acquired,' said the tech. 'Motorcycle has entered the red zone, tracking behind the Honda. Confirmed two on the bike.'

Parata informed her team. 'Target confirmed, estimated two minutes away.'

Watching the feed from the drone, Grace saw Marla's silver car turn into Airport Drive and approach the barrier. The car stopped, Marla took a ticket, the barrier arm raised, and the silver car drove sedately in, heading towards the opposite corner of the car park.

'Target approaching the barrier,' said Parata. 'Remember, shooting's a last resort. We want them alive.'

The motorcycle slowed as it approached the barrier arm. Grace held her breath, the excitement building. At the last moment, it veered left and continued towards the airport terminal.

'Target hasn't taken the bait.' It was the most animated Grace had ever heard Parata. 'Hold in position. No one move a fucking muscle.' She put her thumb over the microphone. 'What are they doing?' she said to the tech as well as to herself.

The tech spoke calmly. 'If they sensed a trap, they'd be hurtling away. They're Sunday driving. Being cautious.'

Parata took her thumb off the microphone. 'They might be doing a recon lap. Hold in position, wait for my signal.'

Grace watched the motorcycle ride past the airport's main entrance and head towards the exit. In the meantime, Marla had parked against the far fence. She hadn't seen her get out, like everyone else, she was watching the motorcycle, but two black suitcases now sat behind Marla's car. She must have put them there as props.

'They're coming back around,' Parata informed her team.

Grace could feel the hairs on the back of her neck bristle. The motorcycle, now the full focus of the drone, approached the barrier. The rider reached out and took a ticket. The barrier arm raised, and they rode sedately into the trap.

The motorcycle turned sharply, taking the same path as Marla.

'Go, go, go,' Parata screamed into the microphone, before ripping it off and wrenching the van door open. A gun appeared in her hand from nowhere as she ran towards the motorcycle.

Not thinking, Grace followed Parata. Cars screeched and slid into position, blocking the exits and securing the trap. The gardeners, tools replaced by guns, weaved through the cars.

The rider, seeing the trap close, accelerated away from the agents, turning a hard left, roaring between a line of parked cars.

At what looked an impossible speed in the confined car park, the motorcycle searched the perimeter for an exit. The agents weaved between the cars, trying to herd the motorcycle into a corner. The motorcycle's passenger had drawn a gun, but the rapid changes of direction meant they were having to hang on to the rider, not aim and shoot.

Without turning around, Parata yelled at Grace, 'Get under a car, Ace.'

'Like fuck,' she said to herself. There was way too much adrenalin in her system for her to realise she should be shitting herself. It didn't get this hazardous for a journalist outside a war zone.

As the motorcycle weaved and sprinted, the agents moved from position to position. Without warning, the silver Honda Fit with its tyres screeching, reversed into the path of the oncoming motorcycle, sending the suitcases flying. The rider, focused on the agents, didn't react in time. As he or she tried to dodge the car, Marla veered into their path, slamming on the brakes.

If it was the movies, the collision would have sounded like thunder, both vehicles exploding with Marla rolling away unscathed. The real-life sound was a short screeching of tyres followed by a dull thud, like a sack of flour hitting the floor. The rider smacked into the car, making a second dull thud. The passenger, as physics demanded, flew over the car, landing in a heap well beyond the impact.

Everyone stopped and for a few seconds the world was silent.

'Fuck,' whispered Grace, as Marla's car rolled into the security fence.

Pouncing, the agents were yelling but it was soon obvious the crash had incapacitated both rider and passenger. They checked for weapons, finding a pistol on the rider. The passenger, who Grace could tell was a man, had let his gun go in the crash, it had clattered into the security fence. As her team secured the scene, Parata called in an ambulance.

While nobody was looking, Grace used her phone to take photos of the action before stealthily putting it back into her pocket.

With the targets neutralised, Parata stalked towards Marla's car, an agent joining her. Grace's eyes widened when she saw it wasn't an agent, it was Detective Fergusson – that wasn't part of the deal. Parata pointed left and an agent moved to cover Marla's car, their gun drawn.

Through the rear window, Grace could see Marla slumped at the wheel, which was odd. The motorcycle had hit the front passenger side of her car, and her car had rolled into the fence at walking pace – she shouldn't be injured.

Parata called out, 'Simmons, come out with your hands on your head.'

Marla didn't move.

'It's okay,' she shouted. 'Our arrangement is solid. We'll get it sorted.'

Marla still didn't move. It was a standoff.

Edging alongside Parata, Grace hissed, 'What the fuck is Fergusson doing here?'

Speaking quietly, her eyes fixed on Marla's Honda, she said, 'I couldn't get it set up without his involvement. It changes nothing.'

'For Marla it—'

Interrupting, Parata's voice reverted to its normal volume. 'Fuck, Ace, now's not the time. I need to get this done and you're getting in the way.'

'Let me talk to her,' said Grace. 'She's not going to hurt me, but she might kill you. I fucking would.'

Turning her head, Parata stared at her hard.

'I know you could take her by force,' said Grace, 'but she might be hurt – and I know she's armed. Let me talk to her.'

Looking back towards the car, Parata said, 'This is against my better judgement.' She called out, 'Simmons, Ace is coming over, she's not armed. We've got her and you covered.' Turning to Grace, she said, 'If she takes you hostage, I'll be insisting she shoots you as part of any deal.'

'Whatever.'

Grace edged towards the car, circling to the right. This way she could walk towards the driver's door so Marla could see it was her and she was alone. The sunlight on the window made it hard to see, but it looked like she was crying. Odd.

'Marla, it's me, Ace. I'm going to open the door. As JP said, we can get this sorted out. Everyone knows you're innocent.'

Sobbing, she kept her hands on the wheel, her head resting on her hands.

As if she was disarming a bomb, Grace inched the door open and crouched down to Marla's level.

Marla turned her head to look at her.

Her eyes widening, Grace muttered, 'I should've known.'

The hair looked right, and the large brown sunglasses were Marla's, but the stubble – what? Grace shook her head and said, 'I should've at least guessed.'

In her normal voice, Grace said, 'Come on out, you're safe now.'

Through the sobs Grace could make out the words, 'They killed him, not me.'

'What's going on, Ace?' Parata's shouted voice sounded accusatory.

'We're good,' Grace called as she stood. 'You're, um … you're not going to like this, JP.'

Gently, she helped him out of the car. When he stood up and saw guns pointed at his chest, he took an involuntary step backwards into the car door. Grace pulled off his wig and sunglasses.

Her gun dropping to her side, Parata said, 'You have to be joking. Western! What the absolute fuck?'

Grace had to grit her teeth to control her laughter as she led a still-crying Western towards the agents.

Parata, looking as if she wanted to shoot someone, said, 'This isn't funny, Ace.'

'I know,' said Grace, still smirking. 'It's hilarious. Besides, you've caught the killers. Marla, and Western, delivered them to you on a plate – as promised. This makes your life easier, doesn't it?'

A smouldering Parata was about to reply when the tech called out from the van. 'New contact in the red zone.'

'Guess who,' said Parata with a roll of her eyes. Turning to her team, she said, 'Keep an eye on these two, you'll need to travel with them in the ambulance. I'll let the police know to relieve you. And cuff Western, he has some explaining to do.'

In the van, the tech had focused the drone on a red car on the main road outside the airport's perimeter. A few metres from the car a single person was sitting on the grass.

Parata peered at the screen. 'How do you know it's a contact? They look like they're having a picnic.'

Grace, who had followed Parata, mumbled, 'Strange place for a picnic.' Parata's was the right question, but they both knew it was Marla, watching events unfold.

'Airport security contacted me,' said the tech. 'They told me we didn't have permission for two drones.'

Her eyes closed, Parata spoke calmly into her microphone. 'Secondary target confirmed at ten o'clock outside the airport perimeter. Team A to pursue.'

Two doors slammed, an engine started, and tyres briefly screeched.

'Contact is now inside the car,' the tech informed Parata.

Grace looked at the screen. Marla had gone but the car remained motionless.

Grace stepped out of the van to watch. It was a slow, circuitous route to exit from the car park. The agents drove rapidly but carefully, mindful they were in a public space. On the screen, she watched the red car drive away at pace.

The agents radioed in that they didn't have a ticket to exit the car park. Parata cursed. Over the radio they asked, 'Can you get them to raise the barrier, or should we crash through?'

Parata put her thumb over the microphone. 'How long can your drone keep the car in sight?'

'About another twenty seconds.'

'Can't you fly after it?'

He shook his head. 'She's driven under NZPM airspace. I can't fly the drone into their take-off and landing corridor.'

Speaking over-calmly, she said, 'Negative. Abandon pursuit, she's off and gone.'

As the sound of an ambulance grew louder, Parata turned to look at Grace, again staring hard.

'What?' said Grace.

Imitating Grace's voice, she said, 'Let me talk to her!' Then, reverting to her normal voice but with an I-am-so-fucked-off tone, she added, 'If I find out you knew ...'

Grace tucked her legs under her and leaned on the arm of the couch, wine glass in hand. Sean, also with a glass of wine, sat next to her as Grace's children and Sean's dog sprawled around the lounge. Without interest they watched the dying moments of *The Chase*, waiting for the news.

'Turn it up,' said Grace when the news started.

The newsreader, impeccably dressed as always, spoke excitedly. 'In breaking news tonight, the police have arrested several prominent New Zealanders associated with the new political party ProtectNZ. Covering the story for One News is Maiki Sherman at Parliament.'

The image changed to a blurry image of a handcuffed man standing by a police car. Sherman took up the action. 'Early this morning the police executed a number of warrants with four of those arrested linked to the ProtectNZ political party.' Images of the police arresting various men cycled through as she narrated the story.

'Prominent businessman Edward Blackwood was taken from a luxury Wellington apartment and into custody.'

Live action showed the police leading a large, scowling, handcuffed man towards a police car accompanied by a myriad of camera flashes. A voice called from out of shot, 'You've forgotten your Trump hat, you tosser.' Blackwood turned his head towards the camera, his eyes burning, but they had bleeped out his long reply.

Grace paused the story, laughing.

'Mummm.' Her son had adopted a parental tone. 'That sounded like your voice.'

'It was. I did enjoy that. I didn't think it'd make the news.'

Sean shook his head. 'You dragged yourself out of bed at three in the morning, in the middle of winter, to drive to Wellington to gloat?'

'Damn straight,' said Grace. 'I'll be in court for his trial too. Wouldn't miss it.'

Everyone smiled but also shook their heads. She unpaused the story.

Sherman voiced over another minute of flashing lights and police cars at another arrest.

The shot changed to Sherman, microphone in hand. 'Grace Marks, a local journalist, has supplied much of what we know. Her story was released after the police operation had concluded and alleges the men arrested were involved in the attempted murder of Sebastian Ball and the murder of Geoffrey Western, whose body was discovered at a playground near Waikanae. Her story documented how the men, using overseas funding from groups associated with alt-right terrorism, had orchestrated the attacks to both enhance and protect the party's image.'

The shot changed to a split screen of the newsreader and Sherman.

'What have the police said, Maiki?'

'They haven't issued a statement, but they indicated they'll be laying a range of serious charges as their investigations continue. The police also took Sebastian Ball, the leader of ProtectNZ, in for questioning but released him later. They said, at this stage, they didn't expect to charge him with any offences. He's scheduled a press conference for tomorrow morning.'

'Are you going to Ball's press conference?' asked Sean.

'Wouldn't miss that either,' she said with a beaming smile.

The newsreader asked, 'How did Grace Marks, our colleague, become so involved?'

Sherman smiled broadly. 'Well, Simon, you may remember she was interviewed about finding hate mail in her letterbox. She assumed it was coming from alt-right groups trying to stop her publishing stories about their activities. It appears the hate mail was most likely in relation to her investigation of ProtectNZ's funding from international alt-right groups. An image she used in her story was of the domestic terrorism unit of the SIS arresting two people at Palmerston North airport a few days ago. Those arrests precipitated the police operation that took place early this morning. The SIS, unsurprisingly, have stayed tight-lipped and I hope to talk to Grace Marks to find out how those threats led to this political intrigue.'

'Ngā mihi e hoa,' said the newsreader. 'In other news …'

Grace froze the newsreader.

Her daughter bounded up, giving her mum a hug. 'You're famous. And those alt-right dickheads are going down.'

'Yeah, well done, Mum,' said her son laconically, as was his style.

'Just doing my job,' she said seriously, before holding up her glass. 'Three cheers for me.'

Grinning, her children disappeared to their rooms, leaving Grace and Sean sitting on the couch, the TV paused. Sean's dog Roxy, not usually allowed on the couch, joined them to be closer to the action.

'You didn't tell me you were part of the SIS takedown team,' he said.

'There wasn't time. Besides, I wasn't allowed to tell anyone, even now. JP said her boss wasn't happy I used a photo from the takedown, though I made sure no one was recognisable.'

Sean's eyes narrowed. 'You've been running around a lot with this one. And the stories you've told me ...'

'Yes?' she said staring at the TV.

'Don't take this the wrong way, Grace, but your actions – how can I put it – they're a little beyond your capability.'

Grace opened her mouth to protest.

Sean carried on. 'Bugging and tracking a car. Using a drone, I've never seen you near a drone. Getting pictures of the ProtectNZ Board at a hotel without them recognising the intrepid "Ace Marks"?'

Holding up a hand, she said, 'There's a logical explanation.'

'How about not being in Wellington the day you took the photos of the board? You were with me. Did you beam yourself to Wellington?'

'I had a little help.'

'The woman who was here. Your colleague from Wellington?'

'Yes.'

Sean licked his lips. 'She looked familiar, but as she was a colleague of yours, I assumed I'd seen her picture on TV or online.'

Grace stayed quiet.

'When I checked,' he continued, 'because I was curious, she looked awfully like the suspect in that Wellington murder case.' He raised his eyebrows. 'You told me she was a former agent who they had framed and no one would see her again. I know you can't tell me much, and I respect that, but …'

Finishing her wine, she held the glass towards Sean, looking hopeful.

Pushing himself off the couch with a sigh, he said, 'When I return.'

Her wine replenished, and having had a minute to think, she said, 'Yes, it was her, Marla Simmons. And yes, she did a lot of the stuff I took credit for so she could stay in the shadows.'

'The police must have known.'

Grace's face scrunched. 'The police didn't know but the SIS, my contact, was all over it.'

She took him through the story from when Marla had arrived to help, culminating in an angry Agent Parata watching Marla drive away. Sean shook his head almost continuously as she recounted the highlights of the past weeks.

When she had finished, he laughed. 'You must have enough material for several stories.'

'I have. I've a dozen angles and JP has promised to feed me more details about Blackwood's involvement. From what I've heard so far, a lot of the money they used came from dodgy overseas sources, American and Russian. Then there's Ball's press conference tomorrow.'

'Is this survivable? For his party, I mean.'

'I doubt it. So much shit is sticking to them now. Even if they try to bluff it out, they'll sink back into the rural mud from where they emerged.'

'And this Marla Simmons? Where's she now?'

Shrugging, she said, 'As I said, she turned up to help me kick the alt-right nutters into touch. I reckon the SIS should pay her. Without her involvement, I doubt we'd be any the wiser about ProtectNZ, not until it was too late.'

'Will you see her again?'

'Maybe. We have a secure comms link, but she said she needs to trash it in a few days in case anyone tries to track her. She's still wanted for murder, and even though the SIS know she was set up, the evidence the police have points to her. Throw in the fact that the US spy agencies are keen to get their hands on her. JP said the two they caught at the airport were likely trying to claim a bounty by killing her.'

'The US has a bounty on her?'

'Not officially, but they're happy to work under the radar to get what they want. They want her alive, but I guess they'll settle for dead.'

Sean shook his head. 'What's the bet part of the money that financed ProtectNZ came from various overseas government agencies?'

'I'd like to think not, but we'll never know. The SIS might find out, but they'd keep that information locked in the bowels of their spooky mirrored building in Wellington.'

Sean kissed her. 'Well done. You've well and truly established your credentials. You can stop risking your life now.'

'What? And let the crims get away with murder? Never.'

'Marla Simmons may not always have your back.'

'That's true.'

'So, what now?'

'What now?' Grace's face lit up. 'Loads of cheap knock-off imitation champagne – that's what now!'

Grace's love-hate relationship with her media colleagues had swung back to the love side. As the throng of journalists stood waiting outside the ProtectNZ offices for Ball, still the leader of ProtectNZ as far as everyone was aware, she received pats on the back, elbow bumps and over-enthusiastic congratulations. Her memory wasn't that short. She had received her share of withering, disparaging glares in the past during her late career move into the journalistic ranks.

Someone nudged her shoulder.

'You're becoming quite the legend.' It was her colleague Zack, the camera operator who had helped her get into the ProtectNZ rally at the Michael Fowler Centre. 'How's the darling of the press this morning?'

'Hung-over,' said Grace, her voice gravely.

'You bloody should be.' Winking, he pushed his way through the crowd looking for a sharp angle.

The fact that Ball was fronting the media in person, not issuing a statement, indicated to Grace this wasn't an admission of defeat, not yet anyway. Aside from those arrested, two board members and four high-profile candidates were implicated in the scandal. According to media reports, ProtectNZ acted immediately, erasing them from the party overnight; all mention of them, their photos and their social media profiles had been removed. The purge sounded Stalinesque, leaving no sign they were ever associated with ProtectNZ.

The front door opened and out came a smiling Ball, together with a way-too-smooth man dressed as though he was walking along a red carpet. Accompanied by a buzz of camera shutters, they didn't walk, they strutted to the podium set up in front of their offices. Two hefty security guards followed them and took up positions either side of Ball. As he took command of the podium, he wasn't displaying the body language of someone heading to the gallows.

'Good morning. I have a brief statement to make before Colin Cromarty, our public relations executive, and I will take questions.'

Ball looked to be back to his confident self, which Grace found strange. Surely their party was in chaos, at least it had been the previous night.

'Yesterday the police arrested several prominent people connected to our party. Other individuals are the subject of ongoing investigations. These people have all voluntarily resigned from the party. At this stage, we don't have the full details of what occurred, no doubt those will come out in the days and weeks to come. I'm here today to tell everyone, especially our party members, that ProtectNZ is stronger today than ever.'

Several members of the assembled media greeted this statement with guffaws.

Ignoring the reaction, a smiling Ball ran a hand over his head.

Grace snorted, he wasn't addressing the media, he was using them to broadcast a message to the party faithful.

'The success ProtectNZ was experiencing was seen as an opportunity for some to advance their own political causes and careers. We have removed this element from the party, it is in the trash where it belongs. ProtectNZ has always had the best interests of ordinary New Zealanders at heart. Our mission is unaltered. We *will* be contesting the upcoming election with all the energy we possess.'

Surveying the assembled media, he said, 'Questions.'

As usual the media voices scrapped for attention and sound bites. In his element, Ball batted away questions about his involvement with those arrested, what he discussed with the police and questions around campaign financing. He said the party's books were, and always had been, open to the Electoral Commission for scrutiny.

As always, Grace waited for the media mud wrestling to die down before firing a question at Ball. Why fight desperate reporters who needed a sound bite for survival? 'If, as you say, an unsavoury element was using the party for their own ends, are you intending any major policy shifts?'

Ball's smile wilted but Cromarty, sensing the danger, stepped forward.

'Allow me, Seb.' He took command of the podium. 'We will be reviewing our policies in the light of recent events, ensuring the party remains committed to delivering on its core strategies and mission while maintaining our core values.'

Giving Grace a well-practised shit-eating grin, he stepped back. It was a business, bullshit, bingo answer. One that uses important-sounding words to say fuck all.

Undeterred, she launched a follow-up question. 'Can you assure people that the agenda of those arrested is not a core part of ProtectNZ's values and policies?'

Cromarty stepped deftly to the podium. 'Absolutely. The ethos of ProtectNZ resides in helping ordinary New Zealanders. At times, the interest of other groups will align with ProtectNZ's goals, but that is coincidental rather than planned or strategic.'

Taking control of the podium, Ball said, 'Are there any other questions?'

After answering a smattering of additional questions, he thanked everyone, saying he looked forward to seeing the media "regularly" in the future. The journalists instantly dispersed, off to write and file their stories. Grace was about to head away herself when she saw the ominous figure of Ms Pilkington heading towards her.

'I'm not up to this,' she said to herself as the stern-faced woman approached. 'What have I done now?'

Ignoring Grace's question, the woman said, 'Sebastian would like a quiet word with you, if you have the time.'

'He does? Okay, where?'

'Follow me please.' Turning abruptly, she headed towards their offices.

As she followed, Zack called out, 'Be careful Ace. Remember Khashoggi.'

Giving him the thumbs up she disappeared into ProtectNZ's offices. Every journalist knew Jamal Khashoggi's horrific story. A loud critic of the Saudis, he was the journalist who had walked into the Saudi Arabian embassy in Turkey where an assassination team had murdered him, used bone saws to cut his body into pieces, taking them away for disposal in diplomatic cars. Despite massive international pressure, not a trace of his body had surfaced. Because of the Saudis' oil, the world had ashamedly turned a blind eye. New Zealand journalists would never consider a fate like that a possibility, but recent events suggested, if the stakes were high enough, who knew?

Ms Pilkington, who Grace could easily picture with a bone saw, showed her through to Ball's office, where he was sitting behind his desk with a coffee. The ProtectNZ offices were as busy as the previous time she had visited; she expected them to be quieter, more sombre.

Ball rose as she entered, offering his hand. Before shaking hands, she paused to look him in the eyes for a long moment.

'Have a seat, Ace.' He shut the door. 'There's a coffee for you, black no sugar.'

Taking a seat, she smiled a thin thanks.

'Whoa,' he said. 'The last few weeks have been a hell of a wild ride.'

She stared at him, waiting.

Straightening himself, he put his elbows on his desk. 'I asked you in, Ace, so I could apologise – in person. I know what happened at your house. I never intended it to get so out of hand but, and you know this better than anyone, they used me too in their plans. I didn't think—'

'You knew what your words would do,' cut in Grace. 'What you didn't know, what you may not still know, is four of the mob your words inspired invaded my house, including the two who shot you and murdered Geoffrey Western.'

Ball's eyes widened. 'I … What happened?'

Grace took him through the attack, crediting Marla's heroics this time to the red-headed police officer on the scene.

'I'm sorry, Ace, I had no idea they intended going that far. I really didn't.'

Staring hard, she couldn't tell if he was genuine. 'The problem with gathering a mob is that it's easy to get them excited, hard to control what happens.'

'Do you think they would've killed you?'

Shaking her head, she said, 'I was going to get the shit kicked out of me, that's for sure – they didn't bring the baseball bats for a game of rounders. The two hired thugs came along to make sure I heard the message and that the local alt-right yokels didn't fuck it up, kill me or get caught.'

He blew out a long breath. 'Will that come out? You know, in print?'

The question had, of course, been in her mind all along though Marla's involvement meant she initially dismissed it as a possibility. She shook her head, trusting her instinct, but tucking the idea away to consider later. Changing the subject, she asked, 'Did you tell the police you knew you were going to be attacked?'

'This is off the record, Ace, okay?'

'Okay. But just so you know, I've more than enough material that's on the record.'

'I expect you have. I told the police everything I knew. And I wasn't meant to be shot, just threatened, but *they*, Blackwood and his alt-right backers, decided public sympathy would play well. It was Blackwood who insisted we go on the attack against the media, and you Ace, after your story came out.'

'Make me an enemy of the people?'

'It isn't rocket science,' he said with a sigh. 'As you're aware, they were using a populist playbook. A single journalist makes a recognisable target rather than the vague concept of "the mainstream media". And they're right. It's like focusing on politicians instead of a single, identifiable politician – the prime minister.'

'It seems to work best if the target identified is a woman. Trump chanting "Lock her up" and the vile, misogynistic shit thrown at Jacinda Ardern. Why is that?'

Ball blew out a long breath. 'You know the answer. It's a societal issue, you can't lay that at my door.'

'You're not helping though, are you.' Grace pursed her lips, letting it slide. 'You keep saying "they". I assume you mean those arrested. Tell me, is the focus going to materially change for ProtectNZ now you've managed to jettison them?'

He sat forward. 'I happen to believe the media has a vital function in a democracy. We'll be focusing on policies that enhance the lives—'

Holding up her hand, cutting off the political slogan, she said, 'Save it for your faithful. You believe the massive hole below your party's waterline is survivable? That moron Blackwood with his stupid hat? The association with murder and killers for hire? The wealthy trying to buy their way into parliament so they can make even more money?'

'They're all gone. And Colin, the PR guy at the press conference, is excellent. I can't tell you how, but he's confident we'll soon be smelling like roses. Most of the blame belongs to Blackwood and co anyway. He spoke about returning the world to what he called "a golden age".'

Grace's eyes narrowed. 'He was a traditionalist?'

'That's right,' said Ball surprised. 'That's what he called himself. I assumed he meant he had old-school values.'

'A lot of deluded, rich, white men are at the bottom of that particular rabbit hole,' she said. 'They believe the world runs on a weird loop which returns to a golden age.' In response to Ball's confused look, she added, 'It's a world run by white men and religious zealots who expect everyone to kneel at their feet and kiss their fat arses. Think pre-Enlightenment and you're looking roughly at their perfect world. To help the world get there, they're busy sowing seeds of chaos. You can guarantee that wherever the world is fucked, leering rich twats like Bannon and Dugin, if they can stay out of jail, will be lurking in the shadows with sweets in their pockets.'

She had lost Ball, who was shaking his head.

'Google them,' she went on. 'You should know who's ultimately backing you. And, if I was you, I'd make sure they have no influence, otherwise they'll have you dancing to their warped tune. They're nutters, no different to Jim Jones or David Koresh. The problem with the current crop of cultists is they have too much money. If they didn't, they'd be famous in their village pub as idiots who predict the next shower of fish for half a pint.'

Listening politely, Grace could tell he wasn't following her.

'Interesting. Anyway, Colin will nuance the messages.'

'I bet he will,' said Grace. 'I've never heard questions avoided with so many redundant words.'

'As I'm sure you're aware,' said Ball chuckling, 'it's part of the game.'

'It *is* a game to you, isn't it? I'm not sure you believe in your party's policies which, unless you change them radically, will benefit wealthy

New Zealanders and not ordinary New Zealanders. You know that. You're playing to win, but what do you want to win?'

Ball held his arms out in a what-can-you-do gesture.

'You could do the right thing,' she said.

'And what's the right thing?'

'Devise policies that *do* help ordinary New Zealanders, not lock in the status quo. Your dad was a train driver, wasn't he?'

'He was.' Ball's eyes glazed over briefly. 'And our policies will help ordinary—'

Speaking over the top of him, she said, 'No, they won't. They'll help rich New Zealanders get richer. You can't turn the world back forty years. Don't let the wealthy, including your backers, wring out every dollar of profit they can before climate change kicks in and people all around the world die.'

'You should be in politics, Ace. It's meant to be a contest of ideas.'

'I agree, it is, but the contest is open to blatant manipulation. In no fair contest is Donald Trump anything but a sad parody of a Simpson's episode.' Tilting her head, she said, 'How much money are you planning to spend on social media?'

Ball shifted uneasily in his seat. 'That's strategic.'

Grace opened her mouth, but Ball didn't let her ask another question.

'Anyway, I do have to crack on. I need to do a lot of damage control before we can get back on point.'

'I appreciate the personal apology,' said Grace as she stood. 'A hundred bucks says your party doesn't win a seat.'

Ball stood up, his hand shooting out. 'You're on. Have you seen the latest polls?'

'I have, but they took those polls before this crapshoot and I have faith in the public, in *ordinary New Zealanders*. Now the truth is circulating, and you look like a bunch of alt-right schoolchildren, I can't imagine anyone except selfish, money-obsessed conservatives will vote for you. You will sink like a stone.'

He smiled before briefly shrugging. As her hand reached for the door, he said, 'Did Trump sink like a stone?'

Leaving her hand on the handle, she looked over her shoulder. 'He should've. Only his money is keeping him afloat. When that runs out …'

'If it runs out,' he said. 'And even then, a new' – he made quotation marks with his fingers – "Trump" will emerge.

With a final glare, she left. Outside his office she considered the range of wealthy gits happy to back right-wing muppets; Theil, Bloomberg, or The Wrights, and she said, 'Fuuuck.' She meant to say it quietly but, judging by the staring faces, she had failed. Mustering a beaming fake smile, she made for the front door.

CHAPTER 48

'She's going to text the location to me,' said Grace. 'You can't blame her for being cautious.'

Parata stared at Grace, weaponising her height.

'And stand a bit further away, I get a sore neck talking to you.'

The SIS agent smirked as she gave Grace space.

Three other cars were at Pharazyn Reserve on what was a cool, cloudy day. They belonged to families with rugged-up children who were playing on the jungle gym while the adults huddled together with their takeaway coffees. Parata had parked her sparkling clean Audi well away from Grace's in-need-of-love Ford.

'I gave her my word,' said Parata.

'I know. I trust you, but my liberty's not at stake.'

The agent puffed out an acknowledgement of sorts.

Grace's phone buzzed. 'There you go. We're meeting where I picked her up from the last time I was here.'

'Where's that?'

'I think the idea is I know, and you don't. That way she's guaranteeing you can't organise a surprise. She'll be there five minutes after us.'

Surveying the sky, the agent said. 'I can't see or hear a drone, but I'd bet there's one up there. That's why she chose here.'

'Hop in. She said to come in my car.' Responding to her hesitant look, Grace added, 'Your flash car's safe here.'

Parata folded herself into the passenger seat.

'You can slide the seat back if you need,' said Grace.

'I already have,' she muttered.

Fifteen minutes later, Parata was rolling her shoulders standing next to Grace on the footpath. 'Here?'

'We were improvising,' said Grace. 'There weren't many places open past ten. Come on, you can buy me a drink. The car you own tells me you're getting far too many of my tax-payer dollars.'

They went into the Pinetree Arms which, because it was three o'clock on a Friday, wasn't doing a roaring trade. Parata bought three ginger beers and they sat at a leaner, well away from the other patrons who were mainly hypnotised by poker machines.

'Well, this is lovely,' said Grace.

'Yeah right. Tell me, before Simmons—

'Call her Marla,' interrupted Grace.

'Okay. Before Marla arrives, did she honestly just turn up to lend you a hand?'

'Scout's honour. I came home and there she was. She frightened the life out of me. As the cards fell, the whole ProtectNZ side of the debacle drew her in.'

'And you didn't know Western was driving her car?'

Grace shook her head. 'The plan Marla laid out to me had her in the car. How the fuck Western ended up driving it at the airport – well, I guess we'll find out when she gets here. Here's a question for you. Would you, the SIS, have let her go?'

Pursing her lips, she said, 'It wouldn't have been my call, but I did give the SIS's, my bosses', word. I kept Marla's part of the sting operation out of official channels so only my boss and I knew about her involvement.'

'What about Fergusson?' cut in Grace.

'He was a necessary complication, but he knew we had what we call "operational flexibility".'

'You're sounding like a politician. You would've let her go – yes, or no?'

'Just to remind you, this conversation never took place, right?' The agent waited for her to nod. 'If she asks, I can only give her a qualified yes.'

'Let's hope she doesn't ask. Does your boss know about this meeting?'

'This meeting is not happening. Strangely, I trust you both, but life is simpler without you.'

The door opened and in walked Marla. Like the other women she had dressed casually in jeans and a warm black jacket. She looked around carefully but casually before heading towards them.

'There's no one else,' said Parata.

'I know, I watched you at the playground.'

'We didn't hear or see a drone,' said Grace.

Smiling at Grace, she said, 'I was sitting with the parents.'

The short, awkward silence that descended was broken by Grace. 'I guess we can't take an usie.' The two women stared at Grace. 'You know, a group selfie. Not to use now but in the future. It'd make a great story when we're—'

'In jail?' offered Parata.

Sniggering at the SIS agent's comment, Marla asked, 'What do you want to know, JP? No, I didn't murder anyone, but I hope you've figured that out by now.'

'We have, but it remains active on the police's books. You're still the leading person of interest – the police's *only* person of interest.'

'Is there any chance you can clear her name?' asked Grace. 'That'd make a great story too.'

'Not without Marla handing herself in,' said Parata. 'And, as the evidence points to her, it'd be risky. The police like to stamp "solved" on murders. It lets the public sleep peacefully in their beds.'

'That's what I figured,' said Marla.

'Are you planning to stay in New Zealand?' asked Grace.

'In the short term. Maybe the medium term too.' Marla turned to Parata. 'I can't go home, can I, JP?'

'Several US agencies have expressed an interest in' – Parata wet her lips – 'chatting to you.'

'Not to mention the unofficial bounty they've put on you,' said Grace. 'Arseholes.'

Marla shrugged. 'It's the dictionary definition of a dog-eat-dog profession.'

'How about letting us in on your Houdini trick?' asked Parata. 'How did Western end up in a wig driving your car? He's not being the most cooperative of witnesses.'

'I'm keen to know that too,' said Grace. 'You left that bit out of the plan.'

Smiling, Marla said, 'Surprises work best when nobody knows. I visited him at his house, to warn him he was going to end up dead unless he smartened up fast.'

'The agent we had on him never saw you.'

'That's how it was meant to be. And you abandoned the tail on him which meant I didn't need to waste time working out how to ditch her.'

'I needed her at the airport,' said Parata. 'Besides, I didn't think I needed eyes on Western anymore.'

'Anyway,' said Marla, 'I convinced him to help me and himself. The two on the motorcycle – how are they doing, by the way?'

'The woman, she's busted up, but she'll recover. The man is in a bad way – he may not pull through. The woman saw the writing on the wall, she's filled in the gaps we couldn't get from their computers and phones. They had enough material to blackmail Blackwood – if they weren't already.'

'Who were they?' asked Grace.

'A couple of former soldiers for hire. Sorry, Ace, we need to keep them out of the media.'

'How do you intend to do that?' asked Grace.

The agent shrugged. 'There's no evidence of their involvement bar your grainy photos. Our official line, if you do decide to run the story, will be no comment. Pick your battles, Ace. There are some keen to throw Marla under the bus for this as well.'

Marla shrugged but Grace opened her mouth to protest, Parata's raised hand stopping her. 'Justice will be done, but they're embarrassing from too many angles. You were saying, Marla.'

'Like the SIS agent on Grace, they were tracking her too, hoping she'd lead them to me. I used that to set them up. The first time Ace and I met for an old-school spy rendezvous, they followed me when I left, but the lane I took trapped them in a small car park next to the supermarket car park where I was parked. The next time they would be ready, waiting in the supermarket car park – as planned.'

Parata's slight grin conveyed admiration.

'They wouldn't want to make the hit with so many witnesses and they positioned themselves where I expected because it gave them a view of most of the car park. Western and I parked next to each other at the far end of the car park, obscured from their view. After meeting

Ace – Western was already in my car wearing the wig and sunglasses – I jumped into his car and he left after ten seconds, driving to the airport on a safe and slow route. I watched them follow him, gave them thirty seconds, then took a different route.'

'Why the airport?' asked Grace.

Parata answered. 'The fencing made a perfect trap, plus, if they thought Marla was getting on a plane, this was their last chance.'

Marla smiled.

'Clever,' said Grace. 'Then you parked near the airport to launch your drone.'

Marla nodded. 'When they rode towards the car park, I launched my drone. I assumed everyone would be watching the action and I was invisible. I needed to know what happened. I hoped you'd take them easily and I sure didn't expect Western to star.'

'He did well,' said Parata. 'He may have saved innocent lives. We were heading for a shootout.'

'Not that I care,' said Marla, 'but what's going to happen to him?'

'The police are still investigating him; it'll take them a while. If he has committed a crime, it won't be serious.'

Grace's spine stiffened. 'What about the threatening notes he posted?'

'As I understand it, you've no evidence it was him. You'd need Marla to appear in court to give evidence and that's not going to happen.'

'He gets away scot-free?' said Grace.

The agent shrugged and turned to Marla. 'What's your take on Western? Bad bastard or a harmless idiot?'

'Definitely not a bad bastard. Angry man, a bit dim and easily led. Put him in a different circle of people and he'd be marching for gay rights.'

'That makes sense,' said Grace. 'I've long thought people aren't falling down rabbit holes, they're being groomed.'

'It's the basic recipe for all gangs, terrorist or criminal,' said Parata. 'Powerful personalities draw in weaker people who feel disaffected. They need to believe in something, and the gang gives them something. Making money, a great cause, even if it is a fucked-up conspiracy theory, or a feeling of whanau.'

Parata raised her eyebrows at Marla. 'After you saw the motorcycle crash …'

'As your agents found out, JP, it's not a quick route out of the car park. It gave me plenty of time to get away under restricted airspace. I parked the car a block away from Western's house and left the keys in his letterbox as we agreed. I took the bus back to town and paid cash for a new car.'

'A *new* car!' said Grace.

Marla smiled. 'New to me. Another reliable, cheap, anonymous second-hand car.'

'Registered to a phantom in Timbuktu no doubt,' said Parata.

'Tokoroa, but the trail's as cold.'

'My turn for a question,' said Grace. 'How did you find out about the ProtectNZ Board and where they were meeting?'

'That's a longer story,' said Marla. 'Let's just say an individual who's still a candidate for ProtectNZ shouldn't be so loose with his technology – and his morals. If he plays up, I might listen in on what he's up to, even send through the material if it's warranted.'

The SIS agent put a range of questions to Marla who answered carefully, not wanting to give away information that might compromise herself. Parata was running out of steam when a familiar-looking man, old and dressed in what might have once been his ballroom dancing clothes, entered the bar. When he saw them, his eyes lit up and he tottered straight over.

'You're here again, my dears. *And* you've brought another charming friend. I didn't expect to see you again, this is a delight.' Moving closer to Marla, he put his hand on her arm. 'Have you looked at the fields today, dear?'

'I haven't had a chance, Derek. We're about to leave but, if we can, we'll swing by later this evening. No promises, mind.'

'Splendid,' he said straightening. 'If you make it, I shall stand you all a drink – from my winnings.' He winked at Marla.

They watched him head unsteadily towards the bar, greeting nearly everyone he saw. Parata looked quizzically at Marla, who held her hand up in a don't-ask gesture, while Grace had to fight from collapsing into laughter.

Marla asked Parata, 'Did you ask the woman why they called in a tow truck?'

Parata frowned. 'That didn't make sense to us either. Why not drive the car to the beach? She said the plan had been to scare Regan Western, make sure he kept his mouth shut. According to her, the conversation with his brother went badly. He pulled a gun; she reckoned he gave them no choice. They didn't want to chance being seen driving the car, so they took the keys but they didn't have enough time to hand them over. Someone, she didn't know who, called in a couple of local towies used to doing cash jobs, no questions asked. If you two weren't following Western's car, they might have pulled off the drug-deal-gone-bad story.'

Grace leaned in closer. 'Who do you think the someone is?'

'We don't know,' said Parata. 'Probably Blackwood, but we'll need to establish a link. It's going to take a while to pull all the evidence together to see who we can charge with what.'

Grace rolled her eyes. 'The arseholes will be on bail for years. Free to drink martinis and watch the sunrise.'

'*The Hurricane*,' said a smiling Marla.

Grace nodded as Parata checked the time on her phone.

Looking at Grace, Marla said, 'Before you go, you need to tell me the "fuck nothing" story.'

'I thought you'd forgotten,' said Grace. 'I'm sure the story comes from David Niven's memoirs; I don't think he made it up. Anyway, he and Errol Flynn—'

'I've heard of Errol Flynn,' said Marla cutting in. 'He was American.'

Grace shook her head. 'He was Australian. Niven and Flynn are shooting a scene for the movie *The Charge of the Light Brigade* that involved one hundred riderless horses galloping across the shot. The director, Mike Curtiz, a Hungarian who spoke pretty average English, calls out "bring on zee empty horses".'

Marla's and Parata's eyes narrowed.

'Niven and Flynn found that hilarious. They rolled on the ground in hysterics and Curtiz snapped. He went over and said, "You lousy bums. You and your stinking language. You think I know fuck nothing, well let me tell you, I know fuck all."'

Heads turned as Marla's laugh broke the hypnotic spell of the poker machines. 'I can't imagine that helped.'

'It sure didn't,' said Grace.

Outside the bar, they stood around awkwardly, not knowing how to finish their unusual meeting. It wasn't a regular occurrence for a journalist, an SIS agent, and a wanted-for-murder ex-agent to get together socially.

'Where's your car?' asked Grace.

'Parked away from here and away from any security cameras. When you two are gone, I'll head home.'

Parata asked, 'If we, I really mean the SIS, need to contact you, is it possible?'

Marla didn't answer immediately. 'I can't see why you would but, before I trash the comms link Ace and I are using, I'll send her an email address you can both use.'

'It'll be like the bat phone,' said Grace.

Parata shook her head slowly.

'I almost forgot,' said Marla. 'I'm sure you could use another story, Ace. And JP, there's another git to catch.'

Grace's eyes lit up. Parata played it cooler.

'Styles,' said Marla. 'He was on the ProtectNZ Board and he's Western's contact into the wider alt-right.'

'Is he?' said Parata. 'How do you know that, and I don't?'

Marla shrugged, then continued. 'There's a stack of illegal plates hidden in his Wellington dealership. He lends them out to other crooks.' In answer to Parata's look, she added, 'Western told me. Said he's been doing it for years.'

'Excellent,' said Parata, 'I'll have to *invent* a probable cause but I'm going to enjoy seeing him again.'

'And I'll be Johnny-on-the-spot, won't I, JP?' said a beaming Grace.

'You're going to get me fired,' said Parata. She turned to Marla. 'Kia kaha, Marla. Be lucky. Let's go, Ace, I've a mountain of paperwork to sort through.'

After a short, awkward silence, Grace said, 'Well … thanks, Marla for, well … everything.'

Catching Grace by surprise, Marla hugged her warmly.

Stepping back, Marla said, 'As much as I enjoy your company, stay out of trouble, Ace.'

Smiling, she said, 'I'll try.'

As they drove away, Grace could see her in the rear-view mirror, sunglasses on, waiting until they were out of sight.

EPILOGUE

Grace lay sprawled on Sean's couch, worse for the one-too-many glasses of wine she had drunk, although what was playing out on TV was keeping her at least feeling sober. As it was his week looking after his children, Sean hadn't drunk anything alcoholic. His logic was that a responsible parent needed to be able to drive to the hospital, just in case. That made her feel like an irresponsible parent, but she figured she was in with the vast majority. She had left her children at home but, at seventeen and eighteen, they could fend for themselves.

'They're asleep,' said Sean, flopping down next to Grace.

'Great work, Dad.'

Sean used his head to indicate the TV. 'With what's happening, how are you feeling?'

Grace wrinkled her nose. 'I'm oscillating between nauseous and suicidal.'

On the screen, Seb Ball, suited and covered in streamers and confetti, was running a hand over his head, playing up to a large crowd. Behind him, beaming, stood Ms Pilkington dressed in what Grace could only describe as fifty shades of blue.

Picking up the remote, he asked, 'Do you want the sound up?'

'God no. I know exactly what he'll be saying. Every second sentence will include, "A victory for ordinary New Zealanders". That would make me vomit for def.'

'How could the polls get it so wrong?' he asked.

Sitting up, groping for her wine glass, she thought better of it. 'The talking heads nailed it. People didn't like to admit they were going to vote for ProtectNZ, not after the scandals. But, as we've seen throughout the world, populist appeal seems …'

'Bulletproof?' he offered.

'Fucking bulletproof,' she said. 'I would've bet they couldn't shake off the alt-right mud they were dragged through backwards.'

'You did bet. Don't you owe Ball a hundred dollars?'

She groaned. 'I do too. Thank Christ I didn't bet an expensive dinner, I would've had to welch. They're now sitting where Peters liked to sit, in the kingmaker seat, except they've twice the seats he ever had. They'll milk it for all they can.'

'Will Ball be deputy prime minister?'

Grace grunted. 'I think so.'

Sean shook his head. 'From being shot, his party embroiled in intrigue and murder to deputy prime minister in less than five months. You couldn't make this shit up.'

'After screwing as much political mileage out of the media as they can,' said Grace, 'they'll form a government with the right-wing parties. Most of the seed funding came out of US alt-right groups, they'll want a return despite losing most of their stooges.'

'Will they have enough power to influence policy?'

Running her hands through her hair, she said, 'Yep, it's not a night the planet will be celebrating. Then there'll be the usual horse-trading on issues, which means all the fucked ideas are back on the table: benefit reductions, diluting climate targets, abortion, gay and trans rights, the voting age, etcetera.'

'Maybe later,' he said. 'They'll focus on the economy and tax cuts to start with.'

'True. It's ironic isn't it, the public vote for our version of the Tories because people think they understand the economy. And, just like the UK Tories who made a dog's breakfast of the UK economy, our lot are clueless about economics. National thinks the country runs like a business − it doesn't. The ACT weirdos think it runs like a household for fuck's sake.'

'Will they take whatever's left of the ACT parties?'

'I would. It's better having the lone nutter raving inside your tent than having him outside, his underpants on his head, weeing on it.'

'You are in a dark place. Will they need you to cover the post-election wrangling?'

'Nope. We've a smart political team who'll be in the thick of the shenanigans. What I am interested in is how.'

'How?'

'How it's possible to run a thinly disguised racist, misogynistic campaign, to sail through a sea of disasters and not only avoid ruin but come out more popular. Most pundits put America's experience down to a combination of religion and rednecks. Brexit played on deep-seated immigration fears. What can we put ours down to?'

'The story you wrote a month ago,' he said. 'Most of the voting population aren't interested in politics.'

'That's right. If they don't vote like Mummy and Daddy, most people make their decision based on the one factor that's impacted them in the weeks leading up to the election.'

'That's part of the how, isn't it?' said Sean, pointing at the TV which had a panel of "experts" shaking their collective heads as they analysed the results. 'We think an election is the culmination of a three-month-long informed debate. But we're watching what? People rocking up to the polls and throwing a dart?'

A half-laugh, half-cry escaped from Grace. 'I wish they were throwing darts. At least that way we'd get a random government. What I think we're watching is the manipulation, maybe the corruption, of the public narrative through the wealthy's ability to have dog whistle political messages regurgitated through the media and amplified by social media algorithms.'

Sean sniggered. 'That's an insightful comment from a journalist who's a little worse for wear. I'd keep that sentence for your next story.'

'I intend to,' said Grace picking up the TV remote and banishing the political experts into darkness.

ABOUT THE AUTHOR

Riley Chance is writing a series of novels set in New Zealand's near future to both entertain and challenge readers to look critically at society. *The Democracy Game* is the second book in the series; the first book, *Surveillance*, was published in 2022.

Since being made redundant, Riley has juggled raising a family, work and life for over two decades. As a seasoned, but unenthusiastic and slightly bitter, member of the precarious workforce, the question – how can citizens change society? – was the spark that ignited a desire to try and make a difference – to change society.

You can find Riley writing, headphones on, in libraries and cafés in Wellington and the Manawatū. Now both children are adults (and currently living in Auckland), when not writing Riley is often up a ladder, at the gym or earning money disguised as a management consultant.